The Book of All Skies

Greg Egan

First Edition, 2021

ISBN 978-1-922240-37-8

Visit the author's web site at www.gregegan.net

Also by Greg Egan

Novels

Collections

Chapter 1

Del sat on the steps of the museum, looking east across the starlit city, waiting for the archaeologists to arrive. Takya's gray disk was approaching the horizon, while Bradya hung seemingly suspended, halfway from the zenith, silhouetted against the constellation she'd always known as the Harp, though many of her friends called it the Crossbow.

The message had told her to expect a delivery no later than Takya's ninth passage, but it was a good thing she had come out early; with the seventh barely over, she spotted the heat blotch of four people approaching together along the main road from the south.

"Jachimo!" she bellowed, a little ashamed of her discourtesy, but she couldn't bring herself to go inside and fetch him if it meant losing sight of the travelers.

"I'm coming!" he called back. When he emerged from the building and joined her, he looked around, confused. "I thought they were already here."

"Almost." Del rose to her feet. "We need to make a good impression. I don't want them thinking we're lax with security."

"Should I be carrying a sword?" he joked.

"I'm sure you're imposing enough unarmed," she replied. Though as the party came closer, she could see that the two guards flanking the archaeologists did in fact have daggers.

She walked down to the road, then forced herself to wait until everyone was in comfortable earshot before calling out a greeting. "Welcome to Apasa!"

"Thank you!" A woman strode forward and shook Del's hand. "I'm Jessica."

"Cordelia. Good to meet you." Jessica was the archaeologist in charge of the excavation at Seena; she had been corresponding with the museum's director ever since the book had been unearthed, but Del had only become fully involved when the last few messages had turned to questions that relied on a conservator's advice.

Del motioned to Jachimo to join them, and they completed the introductions. Jessica's colleague, Lucius, bearing the precious cargo in a sling against his chest, stayed aloof and nodded from a few paces away, as if he were carrying a sleeping infant he didn't wish to risk waking, while the bladed escort, Audrey and Orsino, greeted their hosts with a kind of wary camaraderie that implied that they were all steadfast allies for now, but the situation was always open to reassessment.

Del spread her arms. "Please come in. You must be exhausted."

They followed her and Jachimo up the steps and through the main entrance. When the director had told her there was no fuel to spare for celebratory lanterns to mark the occasion, Del had set about scrubbing the skylights, so at least the foyer's usual gloom had been replaced by a cheerful airiness.

"I have some food prepared," she said, turning to address the guests, "but I won't be offended if you prefer to sleep first." She gestured toward the accommodation wing. "Your quarters are through there; the rooms are all made up, and I've left two pitchers of water in each of them."

Lucius said, "Thank you, but before any of that ... " He glanced down at the box strapped to his body.

"Of course. This way."

Del thought perhaps Lucius would follow her while the other three went to wash and settle in, but instead they set their packs down and accompanied her as she headed for the vault.

"How many people live in this building, normally?" Orsino enquired. They'd entered the corridor lined with statues from the Vitean period, most of them depicting the pets of wealthy families in the act of eviscerating vermin.

"Just Del and I," Jachimo replied. "The other rooms are for visitors."

"And how many entrances are there?"

"Besides the one we came through, two doors at the back."

"They're well protected?"

"Both sturdy, and triple bolted." Jachimo shot Del an amused look, as if he was happy to humor this upstart, but wanted it known that he required no lessons in his job.

They'd come to the end of the corridor. Del took the key tied to her belt and inserted it, then stood aside as far as the string would let her to allow Jachimo to do the same. They turned the keys together, with considerable effort, until the lock squealed and retracted its five metal tongues.

"It could do with some oil," Del admitted, pulling open the door to the vault. The dark within was impenetrable, and the temperature too uniform to be revelatory, but when she lit the lamp at the entrance the long racks of shelves materialized, their shadows flickering for a moment as the flame found its shape.

Audrey and Orsino hung back, taking up positions on either side of the doorway, as if a marauding enemy might charge down the corridor at any moment. Lucius and Jessica followed Del into the vault, and after some hesitation – perhaps worried that he might be seen to be ceding responsibility to the two earnest sentries – Jachimo came after them.

They walked past rows of figurines and pieces of pottery, many of them too mundane in appearance to have been chosen for public display, but nonetheless precious by virtue of their antiquity. Then there were the Palloran death-masks, dazzling works of unquestionable skill in beaten silver, but which were apparently too disturbing for the majority of visitors to stomach. Why the wearers had felt the need to be portrayed half-consumed by insects, when that fate generally ensued with or without an expensive symbolic invitation, remained a mystery.

"We have several Tollean works already," Del said, as they approached the section reserved for manuscripts. "Some complete, some fragments. I can show you a few if you like, as a testament to the excellent conditions we maintain. The humidity in the vault hasn't shifted by more than one part in fifty, for as long as we've been keeping records."

"Maybe later," Jessica replied. She didn't sound as if she was in need of reassurance over her choice of a home for her own extraordinary find, but then, she must have established the museum's reputation among her colleagues well in advance, or she wouldn't even be here.

Del had already labeled the shelf she'd selected for the new acquisition, and she stood aside and let Lucius step forward and lower the box into place.

"Do you mind opening it?" she asked. "I need to make a brief inspection, before I can officially enter it into the catalog."

"Of course." Lucius produced a key and unlocked the box, then lifted up the hinged lid.

Del put on her gloves and took his place beside the shelf. The interior of the box was packed with protective cloth, and she lifted the interleaved layers and laid them to each side, like the pages of two blank books that had conspired to shield the third.

After a time, the cloth remaining grew flatter, and yielded less to the pressure of her fingers as she peeled it back. She slowed down, afraid that she might misjudge the care required at the end of the unwrapping if she allowed her actions to become rote.

Lucius said, "The last four sheets are white like the rest, but the fifth and sixth are vermillion."

Del exhaled in a sigh of gratitude, and the markers soon showed themselves, telling her exactly how many steps remained. But when she raised the final piece of cloth to reveal what lay beneath, a part of her still felt a jolt of surprise, as if a far more likely scenario than the box containing what she had been told would have been an elaborate prank in which the unwrapping went on forever.

The front cover of the volume sitting before her a piece of hardboard, cleaved by three deep fractures, crisscrossed by a dozen shallower cuts and crumbling at the corners, but otherwise more or less intact. The title was carved in grooves and pits that would have been dyed for the sake of contrast, but were always meant to be as amenable to reading by touch as by sight. Time and grit had bleached and scoured the surface, and Del was unwilling to lay even her gloved fingertips upon it, but as she moved one thumb back and forth in the space above the board and watched the shadows distorted by each dip, the letters took shape. This sequence of words in the Tollean language was not unfamiliar to her, even if she had only seen it before in citations. But this was it, the thing itself, as solid and present as it had been to those authors who had casually invoked it, to criticize or praise, a thousand generations ago. *The Book of All Skies* was here, sitting on a shelf in the Museum of Apasa, just waiting for her to render it into a fit state to be read, understood, valorized and disputed all over again.

"That's enough," she decided. Anything more, done in haste, might damage the book. She began replacing the wrapping.

"Now you can imagine how we felt when we found it," Jessica said. "This was part of someone's personal library, judging by what remained of the furniture, though the avalanche pretty much pulverized everything else."

"Did you find any trace of the reader?" Del asked.

"No, but you know what scavenger worms are like."

They withdrew from the vault.

"You mentioned food?" Lucius asked, almost shyly, as if he feared the warm welcome might evaporate now that the main purpose of their visit had been fulfilled.

"Of course," Del replied. "Does anyone else ... ?"

Audrey said, "Believe me, we're all famished."

In the dining room, Del did her best to resist overwhelming the guests with questions, but once they'd slaked their thirst and started on the fish, Lucius and Jessica wanted nothing more than to talk about their find and the prospects for its restoration.

"Don't ask me to say how long it will take," Del pleaded. "With a book that size, I can't even promise it will be finished in my own lifetime."

"Aren't you desperate to know where the Tolleans went?" Lucius asked. His tone seemed light-hearted, but not openly sarcastic.

"I'm agnostic on the question of whether they went anywhere," Del replied. "Plenty of other cultures seem to have given way to successors, without anyone actually migrating."

"But they talked about it more than anyone else," Lucius persisted. "They seemed convinced they knew a way to reach the Bounteous Lands."

"Some of them seemed convinced," Jessica corrected him. "If there was ever a consensus, we've seen no record of it."

"If there was a consensus," Jachimo suggested, "wouldn't we all be there right now? As their descendants?"

Lucius said, "Maybe the people who ended up knowing for sure never bothered coming back; they were more interested in keeping the territory for themselves than having to share it – even if that meant foregoing the satisfaction of telling the doubters they were wrong."

"If they did find a passage, it can't have stayed open for long," Audrey declared. "If it was so hard to discover, it must have been narrow to begin with – and maybe it even depended on them digging their way through. All it would take would be one avalanche, one quake, one lava flow, to seal it up again."

Del looked to Orsino, who was yet to offer an opinion. He was silent at first, but then he ventured, "Maybe the Tolleans were more resourceful than us, or more persistent. But just because no one's repeated what they did, that doesn't mean it's become impossible."

"Impossible or not," Jessica said, "we should know soon enough. If there's a map, we can compare it with our own maps. If there's a strategy for finding a route, we can test it. If there's even just a theory of the world that somehow points to the necessity of a persistent connection with the Bounteous Lands, we can judge it against all the evidence collected since. Whatever they found, or believed, or imagined, this will be the place where it was actually spelled out – not just invoked as something that everyone was assumed to know about already."

Del smiled, still a little daunted, but exhilarated too. *The Book of All Skies* had always seemed like a mirage to her before, but now that it was in their hands, even the things it merely spoke of might turn out to lie within their reach as well.

She said, "I should probably sleep now, and make an early start."

Chapter 2

Del woke, confused, unsure what had roused her. She was certain she hadn't slept for as long as she'd intended, but when she closed her eyes and tried to drift away again, she found herself resisting.

She climbed out of bed and left her room, then walked down the corridor to the foyer. There were faint heat-prints lingering on the floor, leading to the exit; she supposed that one of her guests must have decided to go out for some air. But the fading trail didn't seem to originate in the accommodation wing; whoever this was had wandered about a bit first.

Del crossed the foyer. The glass doors were unbolted, but she couldn't see anyone outside. She went out onto the stairs and peered down the road. There was a figure in the distance, walking north, the coolness of a backpack separating their head from the heat of their arms and lower body. It was hard to be sure from a view like this, but she believed it was Orsino.

She felt for the vault key, and was relieved to find that it was still attached to her belt. But why would Orsino – or any of her guests – depart so abruptly? If a messenger had come, with news of a family emergency or whatever, she would have been the first to wake.

Del contemplated pursuing the retreating figure to ask politely for an explanation, but then it seemed wiser to check with the others first. She went inside and walked to Audrey's room.

The door opened on the second knock; it seemed the cascade of activity was waking everyone.

"Did Orsino say anything to you about leaving?" Del asked.

Audrey scowled and walked past Del to Orsino's door; she tried the handle and it opened, revealing an empty room.

"Why would he just go like that?" Del pressed her. He couldn't have taken the book; the key had never left her side. She ran her fingertips over the thing anxiously, reassuring herself that it wasn't some kind of substitute that had been left in place of the real one by sleight of hand. The shape was exactly right, every notch and protuberance familiar. There was a slight slipperiness to the normally rough surface, but perhaps she'd handled it so much now that she'd coated it with the oils of her own skin.

Jachimo emerged from his room. "What's happening?"

"Do you still have your vault key?"

He followed the string from his belt to his pocket. "Yes. Why wouldn't I?"

"Orsino's gone, and no one seems to know why."

Jachimo nodded in the direction of the vault, and they jogged off together. "He couldn't have opened it!" Jachimo insisted, as they passed the statue of an executioner bird tugging the intestines out of a plump harvest rat. "Pulled the keys off, then tied them back on again, all without waking us?" Del wanted to believe it was impossible too, but neither of them was convinced enough to turn back.

The door to the vault certainly hadn't been left unlocked. They opened it, and Del lit the lamp. As she hurried between the shelves, she spotted the box up ahead, sitting exactly where Lucius had placed it.

She slowed a little as she approached, and turned toward Jachimo, moving aside so he could see what she'd seen. Then she put her hand on the box; Lucius had left her the key, but she'd seen no reason to hide it, and it remained hanging on a peg below the shelf. Any thief could have taken the box unopened, or just smashed it where it sat.

She unlocked the box and lifted the lid. Inside, there was nothing: the book and its wrapping were gone. If she'd taken the key away that would not have stopped the theft, but it might have made the loss visible sooner.

Del's face burned, with shame as much as anger. Somehow, her carelessness had just lost the museum the greatest acquisition of her tenure by far.

"I'm going after him," she said.

"I'll go," Audrey called from the doorway. "Even if you catch him, what can you do?"

Del approached her. "Oh, I'm sure I'll catch him! When I saw him he was just walking down the road, trying not to draw attention to himself."

"But when he sees you coming?" Audrey countered. "He's not going to hold back once he knows he's being chased."

Jachimo laughed. "Del placed seventh in the last sky-to-sky; there aren't many people who could outrun her at the best of times, and I'd be willing to bet that her fury right now is more of a prod than your ex-comrade's greed."

They started back down the corridor. "And what will you do if he draws his dagger?" Audrey asked.

"Keep my distance," Del replied. "Maybe I can tire him out with the chase alone, without getting in harm's way." But then what? Even if he came to a halt, exhausted, far from his intended destination, there was no guarantee that there'd be helpful bystanders around, able to identify the two of them correctly as fugitive thief and righteous pursuer.

"I need to come with you," Audrey said firmly. "If I can't match your pace, at least I should be able to keep you in sight. Then if you can slow him down or corner him, you can wait for me to catch up."

Reluctantly, Del gave her assent. For all she knew, Audrey might be Orsino's accomplice, but who else could she ask to back her up? Jachimo was stronger than any of them, but he wasn't light on his feet, and Jessica and Lucius were no more qualified to confront Orsino than she was.

The two archaeologists were standing in the foyer, looking confused. Audrey broke the news to them, then tried to assuage their anger and dismay by describing the plan, such as it was. "Cordelia and I are going after him. He can't have gone far ... but do you know where he might be headed? Someone he could have in mind as the buyer?"

"No!" Jessica clawed at her cheeks, distraught. "How could I have trusted him?"

"He has no reason to damage the book," Del observed. But she was wasting her time offering comforting words. "I need to get some things," she said.

She ran to her room and slipped her shoes on, then took a mouthful of water and quickly filled a flask. *Was she really going to do this?* But if she didn't, she might never see the book again. If it ended up in a rival museum, that wouldn't be so bad, but if a private collector had bribed Orsino to procure it, the demented narcissist might take its secrets to the grave.

When she returned to the foyer she saw that Audrey was waiting on the steps; Del hadn't told her which way to go, and Orsino would be out of sight by now. Del nodded to Jachimo as she passed, but found herself unable to meet Jessica's or Lucius's gaze. They were the ones who had made the mistake of hiring Orsino, but the book itself had been in her care.

She flung open the doors and bounded down the stairs, calling to Audrey as she went: "North!"

It was tempting to break into a sprint, to swoop down the road toward her quarry like a raptor descending from the sky, but Del brushed aside her fantasies of a swift and effortless victory and settled into a pace that she knew she could sustain indefinitely. Speed wasn't everything: one misstep could leave her with a twist or sprain that robbed her of any advantage – and if she left Audrey too far behind, there'd be no point relying on her help at all.

She glanced back toward the museum, and saw that Audrey was in fact drawing closer. Del sped up a little, and waved to her encouragingly. If they urged each other on, all the better.

There was no sign of Orsino yet, but the road meandered between a sequence of small hills that could easily be obscuring him. And if he'd left the road she'd still have a chance to spot him, as the hills only blocked her view on either side in turn. To the east lay the outskirts of Apasa, with scattered homes and warehouses growing sparser as she moved north. To the west the landscape was dotted with rice fields and fish ponds, shimmering with heat and exuding the pungent scent of subterranean waters.

Then she rounded a bend and there he was, trudging along in the distance. Or at least, it seemed like the same person she'd observed from the steps of the museum, and with Bradya still not set, who else would be on the road? Well ... some early-rising laborers and traders, some innocent travelers eager to be home. The only trouble, if she was mistaken, was that hanging back to avoid alerting someone who was not in fact Orsino might slow her down so much that her real target slipped away.

The only cure for her doubts was proximity. Del maintained her pace, whittling away the gap between them. The road was level now, and almost straight; there'd be no hiding from Orsino if he turned and looked back, but equally, he'd have no hope of shaking her off. Del indulged in a brief reverie where he pondered his fate and cut his losses, leaving his pack on the road so he could flee unencumbered. She really didn't care about bringing him to justice, so long as she had *The Book of All Skies* back in the vault before the director knew what had happened.

As she drew nearer, a bank of clouds began drifting in from the west, leaving the figure casting a strange penumbra in the remaining starlight. The prospect of a clear identification at a safe remove was slipping away. But there were no other candidates in sight; if this wasn't Orsino, she'd simply lost him. All she could do now was keep tailing whoever this was, and wait for Audrey to catch up so the two of them could close in together and settle the matter.

Del slowed to a brisk walk and looked back over her shoulder, but it seemed Audrey was still making her way through the hills. She reached for the vault key to check that it hadn't worked itself loose; it hadn't, but she wished she'd left it with Jachimo instead of risking it ending up on the road. Despite her exertion, running through the cool air had left her hands less sweaty than before, and the residue she'd noticed earlier seemed more clearly to belong to the key, not to her. It felt like ... a thin layer of wax. As might have remained if Orsino, sitting beside her at the dinner table, had gently lifted it, without tugging on the string, and pressed the metal into a block that could retain its shape.

Del's anger was tinged with grudging admiration; it would take some skill, not just to steal the impressions unnoticed, but to use the molds – in a guest room, not a foundry – to form objects solid enough to turn in the lock without breaking. A thug might have slit his companions' throats on the journey to Apasa, to save himself the trouble. She would never forgive him for the theft itself, but craft was craft.

The figure glanced back, briefly, then kept walking. Del's glimpse of the man's face had been so fleeting that she had no sense of having gained any information at all. If this was Orsino and he'd recognized her, he was keeping his nerve, holding fast to his imitation of innocence.

After a while he turned onto a path running west off the main road, heading in among the fields and fish ponds. Del slowed a little, wanting to observe as much of his activities as possible before deciding what to do next. As he crossed onto warmer ground and walked amidst the steam escaping from the springs, his heat pattern blurred into the background, leaving her struggling to keep track of him by the light of the few unshrouded stars.

She turned and looked around impatiently, and saw that Audrey had finally emerged from the hills. Del raised an arm high and waved to her, and after a moment she received an acknowledgment. It wouldn't be long before they were reunited – but Orsino was melting away into the landscape. Del reached the path, and followed him west.

She could no longer see him at all, but she retained a sense of roughly where he had to be. The path split into multiple trails weaving between the ponds; Del tried to mimic the angle with the road she'd seen Orsino take, leading him slightly back to the south.

The ground felt warm even through her shoes, and the sulfurous fog made her eyes water. She stepped up her pace, sure that Orsino could not be far away. Once she caught a glimpse of him, she'd refuse to let him out of her sight – and if she yelled loudly, her voice should be enough to guide Audrey through the heat haze.

"Can I help you?" a woman asked brusquely. Del turned toward the sound, but had to take a few steps through the mist to really see who had addressed her. The speaker was standing by the edge of a pool, holding some kind of netted scoop in one hand.

"Did a man walk by here, a moment ago?"

"No. But if your friend is lost, I expect he'll head back to the road."

Del said, "He's not my friend. I'm chasing a thief."

The woman sighed, though Del wasn't sure if this was an expression of sympathy, or just a weary response to an unwelcome drama. "A thief won't be able to hide here for long; there'll be workers on every path soon."

"Good." Del hesitated; she didn't want to sound ungrateful, but it was far from clear to her that Orsino losing the ability to dawdle by a pond, unnoticed, would be enough to flush him out of hiding completely. "If he chooses not to go back to the northern road ... ?"

"Well, he can head west if he wants to," the woman conceded. "Or north-west, to the western road. There are no fences; the terrain and the stink is enough to deter most people, but it's not impassable."

"Thank you." Del set about retracing her steps. If Orsino's original plan had been to take the western road, he might well decide to make the most of the detour she'd forced upon him by cutting the corner. She'd never track him through this maze of ponds and geysers – but she could probably reach the same destination faster by sticking to the road.

And if she was wrong? If he just doubled back and continued north?

Del emerged from the fog just in time to hail Audrey.

"Are you all right?" Audrey asked, coming to a halt on the road beside her.

"Me?"

"You seem a bit ... " Audrey gestured at her own face, a polite surrogate for Del's. "Bluish."

"It must be the fumes." It was a wonder the workers could endure it for so long. "I lost him in there," Del admitted, "but he really only has two choices: come back to this road and continue north, up to Melus, or go west."

"West? Through the Hoop?"

"Yes."

Audrey winced. "That's all we need."

"Maybe you can watch for him here," Del suggested, "and I'll run on ahead and try to cut him off."

"How many times do I need to remind you that he's armed?"

"Just stay on this road for one passage." Del searched for Takya; it was near the zenith. "Then if Orsino hasn't shown up here, and I haven't come back, you can come after me."

Audrey looked exasperated. "After that much delay, I'll never catch up with you."

"Half a passage, then," Del suggested. "I'm sure I can get ahead of him on the western road, if that's where he's going, but if he's not, someone has to be here to grab him."

"What if he heads due west? Parallel to the road, never meeting it?"

"Then I'll probably never find him. But he's just completed a long walk from Seena, and I doubt he got any sleep in the museum." Del gestured toward the edge of the badlands. "Past the fish ponds, it's igneous plains strewn with cracks and fumaroles, all the way to the Hoop. Whatever reward Orsino's been promised, there's only so much endurance anyone can conjure up from thin air. And if he thinks he's only got one meek conservator to contend with, I'm sure the road will grow tempting very rapidly."

Audrey gave up arguing. "Go on!" she urged Del. "I'll find an outcrop to hide behind."

Del set off north, as fast as she could without inviting injury. To be moving swiftly on the open road was enough to make her hopeful again; she'd be foolish to underestimate Orsino, but he was not going to outrace her by struggling over slippery rocks through clouds of acrid steam. If she really set her mind to it, she could easily think up scenarios that undermined her plan: maybe he had an accomplice working in the fish ponds who could conceal the book, allowing him to emerge empty-handed; maybe he'd confound his pursuers' expectations completely by doubling back and heading south. Anything was possible. But if, as she believed, he'd always hoped to walk out of the museum without waking anyone, granting him so much of a head start that there'd be no point trying to give chase, his first steps before he knew he was being followed would be enough to reveal his intended destination: north to Melus, or north then west, through the Hoop, to deliver the book under another sky to whoever had incited him to take it.

She reached the crossroads and turned left. She could see a couple of people walking in the distance, one traveling toward her, one the other way, but neither bore any resemblance to Orsino. She nodded a greeting as she passed the first, and then veered a few paces off the road as she overtook the second, so as not to startle the poor man into dropping the bundle of dried reeds he was carrying on his back.

The clouds that had moved in from the west were beginning to break up. Del could see the bottom of the northern edge of the Hoop as a sharp line, where part of the cloud bank stretching into Ladalla was abruptly replaced by a clear, star-strewn sky. She glanced back to the east; Takya had almost set, so Audrey would be following her soon. All they needed now was Orsino's cooperation; just let him grow weary of the stink of the ponds and the rice fields, and tired of all the agricultural workers asking him if he was lost.

Del stopped running when she judged she was a little farther from the crossroads than Orsino had been, west to his south, when he'd left the road. If he'd committed to cutting the corner but found it heavy going, it seemed reasonable to suppose that he would have compromised and settled on traveling more or less north-west. She searched the roadside to the north for a suitable place to wait; after a while, she found a low bush she could crouch behind, thick enough to conceal her heat, but sparse enough to peek through.

She squatted down and took a few mouthfuls of water from her flask, grateful to wash away the lingering taste of sulfur.

As she waited, she pictured the scene at the museum. The director would be arriving soon, expecting to find a very different state of affairs. Del felt most keenly for Jachimo, who was sure to bear the brunt of things in her absence. But if she could bring the book back swiftly, the whole disaster could be seen for what it was: a betrayal no one could have anticipated or prepared for.

When she noticed the heat blotch approaching from the east, Del's first thought was that Audrey was making good time. But this runner did not have Audrey's loping gait. Del was torn; was it better to remain concealed, in the hope that Orsino, believing he'd escaped her attention, would slow down of his own accord, or better to start harassing him so he wasted time on her while Audrey closed in?

She had no idea, but she couldn't bring herself to let him pass. As he drew near, she stepped out onto the road.

Orsino stopped dead. "Go home," he said impatiently, wiping sweat from his forehead with the edge of one hand. "This is not your concern."

Del was bemused. "How can you say that?"

"Did you buy the book? Did you pay something for it?"

"No, but the museum had an agreement to restore it, and protect it."

Orsino was unimpressed. "You didn't even dig it out of the rubble. Jessica and Lucius might have some complaint against me, for robbing them of the benefits of their labor. But who are you to interfere?"

"Their intention was to hand the book into my custody. If you acknowledge their labor, acknowledge their wishes."

Orsino laughed. "Duly noted. But to acknowledge a thing is not to defer to it. They invested time and effort in Seena that led to their possession of the book, but in the end they still just took it from the ruined house of its long dead owner. They had no more claim to it than anyone else alive."

Del wasn't sure if he really was trying to construct some kind of moral theory that excused his actions, or if he was just mocking her for thinking she could shame him into handing back the book. But every moment she delayed him would bring Audrey nearer.

"We all have Tollean ancestry," she said, "and none of us can prove we're more closely related to the owner than anyone else. But if I restored the book, the translation would be made available to everyone. And anyone who wanted could travel to Apasa to view the original."

"How do you know it's not headed for exactly the same fate, elsewhere?" Orsino replied.

"Then why not just leave it in Apasa? If the outcome's going to be the same, either way?"

Orsino regarded her with a kind of pity: how could anyone need to ask? "Because I'm being paid much more to take the book than I ever was to guard it." He strode forward and brushed past her.

Del waited for him to glance back and see her staring dejectedly at the ground, and then continue on his way, before she started following him. When he looked back again, he turned and drew his dagger. "Do I really need to hurt you?"

"If you want to be left in peace, you need to return the book."

"The book's lost to you. Just accept that, and go home."

Del said nothing. Orsino started down the road again, and she did too. Suddenly he turned and charged at her, holding the dagger up as he ran; she fled as fast as she could, her skin prickling with fear even though she was easily escaping him, and kept running until she saw that he'd given up the chase and continued his journey. She waited a while, then went after him again, matching his pace as best she could, maintaining a safe distance between them.

The next time, he stopped without even looking at her. He crouched down and massaged his calves, then he turned and headed back toward her.

"We're reasonable people, aren't we?" he yelled. "We can work this out!" So far, he'd kept his dagger in its sheath, and his measured pace seemed intended to reassure her that he wasn't going to rush her again.

Del didn't reply, but she stood her ground as he approached. What was he proposing? Was he going to offer her a bribe? If this was just a ruse to try to come close enough to stab her, she was ready to run.

Orsino stopped a dozen paces away, and put his hands behind his head. "Is this really so important to you?" he asked.

"That depends," she replied.

"On what?"

"Is the book going to another museum, or to a private collector?"

Orsino smiled. "Whatever I told you, I doubt that you'd believe me."

"Then just give it back," she said. "If you weren't paid well enough to guard it, you shouldn't have taken the job."

That amused him even more. He turned his upper body to one side then the other, keeping his hands behind his head, as if he was limbering up in preparation for the next stage of the race. Then he brought his left arm back and threw something toward her, striking her on the knee.

Del shouted from the pain and stumbled, but managed to remain upright. Orsino turned and walked away. After a while, he broke into a run; Del couldn't see his face, but she pictured him smugly exuberant, celebrating his own effortless strides, spared the need to draw blood but certain now that she'd never catch up with him.

She lowered herself awkwardly onto the road. The stone hadn't been all that large, and she didn't think it had fractured the bone, but if she tried to move while her knee was still throbbing she was afraid she'd just exacerbate the problem.

She looked to the east. Finally, Audrey was coming. Del tried to distance herself from her wounded pride, and judge the remaining possibilities realistically. Maybe Audrey could chase down Orsino, unaided. Maybe she should just sit here, resting, and hope that everything would be resolved without her.

She turned to the west and watched Orsino receding. But Audrey wouldn't have him in her sights yet; if he left the road or took a turn, she'd have no way of knowing which way he'd gone.

Del struggled to her feet, keeping her injured leg as straight as she could, then tested its function. She couldn't use it normally, but if she favored her other leg she could walk well enough, with a certain amount of pain. She started hobbling along the road, then she tried a different gait, pushing off hard with her good foot then just bearing the shock of landing on the other, without expecting it to do any work.

Gradually, she increased her speed, running as she might if one limb had been replaced with a crude prosthesis — wary of her balance, and wishing the offending leg really was as insensate as wood. Squinting into the distance, she could still make out Orsino, and when she looked back, she saw Audrey steadily gaining on her. Maybe she could do this after all: keep moving long enough to serve as an intermediary, bridging the gap and showing Audrey the way.

After a while she fell into a rhythm that carried her along at a respectable rate without threatening to send her toppling at the first pothole. The pain had lost its scream of insistence, as if her body had decided to accede to her judgment that what she was doing was important enough that the ongoing insult simply had to be borne.

The edge of the Hoop was almost in front of her, emerging from a fractured hilltop a little to her north. Del followed the arc across the sky — tracing the parts where clouds gave way to stars as if they'd been truncated with a knife — and found herself growing vertiginous, not so much at the familiar sight as at the knowledge that elsewhere there were mountain ranges high enough to block the giant aperture completely. Had the Tolleans found a way through those mountains? Some secret crevice or subterranean river? Half the commentators she'd read discussing the supposed route to the Bounteous Lands had dismissed it as a fantasy, while others had judged it plausible but too perilous to traverse. But she had no intention of letting Orsino rob her of the chance to make her own assessment.

Ladalla lay ahead of her now, albeit a part of it indistinguishable from Thena's own patch of cracked obsidian. But the first town through the Hoop, Paveen, was not far away. If Orsino's buyer was waiting for him there, they could hardly perform the transaction without pause, like runners in a relay race. Del pictured a scene in the tavern in Paveen where the handoff had been intended to take place, with all the patrons – swayed by Audrey's testimony seconding her own – united to hold Orsino back as she approached the stolen package—

An unwelcome datum interrupted her reverie. Orsino had left the road to Paveen, and taken a side road that ran to the north: straight toward the hill at the edge of the Hoop.

Del cursed him, unable to decide if this was an elaborate feint, or just part of the journey he'd planned from the start. If he skirted the edge of the Hoop and then kept on westward, he would remain in Thena, but he might just as easily double back and enter the Hoop from the opposite side, taking him into Beremma.

Had she been uninjured, she might have risked leaving the road and heading north-west, but the mix of scrubland and volcanic rock looked like it would send her sprawling. She raised an arm and gestured right, in the hope that Audrey might take the shortcut in her stead, but when she looked back the signal had had no effect.

Orsino reached the ring road that circled the hill from which the Hoop's edge emerged. To Del's surprise, he turned left – sending him, at least for the moment, into Ladalla, but now offering him the chance either to exit and travel on to Eastern Ladalla, or to pass through the Hoop a second time in the same direction, entering Juthena.

Del tried to move faster, but her leg was firmly committed to her present hard-won gait. Orsino disappeared behind the hill. Whatever choices he made now, unless he turned around and retraced his steps she'd lost any hope of seeing him emerge in the same manner as he'd vanished.

The turnoff leading to the hill was right ahead of her; Del took it, pushing on defiantly through a haze of half-voiced protests that she refused to let crystallize and undermine her cause. The sky before her was bisected, with mismatched tufts of clouds to her left and right, and above them mismatched constellations. Living so close to the Hoop, she was familiar with most of Ladalla's western sky, as some Ladallans were with the stars to her east, but over time people had sown confusion by picking different names for the shared constellations, then learning each other's nomenclature and forgetting who had chosen which.

She glanced back and saw that Audrey had left the western road and was taking her chances with a cross-country sprint. Del reached the ring road and turned left, taking heart that at least the two of them wouldn't be split up. Her fondest wish now was to give Orsino one more chance to sneer at her futile efforts, before he found himself confronted by an uninjured and unflagging nemesis that he'd never even known was coming.

As she circled the hill, her changing perspective revealed progressively more of a bank of low clouds on her right, much as if she were circling any ordinary obstacle – except the "obstacle" was another patch of sky, which in turn was being progressively obscured. Her instinctive, but unwinnable battle to assign roles of foreground and background left her with a sense that either she was skirting a huge, mirrored tower, or – as her gut seemed to find more plausible – she'd eaten something that unhinged her perceptions to the point where her body would be better off discarding it as a likely poison.

As she came halfway around the hill, she switched her attention to the surrounding landscape. Orsino would have to leave the ring road eventually, and that would be her chance to catch sight of him again, fleeing across open ground. Once he was clear of the Hoop he could still swerve and double-back all he liked, but it would be far harder to disguise his actual destination.

The corner of Eastern Ladalla near the Hoop's northern edge was every bit as scrubby and barren as the same part of Thena; the rocks and soil of the two regions were more or less contiguous, after all. It was only when Del lifted her gaze higher that the comforts of familiarity fell away. She had visited some nearby towns in Western Ladalla, but she had never had reason to come around to this side of the Hoop – so she had never seen any of the constellations that now shone in the east. For the first time in her life, she had no idea what anyone called half the stars above her. And for the first time in her life, she'd need to give up the notion that, clouds permitting, Takya was guaranteed to make an appearance before too long. Ladalla had no moons of its own, and from this side of the Hoop, no view of Thena's.

Del let the melancholy sense of estrangement sit with her; unsettling as it was, the fact remained that she could turn around and head home whenever she liked. All the children's stories she'd heard of hapless travelers somehow losing track of the number of times they'd circled the edge of the Hoop had been comically entertaining, but she was a very long way from getting lost herself. The only thing she had reason to fear right now was losing Orsino.

As she scanned the scrubland, she could not rule out the possibility that he had chosen to dig in behind a bush and wait for her to circle out of view. She wanted to believe that he was arrogant enough to have abandoned all caution once he'd slowed her down with the stone, but that was probably wishful thinking. He was smart and skillful enough to have copied the vault keys without her or Jachimo noticing – but still careless enough to have made whatever small noise had woken her as he departed. She just needed him to make one more error.

Three-quarters of the way around the hill, though she still hadn't set foot in Juthena, the third sky of the journey began to show through the Hoop. A delicate swathe of light, which she supposed was an agglomeration of stars too close for her eyes to separate, stretched across the view like an ethereal ribbon.

Del tore her gaze away from the spectacle and concentrated on the land around her. When she came full circle, the layout of the roads to the south might have been copied from that between Thena and Ladalla, but the terrain itself was unmistakably different, with thicker grass and fewer sharp edges to the rocks. Looking toward Juthena, she hoped for a glimpse of Orsino jogging along the western road, but instead she was rewarded with the sight of distant lanterns, and singing carried to her in snatches on the breeze. Some kind of festival, she supposed.

She kept running. The pain in her knee was like a drumbeat to which she'd grown accustomed, and when she thought of slowing down or stopping the prospect was alarming, as if she'd habituated to such a precise set of sensations that disturbing the pattern by resting would be as unwelcome as any other change.

That the hill presented a different profile to her the second time around was reassuring – inasmuch as it reduced any risk of confusion, when she was growing ever less scornful toward the disoriented protagonists of the children's tales. Juthena's stars lit up the ground on her left in exquisite detail, but if Orsino had ever crossed this land, he was already out of sight.

In Sarana the stars were sparser, the ground curiously lush.

In Tethemma there were more clouds drifting by, but even through the breaks a darker sky.

As Del rounded the hill yet again, the light falling on the road ahead was so bright and sharp that she assumed she was approaching a group of travelers bearing lanterns, marching in silence. She slowed down, afraid of blundering disrespectfully into the midst of a funeral procession.

Sarana, Tethemma ... Erema? It was unforgivable that she wasn't sure. There were too many lands to commit every single one to memory, but these were the immediate neighbors that every child in Apasa learned.

Erema it was. And in Erema, famously—

The light striking her face carried none of the warmth of a flame, but the mere act of seeing it was as painful as a needle through flesh. Del tried squinting, but it was not enough. She took a few steps with her eyes closed, but then came to her senses and stopped.

She backed away, her leg throbbing, until only a sliver of the new sky remained in view. The stars were so bright that each one alone was like a lantern; she had to hold up a hand and peer between her fingers to keep her eyes from watering.

Travelers could accommodate to the brightness, she'd heard, by wrapping a long strip of fabric around their head and gradually unwinding it. But when they departed it would take them just as long to readapt to normal conditions. If she'd planned a journey through Erema that entailed merely circling the edge of the Hoop, she would have arranged in advance for a local guide to be here to lead her, blindfolded, from ordinary sky to ordinary sky.

Maybe Orsino had made precisely those arrangements. Or maybe he'd just fled, eyes closed, stumbling across the dazzling ground, sure that no one from Thena would have any hope of following him.

Whatever he'd done, he was out of her reach now. The book was gone, and Erema's stars blazed down upon a road that she had no reason to travel. *And you thought you were going to find the way to the Bounteous Lands, where one star lies so close that it gives life to the entire world?*

Del contemplated sitting and resting for a while, but when she pictured the necessary maneuver her leg interjected with an immediate veto. So she turned and headed back the way she'd come.

Audrey appeared, slowing as she approached, clearly disappointed by the message in Del's demeanor, but not surprised. "We did our best," she said. "I'll vouch for that to your employer, if you'll do the same for mine."

Del was too tired to laugh.

"You can lean on my shoulder if you like," Audrey offered. "Take the weight off your leg. I don't think either of us will be running, and it's going to be a long walk home."

Chapter 3

"I'd like to look at some maps, please."

"Of course." Del took the new arrival's name, Montano, and added him to the list. "Please have a seat. It could be a while."

She pointed to the row of chairs she'd placed in the corridor leading to the map room. Not long afterward, the most recent visitor emerged, frowning resentfully, still awkwardly sliding sheets of paper into the portfolio she was carrying.

"Claudio?" Del called.

"Yes!" The next-in-line rose to his feet and followed her in, his enthusiasm apparently undiminished by the disappointment he must have seen on his predecessors' faces as they departed. But then, if they had found nothing in their research to encourage them, it could only mean that his own idea stood a better chance of being uniquely successful.

"Which maps would you like to view?" Del asked.

"Sadema."

"From what period?"

"The earliest you have."

Del pointed to the map table. "These are mid-Vitean." There was nothing to be fetched or put away. All the would-be explorers wanted the same thing.

She checked that the lamp wasn't short of oil, then turned over the hour-glass. "Don't feel obliged to stay here watching the sand fall if you're already done," she said. Twice, she'd walked in on people who had set the maps aside in frustration, but were waiting out their allotted time, presumably just for the sake of inconveniencing their rivals.

"I won't."

Del left him and returned to her desk, where she started her own timer, then resumed work on the translation she'd been struggling with. If you "broke" a knot, using the same Tollean word as you would if you broke a fence, did that mean you cut through the rope that was knotted, or that you untangled the knot without damaging the rope? The passage she was stuck on offered no clues, but if the meaning was settled she ought to be able to extract it from other examples.

But as she followed the trail through the corpus of fragments she was relying on for exactly that purpose, she just found the ambiguities multiplying. If you "overcame" a conflict with an enemy, did they submit to your superior forces, or was the dispute amicably resolved? And if you "resolved" a plot against you, did the plotters end up dead, or were their grievances dealt with in good faith? Del knew how to discriminate between the possibilities in her own language, but in Tollean the rickety scaffolding of contextual hints and potential synonyms at her disposal was too loose, too unconstrained, to guide her to the correct meaning.

Varro put up the CLOSED sign on the front door, and approached Del. "You want me to empty the queue?" he asked.

"No, it's fine." There were only two people left. "You can leave if you like. I'll lock up."

Varro regarded her sourly. "I'm not meant to leave while there are still people in the building."

"As you wish," Del replied. "I don't want to keep you from your family. But it doesn't seem fair to throw people out. I promise I'll watch over them carefully."

He hesitated, but then seemed to decide that it wasn't worth arguing about. "All right. I'll see you later."

Del was glad not to have to eject anyone, but she paid the price for her promise of vigilance. Despite all the extra locked doors that now lay between the public areas and the most valuable items, it was hard not to be distracted by the possibility that she might glance up and find that she'd lost track of a potential thief.

By the time she led the last visitor down the corridor, all she wanted was to be rid of him, so she could make herself a meal and get some sleep.

"Which maps would you like to view?" she asked.

"Celema," Montano replied.

Del hadn't really been listening. "I'm sorry?"

"Celema, please. I believe the most recent survey is listed in your catalog. You do have it, don't you?"

"Yes, of course. I'll get it." Del carefully placed the Vitean maps of Sadema back in their sleeve and carried them into the storeroom, then returned with the modern atlas of Celema.

She left Montano to consult the maps, resisting the urge to inquire into the reasons for his interest. The theft of *The Book of All Skies* had prompted the Council of Apasa to offer a substantial prize – not for the book's return, which might have been construed as a ransom, but for anyone able to deduce the coveted secret supposedly contained within its pages by their own independent means. It was a way of thumbing their nose at the thieves: take the book, we don't need it! If the Tolleans had found a way to the Bounteous Lands, why couldn't their descendants do the same? And since Sadema was the only land whose terrain appeared to render one of the Hoops impassable, where else could the crucial path lie, but through those formidable mountains?

Del gave up on the passage about broken knots and continued with the rest of the page. She appreciated Jessica entrusting her with even these few loose sheets from the excavation; it was a gracious gesture that made her refusal to lay the blame for the theft at Del's feet more believable than any number of reassuring words. But nothing Del or anyone else had said had been enough to spare Jachimo from the director's anger.

She heard the door to the map room open, and checked her timer; the last grains were trickling down.

Montano approached her desk. "Since there's no one else waiting, I don't suppose there's any chance I could have a little longer, just to finish this?"

Del glanced down at the thick sheet of paper that lay on top of a bundle he was holding; it looked as if he'd copied almost every detail from one of the maps, with great fidelity. "Are you an artist?" she asked.

"I sketch things," he replied. "Maps, machines. I don't know if that counts as art."

Del was growing hungry, but it seemed petty to force him to come back later. "All right," she said.

As soon as he walked away she regretted the decision; she no longer had Varro around to help if she had to drag this man out of the map room. But true to his word, he emerged a short time later.

"Now I realize I've kept you at your post," he said. "In compensation, can I buy you a meal?"

Del was silent for longer than she'd intended; she should have replied at once that such a favor was unnecessary.

"There's also a matter I'm hoping to discuss with you," Montano admitted.

"What's that?"

"I might have an offer of employment, for someone with your language skills." He gestured at the pages on her desk. "You speak Tollean?"

"I read it," she said. "I don't think anyone really knows how it sounded."

"My mistake. But even knowing its structure is sure to be of use."

Of use for what? She had no interest in searching the mountains of Sadema for secret Tollean inscriptions. But apparently neither did Montano. Whatever he had in mind, he deserved a fair hearing.

"I'll need to lock you out while I tidy up," she said, apologetically. "But it won't be long."

When she joined Montano, they set off down the hill into town. "Do you like Ereman food?" he asked, as they approached a cluster of restaurants.

"I don't think I've ever tried it," Del confessed. "But why not? At least the place should be well-lit."

Montano led the way. The restaurant turned out to be hidden down an alley, but its windows really did shine brighter than any of its competitors.

Inside, the place wasn't crowded, and they were quickly seated at a good table and handed menus. Del had no idea what any of the dishes were, but she was too ravenous to waste time quizzing the staff, so she asked Montano to order two of whatever he liked himself.

While they waited for the food, he fidgeted with his portfolio, then finally placed it on the floor, resting against a table leg.

"Did you get what you needed from the maps?" Del asked him.

"I think so," he said. "I would have bought one of the atlases myself if I could, but the publisher made so few that they're almost unobtainable."

Del wasn't surprised. "Celema is a nub. There are geologists with an interest in every corner of the world, but beyond that there's not much demand for maps of an uninhabited region that doesn't even lie on the route to … well, anywhere."

Montano smiled. "And you know all the routes? Without exception?"

Del hesitated, but then decided she wasn't willing to retract her claim just to accommodate an overly generous definition of *anywhere*. "I don't doubt that you could keep passing through the Hoops beyond Celema, if you had some means of moving safely through the void. But even if you ended up beneath new skies, what good would that do you with no land beneath your feet?"

"How do you think the world formed?" Montano asked.

Del shook her head. "Don't ask me to choose between competing theories. Maybe the Hoops collided with a huge body of rock, and the pressure in its interior squeezed it through the apertures, over and over, until it was spread so thinly that it lost the force to keep going. Or maybe the Hoops wandered into a dust cloud, and the dust drifted through, coming together into a solid body much later. But either way, the rock we see now shows no sign of going on forever. If we follow any path, we get to a nub eventually." Well, any path that didn't strike the obstruction in

Sadema, but clearing a way through the mountains would surely just reveal the same situation on the other side.

"I have no quarrel with any of that," Montano replied. "But now, tell me how you think the Hoops work."

"If I knew how the Hoops worked," Del retorted, "I'd be famous in every land."

"You know what I mean," Montano insisted. "Not some deep secret concerning their nature or origin: just the practical matter of discerning when two travelers end up beneath the same sky."

Del grew a little self-conscious. "I know what my mother taught me, what every child I know was told. Take a ball of clay and embed two rings in it, so that parts of each ring emerge from opposite sides of the ball. The ball is like a map of the world as it would be if the Hoops were just ordinary rings – but there's also a simple way to show their true effect. If two travelers set out from the same town, and you trace the routes they take on the surface of the ball, you can't conclude that they'll meet up with each other just because their paths meet on the clay. Instead, you need to take two reels of thread, slip the ends of both of them through a needle that you stick into the clay to mark the home town, and then unwind the thread along each traveler's path. If their paths seem to cross at some point, cut the threads free of the reels there and tie their ends together, making a loop between the start and end of the journey. If you can pull that whole loop through the eye of the needle, without it getting snagged on the rings, then the two travelers must have passed through the Hoops in exactly the same way – so they really did end up beneath the same sky. But if the loop gets stuck on a ring, that will prove that the travelers took such different routes that they ended up at different destinations."

The food arrived. Montano had chosen a dish of fish and vegetables; Del sampled it warily. The flavor from the spices was unusual, but not unpleasant.

"Is it all right?" he asked.

"It's fine," Del assured him. "Are you going to tell me what's wrong with my folksy ball of clay and its threads?"

Montano laughed. "It's exactly the metaphor I learned myself. I'm not going to disparage anyone for putting their trust in it, when it's served us so well. But I do claim that it hasn't been tested quite as extensively as it might have been."

Del said, "Everywhere we've been, the Hoops have behaved the same way: if your path passes through them in a manner that would tangle up a thread, you find yourself beneath a different sky whenever the thread is differently tangled. If we could get through the mountains of Sadema, we could see if the same holds true in all the other lands – but you're not interested in those mountains, are you? You want to go to the nub at Celema, and ... what? *Travel through the void?*"

"Not immediately," Montano said. "Not without encouragement or reason. Not without evidence that the journey would succeed."

"Oh, that's all right then."

He smiled, but then his demeanor became solemn. "I had a sister, Natasha. She died in the plague."

"I'm sorry," Del said. "It took both my parents."

Montano winced. "Everyone I know has lost someone. It was a horrible time."

"Yes." Del waited for him to regain his thread.

He said, "My sister was a student of the natural sciences. More than a student, though she was young when she died and not much heeded by more experienced colleagues. You're familiar with the law of universal gravity?"

"I was born beneath two moons," Del replied. "Whatever people with unchanging skies might believe, I'm convinced by the evidence of my own eyes."

"Natasha studied that law," Montano said, "and the way it should be applied in the presence of the Hoops. The Hoops hide some land that we could see were they not present, but also reveal new land in its place.

When the land that is obscured and the land that is revealed are more or less equivalent, in shape and constitution, the Hoops make very little difference, and the gravity that pulls on Takya and Bradya is almost the same as if they were circling a simple ball of clay.

"But at the nubs, those two things could not be less in balance. The land ends, and through the Hoop there is only void. The precise way the influence of gravity passes through the Hoops can't be neglected anymore, if you wish to understand the situation properly."

"That makes sense," Del agreed.

"My sister wrestled with the mathematics of the problem," Montano said, "and she believed she found the answer. In the presence of the Hoops, gravity does not spread out uniformly; it follows a more complicated rule of disbursement that only yields the familiar law when the contributory masses are suitably balanced. I plan to travel to the nub at Celema and measure the strength of gravity there, to see if her ideas are in accord with the reality."

It was clear from his tone that his aim, in part, was to honor his sister's memory. But that couldn't be the whole story.

"Even if you prove Natasha right," Del pressed him, "where does that leave you?"

"Suppose," Montano replied, "that a twisted thread need not stay twisted. Suppose that if you circled the edge of the same Hoop again and again in the same direction, instead of finding yourself ever more tangled, you reached a point where the thread came free. Or in plainer terms: you found yourself back where you started."

Del frowned. "So you travel to the nub at Celema, and then keep going – somehow – through the void. In the hope that, eventually ... you end up where you began?"

Montano said, "Not literally, though – not if you began somewhere like Thena. We need to imagine a traveler who does nothing but go round and round the same part of the same Hoop."

"All right." Del pictured such a traveler. If you traced their journey backward, eventually you arrived at ... Sadema. "The path you're talking about would need to have come *through the mountains from Sadema.*"

"Exactly." Montano beamed at her as if the two of them were now in perfect agreement.

"But those mountains are still impassable," Del complained.

"Yes. But they only block the path at that point. If the path joins up with its own beginning, it's no different from any other circle. You can't block a circle at one point; you can always avoid the obstruction by going the other way around."

"Oh." So the journey through the void beyond Celema would lead, first, to another nub that no contemporary traveler had ever seen, and from there, across some unknown number of new lands ... all the way to whatever lay on the far side of the mountains of Sadema.

"I think I understand," Del said. "But what if the thread just grows more tangled? What if you can go around and around forever, never ending up where you began?"

"That's conceivable," Montano admitted. "But that's where my sister's work offers us the means to decide if the journey is worth taking. If all there is beyond Celema is void, her law will give one answer for the gravity there. But if, beyond the void, there lies a great mass of land, stretched out toward us but not quite closing the circle, we should be able to discern its influence. Then we can head toward it – blindly in a sense, in that we have no hope of seeing it at the moment of departure – but as confident of its existence as we are of the far shore of any river or ocean."

Chapter 4

"Who would carry out your duties, in your absence?" the director asked.

"I wouldn't be leaving for a while yet," Del replied. "If we could bring in someone to train for the role, it shouldn't take long for them to learn the most pressing tasks. Dealing with the public, and so forth."

"And what about the rest?" the director demanded. "Proper handling of the artefacts? Conditions of storage? Restoration techniques? Your own mentor stood by you patiently, while you learned those skills."

Del lowered her gaze. The director's office was always brightly lit, but now it seemed to be impossible to face her interlocutor while avoiding the glare of the lamps spread out behind him. "When I come back, I'd be happy to do the same for my replacement."

"But you can't even say when that would be!" he protested.

"I can't," she admitted. "Montano's expedition will be subject to all manner of uncertainties." But there were no new acquisitions on the horizon, or other urgent tasks requiring her attention. It was not as if she was abandoning the museum forever, or walking out in the middle of some elaborate project that would fall apart without her supervision.

"You do know they're all charlatans," the director said bluntly. "All these so-called explorers. Of course there are 'uncertainties'. If they were forced to tell the truth without prevaricating, no one would invest in them at all."

Del wanted to speak in Montano's defense; he'd made it clear that he had no need of secrecy, and she was at liberty to expound on his sister's ideas and his own plans in as much detail as she wished. But she couldn't imagine the director finding any of it persuasive; better that he assume she was running off to Sadema with all the other fortune hunters who thought they could dig their way through a mountain.

"I'm resolved to do this," she said. "I'll help in any way I can to reduce the difficulties that might be caused by my absence, but I won't be dissuaded from the choice I've made."

The director regarded her with an expression Del took to be a kind of morose acceptance. She had wondered if he would start haranguing her about the opportunities she'd been given, and the ingratitude and disloyalty she was now displaying. But perhaps he knew as well as she did that at the first invocation of the word *loyalty*, everything she'd restrained herself, so far, from saying about Jachimo's dismissal would start tumbling out, and then there'd be no unsaying it.

"I have no wish to replace you," he said. "Not until you're a great deal closer to retirement – at which point I expect to be long gone, myself. I'll find someone who can act as a stopgap while you're off on this misadventure."

"Thank you." Del felt a twinge of guilt; this was exactly what she'd hoped for, but now her own treatment stood in even starker contrast to Jachimo's.

She left the office and returned to her desk. Varro, who'd been watching over the map room queue, departed to make his usual rounds of the building.

Del glanced over at the line of hopeful cave diviners, mountain pass aficionados, and subterranean river devotees. It was easy to mock their conviction that they'd be the ones to find a route that everyone else had missed for the last thousand generations, but at least they weren't demanding anything more of the world than the unarguable fact that a large body of rock might contain hitherto uncharted passages from one side to the other. An ant might be disappointed when it ran up and down a wall searching for a crack, but it was not deluded merely for having tried.

There was really only one thing that nudged her own assessment of Montano's chances very slightly in his favor. She looked down again at the troublesome passage in the commentary on *The Book of All Skies*, where an anonymous author asked: could a knot be broken? They seemed to believe that it could – but in the context, what exactly did that mean? That a traveler meandering across a mountainside might stumble on a path that cut through the range from one side to the other? Or that a thread that seemed hopelessly tangled from winding around the edge of a Hoop dozens of times could suddenly be pulled free?

The writer didn't say. The meaning of the language and its metaphors relied on clues and shared assumptions that had long since vanished. She might well be hallucinating any connection with Montano's ideas, as surely as the other prize-hunters were ascribing unearned significance to every ambiguous line or cross-hatching on the maps of Sadema.

And even if Montano *had* stumbled on precisely the notion that had raised such excitement across the Tollean world, that wouldn't prove that he, and the Tolleans before him, were correct. But the chance to walk in their footsteps, and to see a new test of an idea that they might have struggled to prove or disprove themselves, was too alluring a prospect to resist.

If the expedition came to nothing, she could return to her job, duly humbled, and go back to puzzling over the same infuriating ambiguities, scattered across the same few fragile pages.

But if it came to fruition, anything was possible. Who knew what was waiting, on the far side of the void?

Chapter 5

When Montano invited Del to a gathering at his house to meet her fellow expeditioners, she arrived expecting a crowd. After all his talk of struggling to raise the capital needed for the journey, she'd imagined they'd be setting out with dozens of crates of equipment and supplies, borne by twice as many carriers.

"This is Silvio, our navigator and surveyor," Montano said. "Clarissa, our architect. And Imogen, who's an experienced diver."

"Pleased to meet you," Del said. There was no one else in the room. She turned to Montano to ask if he was snubbing the less skilled laborers, but then caught herself in time; it probably made sense for them to acquire any bulky materials they'd need much closer to Celema, and to hire a workforce locally, once they knew exactly what was required.

Montano showed her to her seat and lit a second lamp.

"You've walked under the ocean?" Del asked Imogen. She'd heard of such feats, but she'd never met anyone who'd actually performed them.

"Many times," Imogen assured her. "Surviving in the void would be a different challenge, but I believe a diving suit could be adapted to meet it."

"I see."

"Silvio will be in charge of the gravitational measurements," Montano explained. "And Clarissa will design the bridge we need to travel across the gap."

Del decided not to risk a joke about their respective likelihoods of turning out to be dead weight, though she was clearly ranked lowest by that measure. Only Silvio was sure to have a job to do, but clearly Montano considered it worth paying the rest of them to tag along, to spare himself the delay of having to come back and fetch them.

"I suppose I'm here as punishment for losing *The Book of All Skies*," she said wryly. "I would have been content just to read what the Tolleans believed about the way to reach the Bounteous Lands, but now that that's impossible, what choice do I have but to try to make the same journey?"

"I was raised to believe that the Bounteous Lands were just a myth," Clarissa replied. "Even now, if I argue with my parents about it, they say there are hot springs hotter than the warmest air, so what need is there to invoke an unseen star just to warm us?"

"I thought those hot springs relied on tidal forces from that unseen star to keep the world's core molten," Silvio said.

Clarissa nodded in assent. "But if I mention that, they say if tides are to be invoked at all, there are plenty of moons to account for them."

Imogen said, "It can always be both. The world might well be cooler if there were no moons at all, but that doesn't mean they're sufficient."

Del had read of numerous attempts by people to quantify all the possible sources of heat, and the rate at which it was lost to the void, but without a map showing the full extent of the world the whole endeavor was plagued with uncertainty. The idea that the five of them sitting in this room might actually progress from sharing their armchair opinions on the matter to settling such questions once and for all seemed almost comical in its hubris. Still, it would be equally absurd for her to grow more skeptical of Montano's plans every time she thought of another potential benefit.

"These are the personal supplies that each of you should procure before departing," Montano said, handing out sheets of paper. "The expedition will cover the costs, of course."

Del looked over the list: a tent, a sleeping bag, items of clothing meeting various requirements, some suggested categories and quantities of food, and a bare minimum of pots, plates and utensils.

"We'll be able to restock our food and water regularly, most of the way," Montano promised, "but it seems prudent to have some non-perishable food in reserve from the start, just to cover all contingencies."

"Later, though, if we do ... cross over?" Del wondered.

Clarissa said, "There ought to be the same kinds of plants and animals there as we're used to. If there's water, there'll be fish, and if there's soil there'll be roots and berries."

"The mountains in Sadema have kept us divided for a long time," Imogen noted. "Who can say how the different sides might have diverged?"

Silvio was skeptical. "A barrier for us is not a barrier for every last seed, or spore, or insect. And whatever you think of the people hoping to paddle along an underground river, I'd bet you anything that fish have been swimming back and forth beneath the mountains all along."

"If we cross over," Montano said, "our first concern will be to understand the land we've arrived in. If it's full of friendly Tollean traders offering us delicious food, all the better – but if it turns out to be desert and wasteland for a hundred skies, we won't just march on, unprepared. We won't take another step until we're ready."

Chapter 6

"How's the warehouse?" Del asked Jachimo.

"A bit boring, compared to the museum," he conceded. "But they pay me better."

"You can't live on-site, though."

"I wouldn't want to." He shook his head, irritated. "Stop fretting about me! I've landed on my feet. And I'm not here to rake over the past; I'm here to wish you a safe journey."

"Thank you." Del looked around the garden at the families of the other expeditioners, gathered in groups beside the lanterns, laughing together. She'd chatted with them all, and performed the same party trick as she'd done for the investors, reciting a plausible guess at how a greeting in Tollean might be pronounced. But now she was just impatient to depart.

"Try some of the cake," she suggested to Jachimo, pointing to a plate on the table beside them. He obliged, then held out the last piece toward her.

"No. I've already eaten too much, and ... " She found her pack and hoisted it, pretending to stagger under the weight.

"So who's going to guard you against robbers?" Jachimo asked.

"We'll look after ourselves," she replied. "Since Orsino, I'm not sure I'd trust anyone who makes it their profession."

Jachimo pretended to be wounded. "That's my profession, too."

"You know what I mean. And what are they going to steal? My dried tomatoes?"

"Montano must be carrying some gold, to pay for all the workers he might end up hiring."

"No, I think that's all been arranged between the investors and their banks. He does have letters of introduction, but it would be difficult for anyone else to make use of them." Del hadn't enquired into the matter too closely, afraid that any excessive curiosity might arouse suspicion. "His family has done business all over the world," she said. "I'm sure he knows what he's doing, on the commercial side."

"And the geographic?" Jachimo asked pointedly.

"Well, he's trusting in his sister there," Del replied. "And I'm in no position to judge the correct laws of gravity by staring at the formulas she wrote. So I suppose we'll find out exactly how brilliant she was when we get to Celema."

"I want you to be safe, that's all."

"I know. And I promise you, I'll be careful."

Montano climbed up onto a table. "Thank you for coming!" he yelled, then he waited for the guests to fall silent. "Seeing our friends and family here, to wish us well and offer us encouragement, has left us in such ebullient spirits that we will set out with our steps quickened and our loads lightened. When we return, we'll be weary from our travels, but I believe we'll be bringing back answers that have been lost for a thousand generations. Until then, keep us in your thoughts, as we will keep you in ours."

He jumped down and picked up his pack. Jachimo embraced Del, and they parted; she ran to catch up with the others, who were already striding out of the garden.

They walked along the road in silence, past the grand houses of Montano's neighbors. Other people were going about their business, and they didn't glance twice at the group; away from the well-wishers assembled for the party, no one knew or cared what they were doing.

Del looked to the west and found the museum on its hilltop, silhouetted against Ladalla's stars. "If we were standing on Takya," she mused, "the stars themselves would rise and fall in the sky, just as Takya rises and falls for us."

Silvio laughed. "Are you trying to make my job harder? Up there, you couldn't navigate so easily by the stars – but it looks as if Takya turns in a way that keeps one side facing the world. So the world itself would be fixed in Takya's sky, the way the stars are fixed in ours."

"What if the world turned too?" Clarissa wondered. "Would it pass through the Hoops, so we kept finding ourselves beneath different skies? Or would it drag the Hoops along with it?"

Montano said, "I'm not sure that anything could make the Hoops turn." He gestured to the north-west. "My sister climbed the hill once. She stood near the Hoop, and threw a piece of wood straight at it – slicing the wood in two, while the Hoop showed no sign of being disturbed in the slightest. Even the sharpest, tautest wire would be set ringing by an encounter like that, but she couldn't discern the tiniest vibration."

"You think that settles the matter?" Clarissa asked.

"Probably not," Montano conceded. "Still, she said it was the most enjoyable experiment she'd ever done. The main lesson I took from it myself was to keep my distance, so I don't end up in pieces."

They reached the road to Ladalla, and then the stretch where Del had confronted Orsino. She had heard no news of the book turning up in any respectable museum, but she was still clinging to the hope that the recipient would at least take the trouble to have it professionally restored, and not just leave it in a private viewing cabinet to crumble away, unread.

As they approached the edge of the Hoop, Del found it hard not to feel a sense of unease, unassuaged by the fact that she'd suffered far more on her last journey from Orsino's stone than from any violation of geometric propriety. A tangled thread didn't mean she'd be trapped, so long as she could still unwind it; once she started around the hill, she'd retain the same ability as always to change her mind and retrace her steps.

"If we stayed at this edge, and just circled it until we hit the nub ... ?" she joked.

"We could try the same measurements," Montano conceded. "And see if the gap was small enough to bridge. But that would be a lot of work, for no reward."

Del wondered if he'd actually considered it, but then decided not to gamble with his chance of trying for the real thing at Celema. A successful bridge here would have made it easier to attract investors, but a failure might have scared them all off.

At the ring road they turned right, keeping them in Thena so they could enter the Hoop from the west. It hadn't rained for a while in Apasa, and it seemed that the dry spell had stretched at least this far; their footfalls raised a cloud of dust, too fine to see but dense enough to irritate their eyes and throats. When Del looked to her left, the two skies were filled with nothing but stars, leaving the edge almost indiscernible.

They completed the first circuit in silence, save for the occasional cough, but as they came full circle Silvio proclaimed, "Welcome to Beremma!" His parents lived here, but they'd come to the farewell party, so they were probably still enjoying the hospitality at Montano's house.

"How many skies have you seen for yourself?" Del asked him.

"Maybe ... thirty?" he guessed. "I know, that's not a lot, but don't worry, I've memorized the charts for all of them."

Del was astonished. "*All* of them?"

"The ones we can reach," he clarified, though Del had taken that as given.

"Is that something they test?" Clarissa asked. "For your navigator's license?"

"Yes. They put you in a domed room and project points of light onto the ceiling; you have to say which land you're in, and where. Each candidate is shown a dozen different skies to identify."

"And what about the paths?" Imogen challenged him. "If I name any two lands, can you tell me the paths that will take you between them?"

"Of course!"

"My head hurts just thinking about packing that much information into it," Imogen confessed.

"Well, my whole body hurts just thinking about walking underwater," Silvio replied, "so it's a good thing we won't need to exchange professions."

Del decided not to remind him that all five of them might need to don diving suits for part of the journey; she didn't want to dwell on that prospect herself.

Halfway through the second circuit, the ground beneath her feet began to feel less parched, as if there had been rain not long ago. She inhaled deeply and caught a whiff of some sulfurous vent nearby, but that was preferable to breathing in grit. They passed a woman with a wheelbarrow piled with vegetables, coming the other way, followed by several other farmers and traders taking the same route. When one man enquired where they were going, and Montano replied, "Celema", the man laughed as if it was a nonsense word.

The sky over Tullena bore wisps of cloud, and one exceptionally bright star to the north. "Do you know what that's called?" Del asked Silvio.

"No," he admitted cheerfully. "I know the shapes of the constellations, but not their names, let alone the names of the stars. Some of my friends learned all of that, and they say it helped them, but there are so many Hunters and Fish and Ploughs and Castles, in different positions in different skies, to me it just seemed like a recipe for confusion."

They circled through Tullena, Kerema, Sedalla, and Mossema. The names of the lands stretched back beyond recorded history, and they must have meant something to people at the time, but any system behind the choice of syllables had been lost. Del watched the hill changing shape with each circuit, the stars replaced, the clouds come and go. In Mossema, a long stretch of the ring road had been invaded by weeds, mysteriously resistant to the heavy trampling to which the rest of the surface attested.

"Only fourteen to go," Clarissa muttered, as they passed through the Hoop yet again. "I feel like a rat on a wheel."

"Didn't the Viteans train birds to carry messages from land to land?" Imogen recalled. "I don't know why that stopped."

"When the owners fell from power in the Palloran revolt," Del replied, "most of the birds ended up in the wild, and the practice died out."

"If the air wasn't too thin at the gap ... " Clarissa mused.

Montano laughed. "We could send a raptor over with a message, and see if it came back with a reply?"

"Why not?" Clarissa protested. "It might even be part of their natural behavior. Not the messages, but the crossing itself."

"Maybe you can get them to string a rope ladder for us, while they're at it," Imogen teased her.

"Maybe that's what the Tolleans did," Del suggested.

Silvio said, "If someone had the patience to set up camp in Celema and just watch the birds, who knows what they'd see?"

They were in Peralla now. Del looked up and spotted a single moon, cutting a black disk out of a smattering of stars. Silvio could probably tell her the ratio between its passage and Takya's, but she'd be gone from its domain long before the information was any use to her. The only count that mattered now was the count of their remaining orbits around the edge of the Hoop.

The conversation had fallen away again. Del listened to the footfalls of her companions and imagined it was a drumbeat urging her on, even as her own steps did the same for them.

Chapter 7

When the travelers entered Zeruma and turned off the ring road onto a highway running due east, Del half-expected to find herself staggering and giddy, like a child who'd been whirled by a parent too long finally deposited on solid ground. But though her balance remained undisturbed, she did feel disoriented from abandoning the circular course after so many repetitions; she kept glancing to her left expecting to see the hill in some form, and the edge of the Hoop rising from its peak.

"Here's Yarun, up ahead," Silvio announced. Del had already noticed a few lamps in the distance, but she'd kept silent, afraid she might have hallucinated them out of a sheer longing to be surrounded by buildings and people.

"We can rest in the tavern here," Montano said. "Get a meal and some sleep."

"We have our own tents!" Imogen protested.

Montano was amused. "There won't be much more luxury like this along the way, so we might as well take advantage of it."

As they entered the town, a heavy rain began to fall, which was enough to settle the matter for Del. Yarun looked small compared to Apasa, and the residents she glimpsed as heat blotches through the downpour seemed intent on hurrying away to their homes, but the tavern was right on the road, lit up and unmissable.

Inside, half a dozen diners were seated; some glanced at the group with looks of momentary curiosity, then turned back to their meals. Montano placed his pack on the floor beside an empty table, and caught the eye of the landlord.

"Take a seat," the man said. "I'll be with you shortly." As the five of them converged on the table, Del finally realized how weary she was. She had run longer distances than the path here from Apasa, but she'd never walked a tenth as far with a comparable load.

"More Apasans off to claim their prize in the mountains?" a man from a nearby table enquired. The jibe sounded friendly enough, but they were all too tired to respond immediately, and Del felt a growing tension in the silence, as if it might be taken as a kind of haughtiness.

"Not in the mountains," she replied, as cheerfully as she could. "When the tunnel-diggers go one way, we'll go another." That seemed like a reasonable compromise between downright evasion, and stating their intentions so explicitly as to invite a long discussion of their merits. In any case, the man just laughed and wished them luck.

The landlord brought a menu, and Del chose the first thing listed that promised to be hot and drenched in gravy.

"Are most people getting ready to sleep here, or have they just risen?" she wondered, addressing her companions in a low voice out of fear that the question might sound foolish to the locals.

"They look pretty warm to me," Silvio replied.

"What do you mean?"

Now Silvio was confused. "You've never used that?"

Imogen said, "It's not that widely known in Thena." She turned to Del. "Most people's body temperature is lowest when they rise. We follow the moons, but where there are none, people seem to take the cue from each other's heat blotches."

"Oh." Del was embarrassed; she thought of herself as well-read, so how could she have lived so long without knowing how their neighbors decided when to sleep?

The food came, and it lived up to all her hopes for it, leaving her with a glorious warmth lingering in her belly. "A hot breakfast isn't enough to confuse the matter?" she asked Imogen.

"Maybe for a traveler trying to make a quick judgment," Imogen conceded. "But when people get to see more of the cycle, I think they tend to slip into the same pattern without even thinking about it."

Montano spoke to the landlord about rooms; there were only three available, but the floors would be more than wide enough for a couple of sleeping bags.

As the five of them headed up the stairs, Del paused and glanced back toward the diners lingering contentedly at their tables; it seemed obvious now that they were drowsy, succumbing to sleep not emerging from it. Was it a coincidence that even at this remove, people were following more or less the same schedule as she'd been following when she departed? Or was there enough contact between neighbors to maintain a degree of synchrony over every land that could be reached by circling the same Hoop?

But as she turned away and continued her ascent, it struck her that she had no way of knowing exactly how long she had spent on the journey, and where the moons actually stood at this moment in Apasa's sky.

Chapter 8

Del was woken by angry shouting: an unfamiliar voice, yelling commands.

She clambered out of her tent and saw a woman approaching, wielding a dagger. She stumbled back and turned, preparing to flee; the woman screamed, "Stay where you are!"

Del cowered beside the tent while a man entered it and started throwing things out onto the ground. "Where's the money?" the woman demanded.

"You already have it all," Montano interjected. Del turned and saw him kneeling beside his own tent, his hands tied together behind his back. The others were gathered together, similarly restrained, a short distance away. Silvio and Imogen had been on watch while everyone else slept, but they must have been cornered at knifepoint before they had a chance to raise the alarm.

"This?" The woman held up a small cloth bag and shook it, grimacing with derision at the barely audible clinking, though to be fair, Del thought the cloth was probably dampening the sound considerably. "No one travels all the way to Sadema with this."

Montano didn't correct her, but then, stating their precise destination really wouldn't do much to dent the argument.

The man emerged from Del's tent. "Nothing," he grumbled. He approached her and forced her to her knees, then bound her hands with rope.

Del waited for Montano to explain to the robbers about his arrangements with the banks, but perhaps he'd already tried that. If they'd ambushed other travelers from Apasa who'd been carrying more coins, that might have raised their expectations for a similar yield.

"It's inside you, isn't it?" the woman declared. "All of you? Some of you?" She regarded Del with an expression of revulsion, apparently disgusted by her own hypothesis. "I don't want my hands soiled groping around inside your filthy cavities! Just admit it, and we'll let you perform a dignified extraction."

Del gazed back at her, speechless. The woman turned to the others. "Come on! Whoever's carrying the coins, speak up! If we have to search you all, no one's going to be the better for it."

No one spoke. The woman strode over to Clarissa, grabbed her by the hair, and started dragging her along the ground.

Montano shouted, "Stop! I have more coins! Leave her!"

The woman released Clarissa and approached him. "So if I untie your hands and put you in a tent with a bowl of water, you'll do the dirty work and come out with my money, all cleaned up for me?"

Montano said, "Yes, but it might take a while. I didn't shove them up my anus; I swallowed them."

The woman was skeptical. "You'd risk damaging the coins with your digestive juices? Or rupturing your innards on a sharp edge?"

"Gold's not that easily corroded," Montano replied. "And I know how to wrap them so they don't cause any injuries."

The woman's accomplice joined her. "We don't have time for this nonsense," he said. "Just cut him open, and if he's telling the truth we'll be done with it right there."

Clarissa rose to her feet and started screaming: a wild, enraged, animal sound. The two thieves turned toward her, irritated and bemused. "There's no one around to hear you," the woman counseled her. "You're wasting your breath."

For the moment, they had their backs to both Del and Montano. Del briefly contemplated trying to signal her intent to him so they could act in unison, but then decided not to risk the delay; she stood up and ran straight toward the woman as fast as she could, colliding with her and knocking her to the ground. Her plan had been to stay upright – she'd pictured herself triumphant, with one foot planted firmly on her adversary's back – but her bound hands made it impossible to retain her balance, and the two of them toppled over together.

The woman squirmed and tried to dislodge her, but Del placed her knees on the ground on either side of the woman's hips. The woman had dropped her dagger, and it was lying a short distance away, but Del was afraid to raise her head to try to find out what anyone else was doing, in case the slight shift in her weight gave her captive an advantage.

Then she heard the man, muttering and struggling for breath; Montano must have pinned him. The woman had begun to stink of desperation; her heat blotch blazed and her muscles tensed, leaving Del's hold on her more precarious than ever.

Two bare feet came into view. Clarissa, who'd stopped screaming, managed to move the discarded dagger further from its owner by grabbing the hilt between her toes and dragging it – showing more presence of mind than Del, who wondered at first why she didn't just kick it – then she squatted down on the ground, and with some obvious difficulty managed to bring her bound hands close enough to her feet to work her legs through the loop of her arms. Then, with one knee on the handle of the dagger she slid the rope over the blade.

When she'd finished, she knelt down beside Del and prepared to cut her hands free, but Del said, "Can you untie the rope, so we can reuse it?"

Clarissa grunted in agreement. It took a while, with the woman's struggling making it hard for Del to keep her own hands still, but eventually Clarissa got the knots unpicked. Del looked over to where Montano, Imogen and Silvio were all piled on top of the man; they seemed to have him under control for the moment, so with Clarissa's help, she concentrated on tying the woman's hands securely.

She picked up the dagger and remained with the woman while Clarissa went to untie the others' hands. The woman was silent, probably reluctant to threaten or insult her while she was holding a blade. Del's hands were shaking; she was trying to remain alert to any possibility of the woman surprising her, but she was also afraid of overreacting and stabbing her for no reason.

When the man's hands and feet were bound, Silvio came over and helped Del tie the woman's feet.

"So what now?" she asked him.

"Leave them here and move on," Silvio suggested.

"Shouldn't we take them to a magistrate?"

Montano said, "Ideally, we should, but it would be a slow trip dragging them with us to the next town, and then we'd have to stay for who knows how long while the matter was settled."

They discussed it together for a while, but no one seemed keen on trying to transport their assailants either back to Yarun, or on to Welcan, which was even further away. Imogen filled a bowl with water and placed it on the ground so the thieves could drink from it. Del suspected that it wouldn't take long for one of them to work their hands free; the thought of them coming after the expedition unnerved her, but then, wherever they went there'd be the chance of some other band of robbers showing up. She was going to be a light sleeper from now on, and she had no doubt that they'd all be more vigilant.

Clarissa took a pad and pencil and deftly sketched the thieves, then attached a warning sign to a nearby tree, high enough that they'd be unable to dislodge it until they were entirely mobile anyway. "If someone stumbles on them like this, at least they'll know not to trust them," she said.

"They could still claim to be the victims, falsely accused," Imogen protested.

Clarissa laughed. "Anything's possible," she conceded. "But I still feel better to have sown some doubt, and not just left these snakes here to turn on any hapless benefactors."

As they were packing up their tents, Del saw Montano talking with the woman.

"I had no more gold," he said. "So why were you so insistent? Did someone send you to us? Did someone promise it would be worthwhile?"

The woman just muttered curses. When Montano rejoined the group, Del asked him, "Who would do that? Tell someone we're loaded down with coins, just to make trouble for us?"

"There are dozens of groups competing for the prize," he said.

"Sure, but they can't all be plotting to get each other killed!"

Montano said, "Most of them are going to Sadema, so they'll have a chance to keep an eye on each other. But we'll be out of sight completely."

As the expedition set off again, Del looked back at the disappointed thieves lying helpless on the ground. Perhaps Montano was right, but it made no sense to her. If any of their rivals truly believed there was a chance of crossing the gap at Celema, why weren't they out there at the nub already, trying the same approach for themselves?

Chapter 9

They were in the sixth circuit of their second traversal of the western Hoop when Del noticed the world finally growing smaller.

The evidence was subtle, and a little confusing; the ring road didn't seem to be spiraling down like a winding mountain path, but as they progressed, Del could see the edge of the Hoop drawing unmistakably closer to the vertical. Back in Thena it had been tilted about a third of the way toward the southern horizon, and any change throughout the journey had been imperceptible. The eastern Hoop had also stood at a similar angle, for the five circuits they'd completed before coming west again. But now the only way to make sense of the changing geometry was for the ground to be dropping away beneath their feet, allowing the Hoop to emerge at a different depth, a different angle, a different latitude.

"We're moving north, aren't we?" Del asked Silvio, who was walking beside her. "Descending, and moving north?"

"Yes."

"So why does it feel as if we're still just going around in circles on level ground?"

Silvio laughed. "Because the road *is* level, more or less; if you doubt your own judgment on that, just watch the way the water flows next time it rains: it won't rush forward ahead of us, as if we were marching down into a valley. When the rock beneath us was molten, it would have settled into an equilibrium and found a level surface, just like water does; all the mountain-building and so on came later, once it was solid. But since less and less rock flowed through to make up each land as we approach the nub, that surface must have less and less rock sitting beneath it — even if we're never traveling downhill in the sense that would compel a river to follow us."

"I think I understand," Del replied, not entirely honestly. She could follow the logic of his argument, but she couldn't really grasp how nature had reconciled the apparent contradictions. Of course the ball of rock they stood upon beneath each sky had to grow smaller, eventually, if the world was not to go on forever, or come full circle uninterrupted – and it was just a brute fact that neither of these things was true. But for their altitude to drop without gravity treating their path as it would any other descent still felt like some kind of trick or illusion.

Clarissa had been walking a few steps ahead of them; she turned and asked, "So why, exactly, does my body feel heavier?"

"You mean your pack?" Del suggested. "That's just those extra supplies we took on."

"No, it's everything," Silvio declared.

Del couldn't decide if he was joking or not. "First you say the ground is gravitationally level ... but now you say gravity is increasing?"

"For a single, solid ball of rock," Silvio replied, "every aspect of gravity depends solely on how far you are from the center. But by Natasha's account, that's just a coincidence that arises from the perfect symmetry. Once the Hoops are joining up spheres of different sizes, there's no reason why your weight should stay constant just because you maintain a level path."

Del lapsed into silence, turning this new claim over in her mind, trying to find some contradiction in it. That the ground felt level meant that her weight pushed her squarely against it, instead of at an angle, as it did on the slope of a hill. But there was nothing that amounted to a promise that it wouldn't push down harder.

The next sign came with the weather: for three circuits, they looked out upon landscapes strewn with snow – sometimes falling in the distance upon treeless plains, sometimes reaching all the way to the road. At first, a vestigial warmth leaking through around the Hoop took the edge off the chill, with oddly balmy breezes rising up now and then to melt the rime from their jackets, but after a while the breezes stopped coming. It was like being high in the mountains, Del supposed; the only difference was, if she could have tunneled straight down through the rock, the core she reached here would be cold and dead, having given up its heat to the void long ago.

They camped by the roadside. Del shivered in her tent, even with her sleeping bag buried in a nest built from her share of the blankets Montano had insisted on buying in the last town as they'd traveled west. The extra weight hadn't seemed worth it at the time; now she wished he'd bought twice as many.

When she woke, she found Silvio cooking breakfast on an oil stove the size of a glorified lamp.

"There's no firewood?" she asked.

He nodded toward the bleak white expanse that surrounded them. "There might be some dead branches buried out there somewhere. You're welcome to try finding them."

"No thanks." Del stretched her hands toward the stove's feeble flame. She said, "I'm starting to understand why the Tolleans' first response to this theory might not have been to rush straight here and test it. Better to dismiss the whole thing with a couple of pages of philosophizing and spare yourself the frostbite."

Montano had joined them at the stove as she spoke. "All the wood for the bridge will need to be carried in from Derema?" she asked him.

"Yes," he replied.

She'd known there were no forests at the nub itself, but she'd never thought to check just how close the nearest one would be. "So would the whole prize even cover the cost of that?"

He shook his head. "The investors will only make a profit if this leads to a new trade route: new goods they can import from across the gap, new markets on the other side they can sell to. If we make the crossing but there's no one on the other side, the prize will just take some of the sting out of their wounds."

Del said, "If there's no one there, won't people still want to emigrate to the Bounteous Lands?"

"Perhaps. But it could take a generation or two before anyone would see a profit from that." Montano caught the flicker of disdain on her face. "You asked about the investors, so I'm telling you how they'll see it. And I owe it to them to be honest about their prospects. Would I still want to make the crossing, myself, for the sheer joy of discovery? Of course. But I'd be dead long before I'd carried the wood to the nub, single-handed."

Silvio called the others and started serving breakfast. Del ate the fried tomatoes quickly, before the meal lost all its heat.

Imogen picked up two empty water containers sitting by the stove and began filling them with snow. "Do you want a hand?" Del offered.

"Thanks. This might be our last chance for a while." They ended up packing snow into all five containers, even those that still held some water.

When they set off again, Del was dressed in every layer of clothing she possessed, half expecting to find herself walking through a blizzard. But after two circuits of the hill, though the air was probably colder than ever, it was eerily still, and the snow around them was beginning to give way to bare rock. It was possible that the gravity was even stronger now; either that, or she'd grown weary of being weighed down with extra clothes.

"Did you see that?" Imogen asked Del, pointing in the direction of the hill.

"What?" With the sky clear, it was hard to discern the edge of the Hoop. Imogen took a few steps back, and Del mimicked her, looking to the side as she moved. Instead of just the usual slow revelation of a new sky, she saw a star appear with one step, then vanish with the next. And she was not mistaken; walking forward then back, she could repeat the phenomenon as many times as she wanted.

The eastern Hoop, which had once taken a laborious journey to reach, was now protruding well above the horizon. They were looking at it almost edge-on, rendering it difficult to see at all, but they'd chanced upon an alignment where they'd glimpsed a star through that foreshortened aperture, only to lose sight of it again when they crossed the plane of the Hoops.

Del still couldn't quite believe that so much of the rock beneath her feet had dwindled away, but as they continued on into the next circuit, the land gave up all pretense of possessing anything like the shape she was accustomed to.

On their right, the once-far horizon began to draw closer, as if they were entering a valley. On their left, the edge of the Hoop tilted toward them, but the point where it emerged from the ground receded. The hill that, in various guises, had always been there to wrap the edge now separated from it, and where they had been used to its slope rising up and hemming them in on one side, the terrain became flat, stretching off into the distance.

After a while, Del could no longer see where – or if – the Hoop met the ground. There was no ring road to guide them; they were walking across an expanse of bare rock, and the only part of the edge she could make out was above them, as good as horizontal.

They'd been moving in silence since the changes began, but now Montano spoke. "This is Celema. A little farther, then we'll set up camp."

They turned and trudged along beneath the edge, which Del could only discern by making an effort to recall the two most recent skies, then identifying the line where one gave way to the other. As they weaved a little from side to side to avoid a hillock or a rubble-filled depression, a few stars blinked in and out and helped to refresh her memory – though the edge of the second Hoop complicated those cues, as it converged on its once distant partner. The two perfect circles – touching at a point that, in Thena, was buried at the center of the land's rocky sphere – were now entirely unclothed. Del wished she could have risen up into the void and looked down on the twin disks, one enclosing a nub of rock, the other filled with nothing but a smattering of stars. If a traveler between worlds had chanced upon that vision, would they have guessed how many lands were waiting for them, just around the corner?

"Here," Montano decided. "The gravity's not too high?"

No one else complained, and Del had given up trying to disentangle the various causes of her own exhaustion. She set up her tent, unable to drive pegs into the rock to anchor it, but fairly sure that even its modest contents would keep it from moving far in the event that they ever experienced wind again.

It was Imogen's turn to cook. They hadn't been traveling all that long since breakfast, but Del was ravenous.

As they squatted by the stove, she reached down and placed a gloved palm on the frigid ground. Apart from the two rivers they'd crossed by bridge in Zeruma, they had traced an unbroken path across the surface of the world. She could, still, turn around any time she wanted, and walk back home.

Chapter 10

Del sheltered from the cold in her tent, wrapped in blankets in the dark, digesting her food like some mountain-dwelling animal that had retreated to its lair. But too little time had passed since she'd last slept to allow her to doze off again easily, and she soon grew bored with her own ruminations.

When she emerged, no one else was visible at the campsite, but she could see Silvio and Montano some distance away, one with a theodolite while the other positioned a marker on a tripod.

She approached Montano. "You're measuring the gravity already?" There'd be no shortage of variation to record; just walking here from her tent had left her feeling heavier.

"Not quite," he replied. "First, we need to know the precise distances between a grid of well-separated points."

"The maps in the library weren't good enough?"

"They were good enough to let me choose this place to work from, but no one has surveyed a small region in enough detail before."

Del glanced up at the stars. It was odd to recall that it had not been all that long since the map-makers had been here, wandering about entirely oblivious to the secret Montano was hoping to uncover. But then, she could have stared into the sky for a lifetime herself without guessing what one well-trained bird might have discovered.

"Can I help with anything?" she asked.

"Not really; it's a two person job."

Del left him to it, but she watched from a distance as the pair worked their way across the desolate plain. Back in Apasa, the notion that any change in gravity from place to place could be measurable, let alone revelatory, had seemed fanciful to her. But the peculiar shifts in her weight had already proved to coincide with the shrinking of the rock beneath her, and the replacement of one neighboring land with void. So, who knew how far around the Hoop a suitably refined accounting of the same phenomenon might reach?

When Silvio and Montano returned to the camp for a break, the others emerged from their tents, and the five of them sat drinking hot tea made from leaves Imogen had bought in Zeruma. "I was told people working in the mountains used this to keep up their strength," she said.

"Is the air thinner here?" Del asked.

"I don't think so," Imogen replied. "Not right at this spot. But if we end up ascending, that could change very quickly."

Silvio shuffled through pages of measurements, rechecking his calculations. Del understood the geometry a surveyor used to turn angles into distances, and she understood the law of gravity that had been deduced from the motion of Thena's moons, but exactly how all these numbers could come together to determine the expedition's worth remained a mystery to her.

"Did your sister ever travel to any of the nubs?" she asked Montano.

"No."

"So how did she arrive at her theory of gravity?"

"Electrostatics," he replied.

Del wondered if she'd misheard him.

"That's when——" he began.

"I know what it is," she said. "When you rub glass on cloth, and it attracts paper."

"That's one example. But you can shift charge between all kinds of things – and if you control the experiments carefully, you find that the attraction between charges obeys an inverse square law, just like gravity."

"All right." Del had a hazy memory of reading as much somewhere.

Montano said, "Natasha wondered how far it would take her if she assumed the underlying mathematics was the same. If the attraction between small beads with electrostatic charge obeyed the same kind of law as the attraction between balls of rock, then perhaps more complex situations could be mimicked on a smaller scale as well."

"So ... she carried charged beads around the nearest Hoop?"

"No, everything had to be on a smaller scale. She needed a surrogate for the Hoop that would fit in the palm of her hand."

Del was bemused now. "If anyone can make such things, I've never seen them."

Montano laughed. "A surrogate, not an actual Hoop. After thinking on it for a while, she realized that all she needed, to distort the electrostatic force in a manner similar to the way the Hoops distort gravity, was a metal disk."

Del said, "They sound more like opposites to me. The Hoop lets you pass through into a place you couldn't reach without it. A metal disk blocks your way, even though the other side is easily reached with a simple detour."

Montano pondered this objection. "The crucial property of a metal is that it allows its own charge to move freely. If you place a charged bead in its vicinity, the metal's charge will be pushed or pulled along its surface until it's no longer subject to any force that could rearrange it further."

"How is it no longer subject to a force?" Dell complained. "I can't evade the force of gravity just by weaving back and forth."

Montano said, "There are positive and negative charges, with opposites attracting and like charges repelling. In a metal, the positive charge seems to be fixed in place, equally distributed throughout the material — and in the absence of any disturbance, the negative charge sits alongside it, balancing out its influence. But if you place a charged bead near the metal, its own charge shifts, disrupting the balance between positive and negative in each small portion of the metal. And each portion attracts or repels the charge in neighboring portions, and so on ... until it all settles down to a new arrangement, where the negative charge is no longer spread out uniformly, but rather in whatever manner prevents it, in the presence of the bead, from being pushed or pulled to either side anymore."

"That makes sense." Del couldn't imagine capturing all the details mathematically, but it sounded a bit like the way the surface of the water in a bowl might change its shape under the influence of a steady breeze: piling up in places, hollowed out elsewhere, with the slope between the two maintained by the force of the wind.

"The thing is," Montano continued, "any remaining electrostatic force at the surface of the metal must be directed perpendicular to the surface. The charge isn't free to escape from the metal, only to move within it, so a force that tries to drag it straight out of the disk won't succeed in shifting it at all."

Del was prepared to take his word for this, though she still had no idea where the comparison was leading. The Hoop wasn't full of grains of sand, constrained to lie within its plane but otherwise free to slide about.

"Now, suppose that instead of the metal disk, there was a circular aperture leading to an otherwise hidden region. And imagine that you placed a second charged bead in that region: a charge of the opposite kind, positioned with perfect symmetry with respect to the disk – exactly where a reflection of the first bead would appear, if the disk were a mirror."

"I'm imagining it," Del replied. "But I don't know why."

Montano said, "If I measured the electrostatic force at some point in that circular aperture – due to a charged bead, and its oppositely charged mirror image – can you tell me in which direction the force will be?"

Del looked to the others for clues, but Silvio was still intent on his papers, and Clarissa and Imogen seemed happy to remain as spectators to her ordeal. She closed her eyes.

If she faced a mirror, and tugged with one hand on an insect sitting somewhere on the glass, while her reflection – however nonsensically – *pushed* on the same insect with equal strength, in which way would they be compelling the insect to move? Inasmuch as she was trying to drag the insect across the surface of the mirror, her twin would be trying to push it in the opposite direction. But while their efforts there would cancel out, they would both be trying equally hard to shift the insect away from the mirror in the same direction: toward her, and away from her twin. One kind of force would vanish, but the other would remain, redoubled.

She said, "The force will be perpendicular to the aperture."

Montano smiled. "Just like the force if there's a metal disk, instead of the Hoop and the second charge."

"Yes. But ... that's it? That's all you need to find the new laws of gravity?"

"No, it's just the start," he admitted. "It takes more work, and some other analogies, to exploit the connection fully. But the principle is there: you can understand situations where a Hoop is present by studying more mundane scenarios. That gives you a new road into the mathematics – and it lets you test your ideas from the comfort of home, with a miniature world on a tabletop."

Silvio looked up from his calculations. "I'm ready," he told Montano.

Del watched as they gathered a new set of instruments, and walked back to the grid they'd marked with spots of paint on the rock. "Do you follow all this?" she asked Clarissa.

"Well enough to use the answers, once they have them," Clarissa replied. "If you tell me how gravity changes across the gap, I'll draw up the plans for a bridge that can cross it. Just don't ask me to calculate the gravitational force ten turns away around the Hoop, from a few dozen readings of plumb lines and spring balances."

Del hesitated. "Are you sure that anyone can?" She was torn, herself, between a degree of reassurance to hear that Natasha's work hadn't relied entirely on speculation, and unease at the thought that it relied, instead, on a model thousands of times smaller that measured an entirely different force.

"No one can be sure yet," Clarissa conceded. "But once they claim they know what's ahead, we'll still get to build the bridge step by step, checking everything as we go. If the predictions are wrong, at some point we'll see them start to diverge from what we're measuring, and we'll need

66

to decide whether or not the whole endeavor is salvageable. But I don't believe we'll be caught out with no warning."

Del's lips were starting to crack every time she moved them. She excused herself and returned to her tent, hoping to sleep until there was a verdict about the gap, but her head was buzzing with too many speculations and predictions of her own.

It was also her turn to cook the next meal. Since the rhythm of travel and rest had been broken, her sense of time had grown erratic, and she didn't trust anyone's body temperature to guide her when all their skin was like ice. So she lay beneath the blankets and passed the time by picturing herself talking to the Tolleans in the Bounteous Lands, where the light of one star was enough to turn the sky bright from horizon to horizon, to enliven a thousand new kinds of crops and forests, and to banish any trace of chill or gloom from every room in every building.

When she finally convinced herself that she was hungry again, and not merely impatient, she found her store of rice and dried vegetables and went out to brave the oil stove. The small flame took forever even to melt the water she needed to get started; by the time the food was cooking she was sure that everyone would be famished.

Once she added the spices, the scent brought Clarissa and Imogen out of their tents, and whether it wafted as far as Silvio and Montano or not, they soon noticed the gathering and returned.

"How's it progressing?" Del asked, as she handed Silvio a plate.

"We're about halfway through," he said. "Then there are the calculations."

"You should have taught us Natasha's methods back in Apasa," Imogen chided him. "We could have helped, and it would be done twice as fast."

Silvio nodded wearily. "But we didn't, and it's too late now."

When the survey resumed, Del busied herself cleaning up after the meal, trying to remove every speck of food from all the pots and utensils without wasting too much water. She'd thought she'd been prepared, long before they'd set off, for the possibility that the journey would prove to be futile. She would still have seen more of the world than most of her friends. She would still be paid for her time on the road, and welcomed back to her job at the museum. But the truth was, she could never have come this far without hoping there would be more at the end of it than aching feet, unbearable cold, and the simplest tasks made arduous.

The worst task of all had been growing more pressing ever since they'd arrived at the nub, and her dread alone could no longer postpone it. Del set off across the barren plain, with no prospects of finding shelter or soil, until by virtue of sheer distance even the tents were barely visible to her. She squatted on the rock and relieved herself, hoping she'd chosen a spot that no one else would visit for a very long time. She had not seen so much as a beetle since they'd entered Celema, but then, nor had she stumbled on any frozen coprolites left behind by past explorers. Nature would clean up after her, eventually, even if the requisite scavengers were too small for the eye to see.

On her way back she found herself meandering, preferring the bitter cold where it was only to be expected over the dispiritingly meager comforts of her tent. She wanted a hot bath and a proper bed, inside a real building. She wanted to feel safe again: to be sure that she could sleep without waking to the sight of a knife in her face.

When she reached the camp, she saw Silvio and Montano working by stove-light on their new set of measurements.

"If it was up to me," she said, "I'd throw a thousand balls through the Hoop, and if any of them bounced back I'd conclude that they'd hit something solid."

Silvio laughed. "That's not a bad idea! Though getting the trajectory right might take closer to a million tosses."

Montano looked up, clearly annoyed by the interruption. Del retreated to her tent.

She tried to sleep, and failed, then resolved to stay awake until everything was settled, and failed at that as well.

She was woken by the smell of cooking, but then remained beneath the blankets until Clarissa called her. Montano had set his papers aside, but while everyone else began eating, Silvio ignored them and kept calculating.

"What's happening?" Del asked.

Imogen said, "It's almost done. Silvio's checking for errors."

Del didn't ask what the preliminary results had been; she didn't want to hear an answer only to have it retracted moments later. She chewed her food slowly, relishing every mouthful. Imogen made her special tea again, and Silvio accepted a mug from her while his meal sat congealing.

"Does this place have a name?" Clarissa asked Montano.

"The whole part of the nub closest to the Hoops is called the Shoulder," he replied. "I think the Deremans came here hoping there'd be something worth mining, and when there wasn't they lost interest in naming every spot."

"So it's up to us," Clarissa suggested.

Del glanced at Silvio; he was still frowning intently as he moved his pencil across the sheet.

"What do you want to call it?" Imogen asked.

"That depends on the result," Clarissa replied. She lit the stove again, and began thawing Silvio's dinner.

As the odor of the re-enlivened oil and spices emerged from the pot, Silvio put down his work and stretched his arms above his head. "I'm starving," he said. "You've all eaten already?"

"Yes," Del replied. "You'll enjoy it. Clarissa's outdone herself."

He nodded happily, and turned to Clarissa. "I have a suggestion for you. We should name this place after its most famous landmark."

"The Plain of Five Tents?" Imogen joked.

"One that's yet to be built," Silvio clarified. "But sure to be celebrated. *The Bridge of Five Voids.*"

Chapter 11

"You should come with me," Clarissa urged Del. They were seated in the dining tent, sharing a table with a dozen boisterous Dereman carpenters, but Del had grown used to shutting out their banter when she needed to focus on a conversation of her own. "If one complete circuit isn't worth celebrating, what is?"

Del could think of several better candidates, ranging from an actual sighting of land across the gap, through to the moment the bridge finally had foundations planted firmly at both ends, enabling sane people to set foot on it. "You said that about standing upside down," she replied.

"That really wasn't so special," Clarissa conceded. "People on opposite sides of the world do it all the time. But no one's ever built a single structure that wraps all the way around the edge of a Hoop before."

Del felt no obligation to be a witness to every milestone in the bridge's construction, but Clarissa's enthusiasm was sincere, and the invitation was made in a spirit of generosity. She'd grown used to keeping herself busy in the dining tent, working beside the other kitchen hands and listening half-comprehendingly to all the gossip and drama they'd brought from Derema, in a dialect she still hadn't quite mastered. But if she let herself grow too comfortable with this life, it was only going to be an even greater shock when she finally tore herself away and resumed the path she was committed to following.

"All right," she said. "I'll go with you."

By the time they'd finished eating she was already having second thoughts. "Shouldn't we wait until we've digested our food? I don't want to get halfway to the end only to start throwing up."

"No one throws up," Clarissa promised. "You do know you don't actually feel like you're upside down, at any point?"

"Obviously. But still, when you look around ... "

Clarissa rose and put on her coat. "Are we doing this or not?"

Del followed her out of the lamplit tent into the starlight, through the sawdust-spattered village that Montano had summoned into existence. Piles of logs, and more refined forms of lumber were stacked everywhere she looked; the sheer cumulative weight of it made her body ache in sympathy, though the carpenters she'd spoken with insisted that it hadn't been so bad, dragging it here on well-balanced carts.

As they headed across the plain toward the bridge, she felt a growing tightness in the muscles of her legs that had nothing to do with other people's burdens. Her breathing became labored, and she slowed her pace, to accomodate both the greater effort required to complete each step, and the greater concentration needed to be sure she didn't misjudge the new interplay of forces and send herself sprawling. It had puzzled her, at first, that walking while her whole body was uniformly heavier could be so much trickier than carrying an equal load in a pack. But the new gait was not just the old one with extra effort; her various muscles didn't all magically scale up their responses by the same factor, allowing the basic mechanics of the process to remain unchanged. It was more like finding herself squeezed into the anatomy of a different creature, which, however human-like in form, needed to adapt to its greater weight with an entirely different rhythm to its movements.

Clarissa glanced at her, but knew better than to make solicitous enquiries. Del was panting as if she'd broken into a sprint, but they'd both known what to expect. If she'd wanted her first time on the bridge to be easier, she'd had plenty of opportunities to practice the approach.

Before them, the bridge rose up from the ground like a giant wooden fish-hook. It was as if the architect had started sketching a plan for the scaffolding needed to assemble a tall tower, but as the drawing proceeded a mischievous child had slowly slid the page around beneath the moving pencil, bending what should have been linear and vertical into a deranged spiral. They were far enough from the plane of the Hoops to see the structure curl around the edge as it plunged through the aperture, but the view of the current endpoint was blocked, leaving the completed loop to Del's imagination.

There was no one else around; the laborers would be waiting back in the village for Clarissa's approval to continue their work. As they approached the base, Del took comfort in a narrower view: close up, all she could see was a stack of more or less horizontal platforms joined by ladders. It would be like ascending into a loft, over and over. If she could do that once, she could do it a hundred times.

Around the entrance, support beams far taller than she was sloped from the sides of the tower and vanished into slots carved into the rock. "How are you going to carry anything that big all the way across, for the other foundations?" Del asked Clarissa, breathlessly pointing to the beams.

"We won't be," Clarissa replied. "We're making this end deliberately heavier. Perfect symmetry would be very satisfying – but that would require a second construction team working from the other side to meet us in the middle. The way it's actually being built, to keep the work-in-progress stable at every step along the way it needs to be lopsided."

"I see." That the fish-hook hadn't tipped over so far suggested that Clarissa knew what she was doing; Del's own intuition balked at the prospect of even trying to imagine which way it would have fallen if things had gone wrong. Under ordinary conditions, clearly it would have toppled toward the unsupported side that curved away from the base, but given that gravity always pointed back along the spiral, she really had no idea how such a catastrophe would have played out.

"Does the weight of all the segments just ... pile up, as if it was straight?" she asked.

"Sadly, no. That would have made everything simpler. But when the gravitational vertical follows a curve, you can't stack levels and support them with compressive strength alone. There's always going to be a shearing force between them that needs to be resisted."

Del didn't like the sound of that, but it was too late to start expressing her qualms about the architectural challenges of curved verticals. They were at the entrance, and the first ladder was in front of them.

Clarissa said, "The start isn't easy, but I promise you, it gets better." She stepped forward and grasped the ladder, then began her ascent, methodically shifting just one hand or foot at a time from rung to rung, always in the same sequence. Del watched her and memorized the action, sure that it would be better than anything she tried to improvise herself. Once there was room on the ladder, she followed without delay, more afraid of being left behind than anything else. It was hard work raising her heavier self, but it was not impossible, and once she found a pace at which she could tolerate the effort without escalating her discomfort into genuine pain or the threat of injury, she settled into a rhythm, as she might in some kind of training regime. The regularity of the rungs helped; she felt more confident of retaining her balance than she had on the uneven ground.

When she reached the first platform she saw that Clarissa hadn't waited for her like an anxious chaperone – but the fact that she was only halfway up the next ladder probably meant she wasn't charging ahead at her usual pace, either. Del crossed the platform and continued, trying to keep her movements focused and consistent. Through the gaps in the lattice of struts beside her, she could see the starlit ground around the bridge; she didn't want to banish the view from her thoughts, but she tried to find a place for it in her attention without letting it distract her from the need to keep ascending.

Approaching the second platform, she noticed the pattern of mortices and tenons connecting the timber in one segment to the next. She had never seen joinery quite like it: the sides of the abutting pieces had been carved with an array of square holes and pegs that slotted together across a wide strip – presumably so that any attempt to separate them laterally would entail almost as much effort as tearing the bulk of the wood apart. Clarissa had not been joking about the shearing force, but Del tried to feel comforted rather than alarmed. That the weight of the bridge wasn't just bearing down on it, but was actively trying to rip it apart, had been factored into the design from the start.

Platform by platform, the ground receded. Glancing to the side, Del could see directly through the Hoop now, to a portion of the bridge far ahead of her around the fish-hook's loop. Mercifully, she couldn't discern the details of the structure from this distance, and she doubted that even if it had been crawling with workers she would have been able to resolve their tiny heat blotches well enough to visualize people climbing up ladders in a direction that, to her, still pointed down.

When the tower began to bend, she gave herself no time to hunt for a glimpse of the ground tilting; through the Hoop, her view of the rest of the bridge barely changed, and directly away from it all she saw was the stars. If she thought carefully about the constellations, she could deduce what was happening, but the fact remained that every ladder she climbed felt as if it were parallel to the last one, and every platform seemed perfectly horizontal beneath her feet.

It was on her feet that she first felt lighter: the weight of her whole body no longer seemed to put so much strain on her ankles and knees. The climb was still arduous, but after a while there was no mistaking the change there either, as if she'd gone from hauling sacks of rocks up the ladder to sacks of grain.

She called out to Clarissa, "What's the air like here?"

"About a twentieth thinner."

"Do you think we'll need Imogen's suits, later on?"

"I hope not," Clarissa replied fervently. "If the original calculations hold up, we should never go beyond a loss of one fifth. Mountain climbers cope with thinner air than that."

Del had no expertise in the subject, but she'd been dreading the possibility that the atmosphere would cling so closely to the nub that by the halfway point there'd be nothing left to breathe. It might merely be a nuisance to be obliged to cross the finished bridge with your body sealed in canvas and your air pumped up through a tube, but if the builders had to work that way it would be torture, and she wouldn't blame them if they all quit.

The ladders kept appearing before her, barely changing, while the effort needed to climb them grew less. Del thought she was at ease with the whole situation, but then she glanced to the side and saw Celema's barren ground spread out like a vertical cliff face dropping away in the distance – rudely truncated above by the black sky and stars through the Hoop – and suffered her first moment of panic.

She gripped the rung in front of her tightly but refused to look away. The ground couldn't drag her off the bridge, pulling her body sideways between the struts, asserting some kind of claim over her and insisting she pledge fealty to its orientation; if she happened to lose her hold on the ladder, she would drop no farther than the platform below. What had Clarissa said? People on the other side of the world were upside-down to each other all the time. She had spent all her life in Apasa at a strange angle to some other town's roads and fields. The fact that she was currently deprived of any suitably oriented land herself was unsettling, but the platforms would remain horizontal to her, as would the rungs of every ladder. Gravity might be fighting to tear the bridge apart, but it wasn't trying to cast her into the void.

She loosened her grip and continued, recommencing the entrained sequence of movements, falling back into the rhythm that had served her so well. As she passed through the plane of the Hoop, the ground began tilting away from her; on her other side, the new stars shone unblinking in the cold air. Eerily, there was a constellation that resembled the half-built bridge itself: a row of bright stars that started out straight, then curved into a hook.

"We need to name this sky," she yelled.

"Do we?" Clarissa shouted back. "People have only named lands before."

"So far as we know."

"If the Tolleans have already named it, maybe we should wait and ask them what they chose."

They crossed the upside-down point. A portion of the bridge rising up from Celema, visible through the aperture, made the edge of the Hoop easy to detect, and when it was level with the platform Del pictured the plain she had once walked across spread out above her head. But Celema's unseen ground-turned-ceiling was less unsettling now than the lack of a replacement. Above her, below her, there was nothing but stars.

She kept climbing, watching the aperture become foreshortened as she approached the plane of the Hoops, until most of what she could see of the bridge belonged to the semicircle on her own side. Del thought she was prepared for what was coming, but when she climbed the last ladder and found herself on an uncovered platform, she sank to her knees on the rough boards, unable to speak or look up. Clarissa stood nearby, making no attempt to comfort or cajole her.

After a while, Del rose to her feet unsteadily. "I hope those guard rails are attached securely," she said.

Clarissa pushed tentatively against one of the planks, not mocking her or tempting fate but making a genuine assessment. "I believe they are," she said. "The builders are pretty diligent; it's in their own interests even more than ours."

She continued around the platform, testing the rails, then she lit a lamp and knelt to inspect the floorboards. Del gazed at the collection of tools and instruments that had been left in the middle of the floor; she supposed it made sense than neither builders nor architect would wish to lug everything back and forth from Celema, but she couldn't shake off a sense of the precariousness of the stash, as if an unexpected gust of wind might scatter it, or some enterprising thief from across the gap might swing in on a rope just to grab a chisel.

When Clarissa was finished with the structure itself, she set up a tripod with a plumb line and theodolite, and began measuring the angles between the local vertical and several stars. Del watched in silence, not wanting to distract her, but when Clarissa started taking readings with a spring balance, Del couldn't stop herself from asking, "How strong is the gravity?"

"A little less than it was back in Apasa."

"Maybe I could stay here?"

"If you can talk the builders into bringing you food, be my guest."

Del approached the guard rail and gazed down into the sky. She'd always had stars beneath her feet; it just hadn't been quite so easy to see them. "I would like to come here again, though. If I'm going to make the crossing, I should get used to this."

Clarissa said, "Of course. You're welcome to accompany me any time."

"*Pesh delam va,*" Del decided.

"I'm sorry?"

"That's Tollean for 'The First Landless Sky'. Give or take everything that could be wrong with my pronunciation."

"*Pesh delam va,*" Clarissa repeated. "That should do for now. If the first people to walk beneath this sky were the Tolleans, we can ask them what they actually called it."

"And if we're the first?"

"Then we might as well keep the name," Clarissa replied, "since there'll be no one to object. There's nothing like a long-dead language to make the most literal phrase seem profoundly romantic. Naming it with something we can understand ourselves would be like begging for our own culture to vanish into obscurity, so people in the future can point to their charts and whisper some garbled version of what we said, marveling at how exotic it sounds."

Chapter 12

At first, Del worried that her newfound resolve to keep visiting the bridge would fall prey to either laziness or fear, but once she had gone up with Clarissa half a dozen times it began to feel like part of her routine. Any kind of movement under higher gravity remained physically demanding, but after a slip on a ladder left her with nothing but a bruised shin, the vertiginous views of the ground – and the groundless sky – lost much of their power to unnerve her. She did not grow reckless, and her admiration for the builders' skill and courage remained, but her own particular activities seemed less and less perilous, demanding reasonable care but no superhuman feats of attentiveness.

As the bridge curled its way around the second loop, it stopped following the local vertical, which would have sent it spiraling out into the void. Instead, each segment was displaced "horizontally" from the preceding one, with cantilevers supporting the platforms, while the ladders became less steep, and were eventually replaced by stairs. Del worried that the structure was jutting out in a manner that would surely have led to it snapping, had it been reaching across an equally wide canyon under normal conditions, but Clarissa was adamant that the cyclic change in the direction of gravity was working in their favor, with the different forces on different segments partly canceling each other – all the more so as the curve approached a full circle again.

By the third loop, the stairs vanished: the bridge became a series of mildly sloping platforms joined end to end, following a grand arc around the edge of the Hoop. The bulk of the structure was now devoted to the cantilevers, and Del looked on with renewed anxiety as Clarissa attached a safety harness and clambered down to examine the supports.

"If someone fell here ... ?" she asked, once Clarissa was safely back on the platform.

"I think you'd hit the edge and get cleaved in two," Clarissa replied cheerfully. "But first, the gravity would squeeze you into a paste."

"I don't understand that," Del confessed. "Back home, the edge can cut you if you're foolish enough to run straight at it, but it can't drag you toward it."

Clarissa removed the harness and began setting up her theodolite. "The way Montano explained it to me, the Hoop produces no gravitational force of its own. But the geometry around the edge affects the way the gravity from other things 'flows', the way a sharp bend in a river's channel can make the water behave differently. By itself, a bend in a dry river bed can't dash you into the bank, and if the water's placid it can't do you much harm either. But if the water's rushing downhill and then it's forced to turn suddenly, that's when things get dangerous."

"Hmm." Del was about to joke that her own grasp of the matter was now three times removed from the theory's originator, but then the woman's absence seemed too poignant to be the subject of levity. "I wish Natasha could have seen this," she said. "Imagine being doubted and dismissed like that, only to be vindicated when you're no longer around to enjoy it."

Clarissa didn't reply; she was attending to her measurements. Del gazed toward the end of the bridge, where three lengths of rope strung between the side rails were the only barrier between the platform and the void. But when she turned and looked back the way they'd come, the view was no less dreamlike: the curved deck rose up from a kind of horizon, hiding everything beyond and beneath. From this vantage, nothing in her sight could refute the proposition that she was completely adrift among the stars.

She walked over to the side rail and looked down at the supporting beams, which made her feel a little less unmoored. The edge of the Hoop lay almost directly below them now, and once they reached the point where that was exactly true, she believed the changes in the gravitational force – if not the details of the bridge itself – would be a mirror image of everything that had come before. "Once we cross the halfway point and it's all as we expected, there has to be a second nub, doesn't there?" she asked. "If the void went on forever, the geometry couldn't reach a point of symmetry and start playing out in reverse."

"I think that's right," Clarissa agreed, jotting down a final measurement. "Though I won't treat anything as certain until I've confirmed it with my own eyes."

"Well, at least Montano should see his own hypothesis confirmed."

Clarissa folded up her tripod. Del couldn't quite make out her features, but she seemed to be fighting an impulse to correct some misapprehension. Del's impression had always been that it was Natasha who had developed the theory of gravity in the presence of the Hoops, but her brother who had made the further supposition that a winding path around an edge might turn out to be finite. Montano had always given Natasha full credit for the larger contribution; why would he cheat her out of due recognition for that one extra step which, in any case, the Tolleans might have reached long before either of them?

"What am I wrong about?" Del asked finally.

"I think Montano used to *be* Natasha." She shook her head. "Anyway, never mind, it's not important."

She set off back along the bridge.

Del followed her, unsure whether she should try to pursue the subject further.

"Why wouldn't he tell us?" she asked.

"Is it any of our business?" Clarissa replied.

"I suppose not. But then, why not take credit for his own work?"

Clarissa said, "If he was known as Natasha when he came up with those ideas, his teachers and colleagues might still associate them with that name. But who knows? Maybe he'll take us into his confidence eventually, or maybe we'll just have to accept that we'll never hear the whole story."

Del said, "When the thieves were threatening to cut him open, and you started screaming at them, I thought maybe you and he were lovers."

"That was just a tactic," Clarissa said, amused. "Someone had to distract them."

"I see."

"If I lusted after anyone," Clarissa mused, "it was Silvio. But I got over it."

"We really don't have to talk about that," Del assured her.

"So did you leave someone behind in Apasa?" Clarissa asked.

"No. One good friend, who was like a brother to me, but no one else. What about you?"

"No one I hadn't been betrayed by."

Del got all the talk of cheating lovers she needed from her fellow kitchen hands. "I hope you're right about Montano," she said. "It would be a happier ending than Natasha dying without a chance to see what she made possible." She spread her arms to take in the whole hallucinatory vision. "Along with the architect, of course."

"I won't be happy until it's finished," Clarissa replied. "A bridge into the void might be a marvel to behold, but if I ever want to work again it had better hit land soon – and then show that it can stand up to traders lugging their carts from end to end."

Chapter 13

Del had just begun her shift and was chopping vegetables when the cook, Elledo, approached her. She looked up, expecting another gentle admonishment for failing to dice the onions finely enough, and saw that he was beaming at her as if she'd just invented a new way to braise turnips.

"Congratulations!" he said.

"For what?"

"You haven't heard?"

Del said, "If you tell me what you're talking about, I'll tell you if it's news to me."

"*Land!* I just spoke with my sister Fera, and she told me they've finally seen land."

Fera was a carpenter, but as far as Del knew she worked entirely in the village, preparing pre-cut pieces that the building teams carried up onto the bridge.

"Who told her that?" Del asked Elledo.

"Sama. I think it was Sama."

Sama, at least, did work on the bridge.

"I thought you people were wasting your time here," Elledo admitted, with cheerful candor. "But you've done it. You've won the prize!"

Del hesitated, then put down her knife. "You don't mind if I ... ?"

Elledo said, "Go!"

Del walked out of the tent in a daze, her body protesting at being plunged into the icy gloom after such a brief respite. She stood in the street for a moment, then headed for Clarissa's office.

Clarissa looked up from her drawing board, surprised to see her, then concerned. "Are you all right? Has something happened?"

"I'm fine. No one's told you?"

"Told me what?"

Del said, "I just heard a third-hand report that the builders have spotted land."

Clarissa frowned. "I wasn't expecting it yet, but I suppose it's not impossible."

"I'm just telling you what I heard."

"Are Silvio and Montano back from Derema?"

"Yes, but they're probably still asleep."

Clarissa said, "The first land sighted should be far from the Hoop; you'd barely be able to tell the difference between it and a dark patch of sky. Do you know who actually saw it?"

They found Sama in the dining tent, spreading the news to her friends. Clarissa waited patiently for a chance to press her for details.

"It wasn't black, it was reddish-gray," Sama insisted. "And it wasn't a cloud, or anything else in the sky. It was some kind of outcrop, poking down behind the edge of the Hoop."

When they left, Clarissa still seemed unconvinced. Del was shivering; she'd just realized she'd left her overcoat in the kitchen. "What do you want to do?"

"I'll go up at the normal time, when the builders are taking a break," Clarissa decided. "If I barge in now and they're all slapping my back, but then it turns out that I don't believe it's land ... "

"All right."

Del returned to the kitchen, assuring Ellado and her coworkers that she was thrilled with the news, but that no one from the expedition wanted to interrupt the builders' routine.

She resumed her usual tasks, doing her best to suppress her impatience. If there really was land, they'd be sure of it soon enough.

When she met up with Clarissa in her office again, Montano and Silvio were there.

"Has anyone told Imogen?" Del asked.

Clarissa said, "I've invited her onto the bridge before, but she's never been interested."

"This is different!" Del said.

"You can try if you want to," Clarissa replied. "Catch up with us."

Del went to Imogen's tent and shook the door chimes, but there was no response. "It's Del!" she called. "Can I come in? I've got some news!"

There was a long silence, then a grunt that could have meant anything. Del opened the flap and entered, closing it behind her quickly to keep the cold out.

She could just make out Imogen's form from her heat blotch, emerging through a heap of blankets. "One of the builders thinks she saw land," Del said. "Some of us are going up to check on it now. Do you want to come?"

"No." Imogen's tone was flat beyond indifference, as if the words had barely made it across the gulf from thought to speech.

Del hadn't seen much of her since work on the bridge had started. She could understand why she'd stopped turning up for discussions about the logistics of the building process, once it was clear that the workers were unlikely to need any kind of supplementary air supply, but she'd withdrawn from most other contact as well.

"We should all be there," Del said. "We've all come this far."

"I'm tired," Imogen replied. She stated it as a fact, without a trace of rhetorical vehemence; she didn't care if Del believed her, or considered this a good enough excuse.

Del didn't think this was the time to offer an earnest speech about Imogen's worth as their friend, regardless of the expedition's need for her skills. "I'll talk to you later," she said.

She left the tent and jogged across the plain toward the bridge, reaching the others as they were approaching the entrance. No one asked why Imogen wasn't with her.

"Have you claimed the prize yet?" she teased Montano.

"No," he said. "But if this isn't land I don't know what else it could be."

"A mirage?"

Silvio said, "A mirage that looks like land would just be land that's not quite where it seems. So maybe it's exactly that: some kind of atmospheric effect that's showing us the land sooner than we expected."

They made the ascent in silence; it was too awkward yelling to each other as they climbed the ladders in single file. Alone with her thoughts, Del found herself growing more hopeful. Every measurement since they'd arrived at the nub had pointed to the presence of land across the gap; a premature sighting posed a mystery, but it hardly lessened the chance of success.

When they reached the bridge's third loop, with room to walk side by side, Del could hear the boards groan beneath their feet. She'd never been up here with anyone besides Clarissa before. But each team of builders comprised eight people, usually loaded down with timber; the four of them were not subjecting the bridge to anything new.

They passed through the Hoop one more time, and began their descent. After a while, Del let the others take the stairs ahead of her; the latticework that enclosed each flight was thinner and more open than the corresponding structures in the ascending stage, and she felt uneasy pressing against it to avoid a companion's elbows.

"I hadn't seen any of this before!" she heard Montano remark from the flight below. "When you're on a staircase leading down from an arch, how can you believe there'll be nothing at the bottom?"

Del understood what he meant, but it wasn't long before the stairs did, in fact, end in thin air.

They crowded together on the landing, roped off from the hole where the next flight would be added. Del looked across and found the edge of the Hoop; it was easier to locate than usual, with a dense band of stars visible through the aperture brought to an abrupt, geometrical end. But as she followed the edge past this clear marker, she could not see anything that looked like rock.

"Is it just me?" Clarissa asked.

"No," Montano replied. "I can't see it either."

He'd brought a pair of binoculars, and now he raised them to his eyes. After a while, he said, "It's there! Just barely. Unless I've lost my mind and I'm only seeing what I want to see."

He passed the binoculars to Clarissa, who confirmed the sighting. "Do the Deremans have superhuman eyesight?" she marveled. "I don't know how anyone could have seen that unaided."

Silvio said, "If it's an atmospheric phenomenon, it could be bobbing up and down as the conditions shift."

Clarissa gave him the binoculars. When he spoke, he sounded puzzled. "I would have expected it to be blurrier, if that were the case. This looks crisp to me."

Finally it was Del's turn. She aimed the binoculars at the part of the edge she'd identified before, then she swept her gaze along it, following a now easily-perceptible shift in the distribution of the stars. The outcrop was at the very top of the aperture, poking down according to her sense of the vertical: a tiny sliver of reddish rock, presumably just high enough above a whole plain on the second nub to show from this angle.

"I see it," she said. She lowered the binoculars and peered at the same part of the edge. "But even if Sama has better eyesight than all of us, there's no way she wouldn't have warned us how hard it would be to find."

"Could the bridge be ... sagging?" Silvio asked tentatively.

"Not that much!" Clarissa replied, clearly more amused by the idea than offended. "For this end to move so far would take all the joints well beyond their tolerance. Things would have torn and snapped first; we wouldn't be standing here alive."

"Well, that's a comfort," Del joked.

"So, it has to be atmospheric refraction?" Montano sounded dubious, and Del was too; there was nothing shimmering or hazy about the rock as she'd seen it.

Clarissa said, "I never saw much variation in the sightings I took at the other end. But the temperature profile could be different here. Maybe the other nub's significantly warmer?"

They both looked to Silvio, but he just frowned and stared unhappily at the edge.

Del handed the binoculars back to Montano. He raised them again, and made a sound of disbelief. "It's shifted!" he declared. "The first time I looked, the rock spanned about a fifth of the field, but it's less than that now. Maybe an eighth."

He passed the binoculars to Clarissa. "You're right," she said. "More of it's hidden by the edge."

"Are you sure the bridge can't be vibrating?" Silvio pressed her. "Not permanently sagging, just bouncing around a bit?"

"Oh, I'm sure it's vibrating," Clarissa replied. "But the time scale is completely wrong: one cycle would be about as long as it takes for sound to travel through the wood from one end of the structure to the other. If those vibrations were strong enough to make the rock seem to shift against the edge, we'd have seen it wobble a dozen times before we looked away."

"If it's not the air playing tricks with the light," Silvio said, "and it's not the bridge, then there's only one thing left: the world itself."

Montano laughed, but then his smile drained away. Clarissa took a little longer to respond, but then she did not look happy either.

Del wanted to be sure she'd caught Silvio's meaning. "You're saying the whole world is vibrating? Enough to change the distance across the gap?"

"Yes," he replied.

She was about to object that, with due deference to Clarissa, a wooden bridge seemed far more likely to be swaying than anything made of solid rock. But however much more rigid it was compared to the bridge, in size it outdid it by a vastly greater factor. The tiniest deformations in all the different lands that separated the nubs by the long route would add up, but the only place they would be rendered so starkly visible would be here: where the bridge allowed the motion of one free end to be compared with the other.

Silvio said, "That might even explain why the gap's so small. If the molten rock ran out of pressure when it was flowing through the Hoops, that could have happened anywhere. Why only a few skies away from the other nub? But if it actually flowed all the way around, it might have partly solidified like that, only to snap later at a weak point, to relieve the stress of trying to maintain a closed loop."

"That's all very nice for geologists," Clarissa replied irritably. "But what are we going to do? I can't turn the bridge into a concertina that stays intact while it's stretched and squeezed. Not without starting again from scratch – and probably not ever."

Montano said, "The bridge is designed to be stable under construction, right? It doesn't need to be complete to be safe to traverse."

"That's true," Clarissa agreed reluctantly.

"So we extend it as far as we can without risking it scraping across the ground," Montano suggested, "and then we trail a rope ladder from the bottom, so people can come and go."

Clarissa was dismayed. "This is your highway, opening up trade with the Bounteous Lands? A rope ladder hanging from a constantly shifting platform?"

"We don't know yet that there's anyone to trade with," Montano replied. "If there is, we can look for a better solution. But for now, all we need is to get the expedition across the gap and back again."

Del watched Clarissa struggling to contain her disappointment. No one had told her that her glorious helical arch – asymmetric, but perfect in its own way – would be doomed to have one end perpetually hovering over a landscape that heaved like the deck of a storm-tossed ship.

"We've found land!" Montano reminded them. "While everyone else is swarming over the mountains of Sadema, looking for a secret passage, we're as good as through to the other side. The Demerans are already celebrating. Let's go back and join them."

Clarissa said nothing, but Silvio concurred.

"Eat, drink and be merry," he said, "because soon there'll be a thousand new measurements to make."

Chapter 14

Del and Imogen worked together to pack the basket, then Del began lowering it.

"If the bridge had gone all the way to the ground, we would have had to carry this down the ladders," she mused, cranking the handle of the ratcheted winch. "It would never have crossed anyone's mind to make it easier." The basket swayed a little at the end of the rope; she paused to let the motion damp down before continuing.

"Not to mention lugging everything across the ground to get the supply drops spaced out so nicely," Imogen added. "A world that writhes like a decapitated snake is clearly the best of all possible worlds."

The winch's rope slackened: the basket was sitting on the ground. The hook that had been kept closed by the tension sprung open, allowing Del to wind the rope up.

She gazed down at the bare rock of the nub, craggier than its Celeman partner, but every bit as dry and barren. Montano had decided that no one would set foot on the ground until there was enough food and water in place to sustain them for a reasonable time, in the event of some mishap preventing their immediate return. But this tenth drop was the last, and now there were more tools, clothes, tents and even writing materials sitting on the rock than the expeditioners had had access to for most of their journey.

"Still no welcome party from the Tolleans," Imogen noted.

"This place must be as attractive to them as Celema is to us," Del replied.

"If they built a bridge of their own, shouldn't there be ruins?" Imogen suggested.

"Maybe. But it wouldn't have to be in precisely the same spot, and no one's ever done a thorough search, even at our end."

Imogen walked across the platform to the rope ladder, rolled up but complete, just waiting to be unfurled.

"We should go down there," she said. "What's the point in delaying it? Is Montano so proud that his feet need to be the first to touch the sacred ground?"

Del laughed. "That's unfair." She tried to judge Imogen's demeanor; was this a conscious attempt to goad her into ranking everyone's contributions? "We agreed to wait," she said. "And it won't be much longer."

Imogen rested a hand on the coiled ladder. "What if the Tolleans show up and start plundering the supply drops?" she joked.

"In that case, you'd be welcome to go down and try to reason with them."

"You're the one who speaks their language."

"I'll be lucky if I can even write it, but I'm prepared to wave a sign at them asking them to leave our water bottles alone."

Imogen fidgeted with the rope. Del said, "If you're bored hanging around here, we could walk back along the bridge and meet the others halfway."

"No thanks. I prefer to have ground beneath my feet, even if it's this far below them."

Del was eager to get moving, too, but she could understand if Montano and Clarissa had been caught up in the final stages of settling their affairs with the departing workforce. When Del had said her goodbyes the village had already been half-disassembled, but making sure that all the Deremans' wages had been paid and that all the equipment the expedition had hired would be returned without penalties owing was not a job that could be rushed.

She said, "I bet they're still trying—"

The platform shuddered, dropping what felt like half a pace then rising up again. Del kept her footing, but the motion took a while to die away, as if the bridge were a supple twig, struck once but then rebounding several times.

"What was that?" Imogen demanded. "Are we picking up earthquakes in Zeruma now?" The blood had drained from her face.

"I don't know," Del replied. She'd never experienced anything like it; she wished Clarissa was with them to explain why the incident was entirely innocuous.

A creaking sound rose up from the platform, a low, groaning noise entering her body as much through her feet as her ears.

She said, "Drop the ladder."

Imogen stared at her.

Del walked up and grabbed it from her, then ran back across the platform, unrolling the ladder as she went. She tossed the remaining cylinder over the edge and watched it uncurl. If this was nothing more than Imogen had suggested – the bridge acting like a `pendulum, set swinging by a distant seismic event – all her friends could have a good laugh at her timidity. There were worse things than looking foolish.

She turned to Imogen. "Go first, I'll follow you."

"You go first!"

Del said bluntly, "I don't trust you not to lose your nerve."

Imogen scowled and approached the edge of the platform. She knelt down with her feet toward the ladder, then lowered herself onto it and began descending.

Del followed close behind her, all but treading on her hands. The ground was barely two dozen paces below them, but the gravity was strong; if they slipped here, it would not end with a mild bruise. Half the ladder was lying slack across the rock, helping to anchor it against any tendency for its hurried occupants to set it swinging.

"Are you all right?" Del asked Imogen.

"Yes," Imogen replied, breathless and curt, but not panicking.

Del glanced up at the underside of the bridge. She'd never seen this part of it from the same angle, but it did not look deformed or damaged to her: the timber was all neatly slotted together, with nothing visibly broken or buckled. "This is probably a false alarm," she admitted. "But you wanted to beat Montano to be the first to set foot on Fallamva, and now we have a good excuse."

Imogen didn't reply, but Del felt her pause and alter her grip, each shift in her weight twisting the ladder slightly.

As they resumed their descent, the ladder grew taut. Del looked down, confused, expecting to find Imogen doing something that might explain it. Instead, she saw the ground retreating. They were ascending. *The bridge* was ascending.

"Go faster!" she yelled.

Imogen emitted a wail that sounded as frustrated as it was fearful, but she doubled her pace, and Del followed her. Del could see the loose portion of the ladder being gathered up from the rock, but they were outracing it, coming lower with every step.

They were almost on the ground when the ladder lurched and jerked upward sharply. Del jumped, saw Imogen rising, bellowed at her, saw her jump as well.

Del hit the rock feet first, jarring her knees but remaining upright. Imogen struck the ground nearby and toppled over. Del walked over and knelt beside her, wincing.

Imogen said, "I'm all right." She was staring past Del in horrified wonder; Del followed her gaze and saw the curve of the bridge crumpling, cantilevers snapping and falling even as the spine of the thing was drawn up and back through the Hoop.

Pieces of wood spun down in the starlight. Del covered her head with her hands and crouched protectively over Imogen, then she heard the broken beams begin striking the rock around them: thudding, splintering, rebounding, scraping the ground before coming to a halt.

When it was silent, she stayed as she was, trembling, half convinced that if she turned and looked up again, a piece of timber would smash into her face.

"Are you hit?" Imogen asked her. "Are you injured?"

"I don't think so." Del climbed off her. The closest piece of wood was a few paces away. There was a lot of it, scattered about – but nowhere near as much as if the full portion of the bridge that had once hung above the plain had simply fallen here. She had no idea what part of the structure had been the first to fail, but it was clear that a different notion of *down* had won the tug of war for the majority of the spoils.

She rose, and helped Imogen to her feet, then they hobbled together away from the debris. Del stared up into the Hoop; there was nothing visible through the aperture now but stars.

She said, "Maybe the others were still in the village." Who knew how long Montano had been delayed, dealing with all the loose ends? And Clarissa and Silvio would have waited for him.

Imogen said, "Maybe."

Del sat down on the rock, but it was so cold she could feel it through her clothing, so she clambered to her feet again. She started sobbing. Imogen clasped her shoulder, then put an arm around her and drew her against her.

"It's all right," Imogen said. "They'll be fine. We'll be fine. It's all right."

Chapter 15

When the cold became unbearable, they set up tents and a stove, made tea, took shelter, and tried to sleep. Del knew that the only practical strategy would be to travel away from the nub, but when she emerged from her tent and saw the fragments of the bridge scattered across the rock, it still felt wrong to walk away, as if they would somehow be betraying their friends by not staying and waiting for them.

If Montano was alive, he might try to rebuild the bridge. But as plentiful as their supplies were, it would be hard to stretch them out that long, and foolish to attempt it when there was no guarantee that anyone would be coming from Celema. To survive, they would need to use what they had to search for a longer-lasting food source.

"Was it a quake?" Imogen wondered, as they huddled by the stove eating breakfast.

"I don't know." Del could imagine other possibilities, but she had no intention of putting the blame on Clarissa or the builders, when she had no evidence that either were at fault. "I always thought the nubs were the least seismically active places," she said, "but that might be naïve. Just because they don't have molten rock beneath the ground doesn't mean they're not subject to other forces."

Imogen said, "The timing seems suspicious."

"What do you mean?"

"If there was a saboteur among the Deremans," Imogen suggested, "they might have waited until everyone they knew was off the bridge."

"But why would they want to damage the bridge in the first place? I never heard of anyone with the kind of grievance it would take to want to smash the thing they'd built with their own hands, let alone kill people in the process."

"For a bribe," Imogen replied. "Wasn't someone paid to steal the book from your museum? Wasn't someone set up to attack us for our 'gold' in Zeruma?"

Montano had certainly believed the latter, but Del let it drop; they were both still in shock, their thinking wasn't clear.

"We should rest here for a while," she said. "We need to build up our strength." That could do no harm, if they didn't delay too long. And in the process, she hoped, she would give up the lingering delusion that at any moment, Montano, Clarissa and Silvio might come striding across the plain toward them, not only having survived the destruction of the bridge, but having found an entirely new way to continue their journey.

Chapter 16

Walking in darkness through the blizzard, the skin on her face numb with cold, Del felt hopeful. Snow could only be falling around her if moisture had risen into the air elsewhere. The raging wind slamming against her body could only be driven by differences in temperature and pressure. Somewhere not far away, she decided, there had to be the same kind of hot springs that the fish of Apasa thrived in.

She trudged around the edge of the Hoop, joined by a rope to Imogen so they wouldn't lose each other, advancing almost blindly but judging their path by the slope of the terrain. Beneath the snow, the ground was uneven, untouched by any road-makers as far as she could tell. But they didn't need people in order for there to be food.

Del kept moving long after she was exhausted, afraid that if they stopped and tried to camp the snow would simply bury them. The weather had to change eventually; it could not be snowstorm after snowstorm forever.

Her foot struck something and she lost her balance; for a moment she thought both of them would end up face-down in the snow, but Imogen managed to keep her from toppling. Del prodded the obstacle with her boot; it did not feel like a rock, or compacted snow.

She drew closer to Imogen and yelled in her ear, "I think it's a tree root!"

Imogen tried kicking it herself. "It could be!"

Del swayed, letting the wind-driven snowflakes enter her hood at new angles, striking parts of her face that could still feel. She had never believed that the lands across the gap could be entirely barren, but if this was part of a plant, it was the first living thing they'd encountered. Or at least, the first thing that had once been alive.

As they continued around the hill, the wind began to drop, and a landscape of starlit snow emerged from the darkness. When they approached the Hoop, the transition was impossible to miss: parts of the new sky were completely clear. Del tried to memorize the constellations, as Silvio might have done: there was a snake, and a bird, and a ruined castle. She tried to bind them together in a story; she wanted to be able to recognize this place again, without counting circuits around the edge.

Imogen bumped shoulders with her. "See that!"

Del followed the direction of her gaze. In the distance there was a small forest: just a few dozen stark black trunks, but every tree had to be drawing water from the ground, and feeding on subterranean heat.

"We should rest," Imogen said.

They set up their tents. Del crawled inside and fell asleep at once. When she woke she felt refreshed, though she was thirsty and famished.

She emerged from her tent and set up the stove. When she called to Imogen she received no reply, then she noticed her squatting in the forest and looked away.

While breakfast was cooking, Imogen returned to the campsite, holding something in her gloved hands. She held it out toward Del: it was a small bird with black and white feathers, its head lolling, certainly dead but as yet uncorrupted by decay.

Imogen didn't need to explain; this wasn't a supplement for their meal, or a keepsake acquired on some morbid impulse. It was a sign that every form of life they were familiar with was likely to be present here. The mountains that had blocked the way for all of recorded history meant nothing. This land was a part of their world; they had left all the maps behind, but they were not lost. Not entirely.

Chapter 17

Del took the seeds she'd extracted from the last of the dried tomatoes and pushed them into the holes she'd made in the soil. Her previous attempt at raising a garden from portions of desiccated vegetables had come to nothing, but it seemed worth persisting on the chance that some seed or cutting might yet turn out to be viable, in spite of its unfavorable history.

Back at the campsite, Imogen was baking some freshly caught fish over a wood fire. The springs appeared to be inexhaustible, but they couldn't live on fish alone.

"I could bring more food from the nub," Del suggested. "If the weather gets too obnoxious along the way, I'll turn back and try again later."

Imogen said, "There must be something edible growing wild. If we keep looking, we'll find it eventually."

"Maybe." The closest thing they'd chanced upon so far was a kind of herb that improved the flavor of the fish, but it was no more credible as a source of nutrition than parsley.

They ate the fish, then Del cleaned up, and they sat by the dying embers of the fire.

"We can't keep relying on the nub," Imogen said. "Nothing we left there will help us in the long run. We need to go further and find better land."

Del agreed, but the details still worried her. "What if we made a few trips to bring the remaining food here? Then at least we'd have it all on hand if we need it."

"If we need it, what will we do when it's gone?" Imogen countered.

"I meant that we might need it for longer than we hoped," Del replied. "Not forever. But if it lets us make one more exploratory trip to look for a place that can feed us properly, that could still be the difference between finding that natural garden and succumbing to scurvy first."

Imogen didn't reply. Del hated the idea of the two of them separating, but she couldn't drag Imogen back to the nub if she didn't believe it was worth it.

When Imogen retired to her tent, Del packed her warm clothes and some water. She decided not to take any food; with no detours, the trip shouldn't last that long, and there'd be far more than she needed waiting at her destination.

She left the camp and set off around the hill. The weather was mild, and the ground here was not too difficult to cross. None of that would last, but having a rough idea of the conditions to expect made the prospect easier to face than when they'd been stumbling constantly into the unknown.

As she walked, she found herself thinking ahead. If they could feed themselves properly, what then? Just wait as close to the nub as possible, and hope that the bridge would be rebuilt? Or push on, toward Sadema? Of all the miracles Natasha's theory could perform, it had offered no way of estimating how many circuits of the edge there would be in total before any path came full circle. Sadema could be a dozen loops away, or a thousand. And if they reached the land adjacent to it, there would still be no guarantee that any passage through the mountains would be easier to find from this side than it had been from the other.

Still, none of this was reason to lose hope. Whatever had happened to the bridge, there had been dozens of witnesses to the finitude of the gap. Even if Montano's investors were weary of the venture, word would spread, and one failure would not deter people forever.

She passed through the Hoop a third time; it had started to grow chilly, but there was still no snow. Above her, frozen in the stars, a butterfly was approaching a lily, and a sailboat was skirting a promontory complete with lighthouse.

Then she glanced down at the ground and saw a pair of furrows in the soil, about two paces apart.

She stopped and knelt for a closer look. Neither she nor Imogen had noticed anything like this when they'd been coming in the other direction, but that didn't mean that the furrows were recent, or that they lacked a natural cause. Most carts or barrows had more closely spaced wheels than this, but in any case, who was to say that two heavy stones hadn't fallen from the hillside and ended up gouging parallel grooves in the soil?

Del traced the furrows back the way she'd come. They weren't the product of anything rolling down a slope; they circled the hill, taking much the same route as any traveler between lands might choose.

Eventually the soil gave way to rock and the trail vanished. So she reversed course and followed the tracks in the other direction, past the point where she'd first noticed them. Where the ground was soft they were very deep, and the edges sharply defined. Del couldn't imagine fewer than four people being able to push a cart as heavy as this, and to keep it moving so steadily and smoothly.

About a quarter of the way around the hill, the tracks veered away from the edge of the Hoop and led off across the scrubland. Del peered into the distance, hoping she might see lights, or a building, but nothing stood out.

She felt a burning sensation in her limbs, urging her to break into a sprint that would carry her swiftly to the end of the trail. But if she pursued this now, alone, anything might happen. Even if the cart's owners were entirely friendly, she was certain to face a struggle to communicate with them; interrupting the process midway to go and fetch Imogen would only complicate matters. They needed to be together from the start.

She searched the hillside for markers, and settled on some distinctive rocks whose shape and disposition she committed to memory. Then she stared at the constellations on either side of the Hoop, scrutinizing the precise division between the skies. *Silvio would be proud of me*, she thought. With luck, she might even get a chance to joke with him about her rudimentary navigational skills.

Then she turned and started running, back around the hill, back toward the campsite.

Chapter 18

The fifth time they stopped the pursuit to rest, Del found herself contemplating the possibility that they would have to turn back. They were low on food and water, and they hadn't encountered any springs or streams since they began following the cart's trail. Nothing could be more important for their long-term survival than trying to make contact with this land's inhabitants – but nothing would be more foolish than killing themselves in the process, out of sheer stubbornness and impatience.

When Del woke, Imogen was already folding up her tent. Del drank half a cup of water and started on the same task.

"These people must be indefatigable," Imogen complained, as they picked up the trail again.

"Unless they've harnessed giant rats to the cart," Del joked. She was sure that happened in a children's story, but she'd forgotten which one.

"Where are their paw-prints?" Imogen retorted.

"Paws are softer than wheels."

"True. Now that I think about it, everything's softer than wheels." They'd seen no footprints of any kind: human or animal, naked or shod.

They walked side by side, their eyes to the ground, each of them concentrating on a single furrow. As the terrain varied, one or the other indentation would sometimes vanish, so it was helpful to be able to rely on their partner to keep guiding them in the right direction, without the distraction of having to switch attention to the other track. But even when both furrows disappeared for a stretch, the cart had generally followed such a straight path that it was easy to pick it up again.

Del felt moisture on her cheek and glanced up at the sky, but there were no clouds in sight; a drop of sweat must have followed a strand of hair from her temple then fallen. "Maybe we should dig for water," she mused. Excavating a well might take as long as walking back to the spring they'd left behind – but at least it wouldn't cost them the extra time needed for the return journey.

Imogen said, "What's that?"

They had just come over a rise, revealing a new stretch of scrubland ahead of them. In the distance, Del could see a forest. But beside the forest was a boxy structure, pale gray in the starlight.

She said, "I think it's a tent."

They approached slowly, as much out of weariness as caution. As they grew nearer, Del saw what she supposed was the cart they'd been following, standing motionless behind the tent. At least, it was a thing with four wheels and an enclosed section that would hold a substantial quantity of goods, but she could see no handles or harnesses.

When they reached the tent, there was no one in sight. It was made from a fabric Del didn't recognize, and there were clear sections in it, like windows, but when she touched one gently it felt softer and lighter than glass. Too little starlight entered to really dispel the gloom, and the windows were opaque to radiant heat, so it was impossible to tell if there were any occupants.

"If someone's in there sleeping, do we really want to disturb them?" she asked Imogen quietly. If these people were as wary of bandits as she had become, they might emerge with weapons drawn and strike first for their own protection.

"Probably not," Imogen decided.

They retreated to a respectful distance, and placed their packs on the ground as seats.

"The separation must have bred something stronger than us, if they can push that thing around," Imogen said, nodding toward the cart.

Del wasn't so sure. "Maybe it's lighter than it looks. I can't even tell if it's wood or metal, and that tent's made of something I've never seen before."

"What if we're like animals to them?" Imogen fretted. "Maybe they ate all the Tolleans who came here, and that's why people gave up trying to trade with them."

Del had no idea anymore what was or wasn't possible, but having come this far, she wasn't interested in talking up her fears. "Animals don't wear clothes or sleep in tents. And we seem to have at least the latter in common."

She heard footsteps, and looked toward the sound. A man was approaching the tent, striding briskly across the scrub. Del couldn't swear that he shared every last trait of her own species, but his heat blotch certainly appeared human, and even his clothes did not look particular strange.

He noticed his visitors, and stopped, gazing toward them, clearly startled. He called out, in a tone that seemed mildly wary but not hostile.

Del couldn't understand a word he'd uttered, but she rose to her feet and raised a hand, then greeted him in her wholly hypothetical pronunciation of Tollean. "Good wishes to you! We've come across the landless skies, seeking friendship, knowledge and trade!"

The man stared at her, bemused, then replied to her gibberish with some more of his own.

"What's he saying?" Imogen asked.

"I have no idea," Del confessed.

She knelt down and extracted a pencil and drawing pad from her pack, held them up so the man could see that they weren't weapons, and began walking slowly toward him. His expression remained guarded at first, but then suddenly he broke into a baffled smile, as if he found the whole encounter so strange that he couldn't help but treat it as amusing.

When Del came close enough for him to see the pad clearly, she started writing on it, spelling out her Tollean greeting, on the chance that the barrier between them was purely phonetic. The man squinted at the paper, then took some kind of lamp from a pocket in his coat, lit it too quickly for Del to see quite what he'd done, and held it up toward her message.

When she was finished, she looked to his face, but there was no hint of comprehension. She offered him the pad; he hesitated, then took it, and wrote a short message in an entirely different script – neither Tollean, nor anything she had seen before.

Del accepted the pad back and turned to a fresh page. She made a rough sketch of the nub at Celema, then drew a helix to indicate the travelers' path through the void, then the second nub, and a continuation of the helix for the nine turns needed to bring them to this land. She continued the line as far as she could away from the last turn, then drew three figures at the end of it, and gestured at the three of them.

The man scrutinized the drawing for a while, then laughed. He pointed to the helix crossing the void, then looked at Del with an expression of unmistakeable skepticism. *You did this ... how?*

She sketched in the bridge, adding as many cantilevers as she could to make the nature of the structure clear, without spending an eternity turning it into one of Clarissa's architectural drawings. The man pondered this attempt at an explanation, but it only seemed to exacerbate his incredulity.

Imogen had approached quietly while Del had been drawing. She whispered, "So what does he make of us?"

"I don't think he believes we crossed the gap. Either that, or he has no idea what I've been trying to tell him."

"Where are all his friends? Where's his village? It can't just be him, with a tent and a cart."

Del offered the man the pad, pointed to him, and mimed walking with two fingers. He laughed at the gesture, but seemed to understand it. He drew his own path in the same manner as hers, showing a route that circled the edge of the Hoop more than a dozen times from the other direction, then led back across the landscape. He drew in some hills, a river, and a crudely rendered collection of buildings.

"So he's come a long way to be here," Imogen concluded. "If this land is a wilderness, there might not be anyone but him and his companions."

Del took back the pad and pointed to the man, pointed to her sketch of him at the end of her path, then tentatively drew in three more figures beside him: the very least required to make the cart move.

He frowned, puzzled, then looked back the way she'd come, as if he expected to find that she and Imogen were the ones with more companions.

Del pointed to him again, then to the tent and the cart: it was the size of *his* party she was asking about.

He took the pencil from her and scribbled over the extra figures. He placed his hand on his chest, then pointed to his campsite. He was here alone.

Imogen said, "Then he really must be insanely strong."

The man's build didn't seem unusual to Del. Could his physiology be so different that someone with such a slender frame really could propel the cart all that distance?

Del didn't think it would be polite to dwell on the matter, but Imogen walked over to the cart, stood behind it, then pushed on it with both hands. She grimaced and strained, digging her feet into the soil, but it didn't budge.

The man looked on with a kind of forbearance, as if he found her behavior utterly bizarre, but was prepared to make allowances for his guests' eccentricities. Imogen stepped away from the cart, then motioned to him, inviting him to take her place.

He laughed, but then she repeated the gesture, with an air that Del supposed even he could interpret as a challenge. *You say you're alone, you say you brought this here yourself? Then prove it!*

He thought for a while, then he approached the cart, but he went, not to the back, but to the side. He climbed up and took a seat in front of the enclosed section.

"Does he think we're going to push it for him, while he sits there like a king?" Imogen asked scornfully.

The man reached down and grasped a lever beside the seat. When he pulled it up, the cart lurched backward slightly, then came to rest again. So it had a brake; that seemed like a sensible precaution, to keep it from rolling away on a slope.

Then he started moving another lever that protruded from the floor in front of him. Suddenly, Del heard a sound like repeated hammer blows, metal on metal, loud and growing ever more frequent, until the individual strikes blurred together into a continuous, oppressive drone.

Imogen yelled, "It sounds like a steam-driven pump, but where's the fire?"

The cart began to move forward slowly across the grass. The man turned and looked back at them, smiling. Then the drone rose in pitch, and he sped away. Del thought he might easily vanish from sight, but then he made a turn and circled back toward them.

When he came to a halt, with the cart more or less back at the place it had departed from, he jumped down and gestured to them to climb up onto the contraption themselves.

Imogen turned to Del. "What do you think? It might kill an ordinary person to move that fast."

Del thought it over. "We're the ones who walked through the void on a bridge that this man refuses to believe in. And you've walked under the ocean, with the air pumped to you from above. Maybe we have a few tricks he's never seen, and he has a few, likewise. But I don't think we're all that different."

She clambered up onto the cart, and then offered a hand to Imogen. The man joined them, clearly delighted that they'd accepted the invitation, then he took his seat and began to work the levers.

Chapter 19

Del and Imogen set up their tents, not far from the man's campsite. He watched them for a while, but did nothing that expressed obvious displeasure at this sustained intrusion into his solitude. When they had finished, he approached, carrying a container. He took off the lid and made a tentative pouring motion; he was offering them water.

Del brought one of their own empty containers, and held it while he filled it up. She smiled and bowed her head briefly; it was not her custom, but she hoped it signaled gratitude. Then she pointed to his container and swept her arm around, wondering where he'd obtained the water. The man mimed drawing; she fetched the pad. He drew a stream cascading over rocks, surrounded by trees. Then he pointed to the forest.

After they'd slept, Del and Imogen went to explore the forest. The trees weren't tall, but they looked healthy, with lush foliage that felt warm to Del's touch. The undergrowth was thicker here than anything Del had encountered since Zeruma, and Imogen spotted a bush with purple berries that proved more than palatable.

They found the stream, and Imogen succeeded in catching half a dozen small fish. "We'd probably be all right here for a while," she said. "I think there are some root vegetables we could eat as well."

Del was relieved that they wouldn't be compelled to beg the man for food. Judging from his actions so far he would probably have been willing to share as much as he was able, but the difficulty in communicating the nuances of their respective situations made the prospect seem more humiliating.

"I can understand if the Tollean language didn't survive here," she said. "But if they came across the gap, surely everyone would still know about the crossing?"

"I'm sure they would," Imogen replied, unhooking another catch and tossing it into her bucket.

"So ... ?"

Imogen said, "Just because we succeeded – barely — that doesn't mean the Tolleans did. They talked about some kind of plan to travel here, and debated the pros and cons, but we have no proof that they ever pulled it off."

Del couldn't dispute this, but it was hard to regain her original agnosticism about the Tolleans' claims while standing on land that the naysayers had so fervently declared to be inaccessible. "I can't believe the people who were right about this place never got to visit it."

Imogen was amused. "One side or the other had to be right. The ancients said so many different things about the world that they more or less covered every possibility."

On their way back to the campsite, Del saw the man standing in the forest. He was staring up intently at the branches of a tree, holding what appeared to be a notepad and a writing implement. She paused to try to see what he was so interested in; there were several small, colorful birds flitting from branch to branch, but nothing unusual she could discern. Had he come so far from his home just to study the birds in this forest? It was not inconceivable; she had met naturalists in Apasa who would have made a trip like that for the right opportunity. But it was sobering to think that she and Imogen might owe their survival to an act of esoteric scholarship, or even just whimsy.

Later, when they were cooking the fish, the man approached, carrying a large pot. He paused some distance from the fire, but Imogen gestured to him to approach, and he opened the pot to show them four cleaned and gutted raw fish and an assortment of vegetables.

Del wasn't sure if this was meant as a gift, or if he wished to join them, but she thought it would be better to err on the side of politeness, so after accepting the pot she motioned to him to sit by the fire, and proceeded to merge its contents with their original meal.

The three of them ate together, just enjoying the food, communicating everything they needed with gestures no more elaborate than Del would have used if she'd been alone with Imogen. But when they'd finished, the man took out his notepad and drew the same path he'd drawn when they first met, in reverse. He was going home.

Imogen turned to Del. "I'm sure we could survive here. We're a long way from the edge of the Hoop, but we could leave a sign there with a map, so if anyone else makes the crossing they'll know where to find us."

"Is that what you want?" Del asked.

"No," Imogen replied. "But I thought someone should make the case."

"Then I'll make the other case. The more people we meet on this side, the better our chances of finding a way home, even if no one comes after us."

Imogen smiled. "You didn't say a word about solving the mystery of the Tolleans."

"That seems like too much to ask," Del admitted. "I'd be happy doing anything that keeps us alive and gets us back to Apasa. But if the best hope of that also means learning everything we can about this place and its history, all the better."

The man had been waiting politely while they discussed the matter, but once it was clear that their conversation was over, he passed the notebook and pencil to Del with a questioning look. He'd sketched his self-propelled cart, and drawn himself in the front seat. Del drew two more figures behind him.

"Yerada!" he proclaimed happily.

"Yerada," Del repeated, without even thinking; if it was the wrong response the man showed no sign of amusement, or any urge to correct her.

Imogen said, "I hope that doesn't mean 'My cannibal brothers will be delighted when I bring them this exotic meal.'"

"That's absurd," Del protested. "No language could communicate that much in so few syllables."

Imogen seemed on the verge of conceding the point, but then she changed her mind. "If it's a common sentiment, it might have a compact expression," she insisted.

"So let's pack up the tents," Del replied, "and prepare to meet the cannibals. On the journey, I'm sure we can think up some way to charm them into holding off for a while."

Chapter 20

The cart rattled over the scrubland, back toward the edge of the Hoop, with a velocity that left Del feeling as if her and Imogen's long struggle across the same territory had been a kind of dream. As hills and dips and outcrops that she recalled as bleak, lingering signposts on their famished march came and went, the only explanation that made sense to her was that she'd been walking in a trance.

Their present journey, for all its strangeness, wasn't dreamlike at all; the shuddering machine set her teeth clattering, banishing any possibility of her mind drifting off into oneiric reveries.

"It must be burning something!" Imogen yelled. "I can see the heat. But a steam engine would have burned through the whole thing's weight in wood by now, and I can't smell any smoke."

Del couldn't smell fish oil either, so that couldn't be the fuel. "Once we learn the language, we can start asking questions," was the best she could offer.

Imogen said, "I'd rather just take the thing apart, so I can see how it works with my own eyes."

"Maybe he'll let you do that, once we've reached our destination. But I'm pretty sure you'll have to put in some work first, to learn how to ask nicely."

They reached the hill, and turned to circle it. Steering the cart looked trickier now; before, the uneven ground had diverted them to and fro at random, to no great effect, but here the slope and curvature of the terrain seemed intent on diverting them from their chosen course if they tolerated more than the slightest meandering. But they still made steady progress, sending the Hoop sweeping across the sky, dredging up constellations that Del recalled from earlier journeys as if she were flicking through the pages of a diary.

They passed the site where she and Imogen had set up camp. Then, with no hesitation or ceremony, the cart carried them through the Hoop yet again, to a land they had never set foot upon.

Two circuits later, the cart lurched briefly, then the jittering that Del had grown accustomed to all but died away. The man turned and smiled at them, and Del nodded happily in acknowledgment at the smoother ride. She looked down and tried to scrutinize the surface; the paving stones passed by in a blur, but her impression was of neat, broad polygonal slabs – the kind that in Thena would only be used in a city. Every now and then the cart still juddered; no road was perfect at this speed. But they had left the wilderness behind.

"If we'd explored a little farther, we might have been on this road a long time ago," Imogen mused.

"But we wouldn't have been moving so quickly," Del replied, then she laughed at her own defensiveness. It didn't matter what series of choices and accidents had brought them to this point. After all their tribulations, they were on their way to civilization.

A second cart appeared from behind the hill, traveling toward them. Both slowed down a little as they approached; Del could see two people sitting side-by-side in the front. She tried to read their faces, and wondered if it would be polite to make some kind of gesture in lieu of a verbal greeting as they passed. But their host paid no attention to them, so Del just averted her gaze.

Clouds spread across the stars, and rain began to fall. The man stopped the cart, then clambered back between Del and Imogen and pulled up a kind of hood: a hinged frame with the same kind of material as his tent's windows. When he started the cart again, three lamps lit up below him at the front, illuminating a stretch of the road ahead. Del couldn't see what the lamps were burning, or how they'd been ignited, but from her present vantage she had no way to get a better look.

She turned to the side, away from the hill. There were half a dozen patches of light in the distance – nearby towns, she supposed –

shimmering through the rain. Exactly what was bounteous in these lands remained unclear, but there certainly seemed to be an abundance of fuel.

They passed another cart coming the other way, lighting up the road in the same fashion as their own, but between the rain and the opalescent glass of the lamp housings Del still couldn't make out any details of the flames.

"If these people can travel so effortlessly, why did they never bother visiting us?" Imogen complained.

"We stared at the gap for generations without realizing how narrow it was," Del replied. "If the Tolleans didn't cross it, maybe no one ever grasped the possibility before, on either side." As they spoke, three more carts passed them, all equally swift and luminous, dispelling any notion that these contraptions might be rare.

"So if the Tolleans were only ever talking about a path through the mountains ... do you expect to meet up with some of our competitors soon?" Imogen asked, with just a trace of sarcasm.

Del said, "Nothing would surprise me any more. If there are two ways here, maybe the other route also just needed fresh eyes to reveal it."

As they continued around the hill, the number of carts traveling back and forth along the ring road increased, as did the number of turnoffs feeding and tapping these flows. After a while, Del no longer needed to look out for the side roads themselves; she could see them from afar, painted across the landscape with the light from the carts.

The man leaned back in his seat and yawned. Del didn't want to think about the consequences if he dozed off while the machine was moving, but it was hard to know how to engage with him politely without distracting him from his task. After fretting for a while, she bent forward and touched his shoulder gently; he glanced back enquiringly, unoffended.

"Thank you for all the help you're giving us," she said, hoping that some of her meaning would be conveyed by her tone and demeanor alone. In any case, he smiled amiably and returned his gaze to the road.

The rain stopped pelting the hood above them, and though the sky remained overcast it barely mattered: the carts were present in such numbers now as to far outshine any stars. Glowing towns and cities came and went in the distance; Del wondered if the people here had learned to navigate by these terrestrial lights, instead of relying on the constellations.

As they passed through the Hoop, the man announced gleefully, "Yerada!"

"It's the name of his homeland," Del realized. It even sounded like a land to her foreigner's ear. However long the two groups had been separated, the whole system of nomenclature might well have dated from a time when Sadema had presented no obstruction to travel. But if the hint of a shared history was comforting, that the world had then raised mountains high enough to sever all ties, and that enough time had passed to erase all memories of their prior common experience, induced a kind of temporal vertigo that she couldn't outstare; she could only look away.

After one more quarter-circuit of the hill, the man slowed the cart and turned onto a spoke road that stretched out across the gently undulating ground. Carts traced out the highway in light, and flowed along the side roads that Del could see ahead of them, but even away from these trails, everywhere she looked there were buildings lit up like the most extravagant palaces in a children's tale. Her eyes were beginning to water from the endless dazzle; this wasn't an assault as painful as Erema's sky, but it was still far more intense and relentless than anything human-made that she'd encountered before.

"Our friend might not have been bird-watching," Imogen suggested. "He might have traveled that far just to have a chance to see the stars without all of this glare."

The cart took one of the side roads. Del saw a group of people on foot, deferring to the perilous machinery by confining themselves to a narrow path along the road's edge. It turned again, then after traveling a short way down another street, it left the road and entered a small courtyard in front of a house of dark bricks.

The man gestured to them apologetically with a raised palm then jumped down and walked into the house. "He's going to have to explain to someone that he's come home with a couple of unexpected guests," Del conjectured.

"We still have our tents," Imogen replied. "If we're not welcome here, there'll be somewhere we can camp."

Del admired her self-sufficiency, but comfort aside, she was fervently hoping they wouldn't end up adrift in this strange culture. The man might have been skeptical about their claimed origins, but at least he knew exactly where he'd met them; to anyone else in the city, they'd just be a couple of oddly-dressed travelers who might or might not be faking their inability to speak the language.

The man emerged, looking slightly chastened but relieved, and motioned for Del and Imogen to follow him. They grabbed their packs and walked after him into the house, down a corridor then into a brightly lit room with four chairs and a table. A lamp was hanging from the ceiling, but when Del glanced up to try to examine it she had to turn away.

She could smell fish cooking and looked around for the stove; this time, there was a strong heat blotch but no light apparent at all.

A woman entered the room and inclined her head briefly, regarding them with a mixture of curiosity and irritation. Del returned the gesture awkwardly, wishing she'd made more effort back in the wilderness to learn some basic greetings and etiquette.

The man dished out the meal onto four plates and they all sat together. He offered them no utensils, but Del watched him using pieces of bread from a stack in the center of the table to pick up the food, which was already finely cut, and she did her best to mimic him. The fish tasted glorious; it was kind of the couple to share what had clearly been prepared for the two of them.

"I think they're fattening us up for later," Imogen whispered.

When they'd finished eating, the woman showed them a room where they could wash and excrete in private, and Del let Imogen have use of it first.

"Thank you," Del said to the woman, who replied with a curt phrase that might have meant anything.

Suddenly, Del found herself smiling. It was all she could do to keep herself from reeling around, staring up at the blinding lights on the ceiling. The two halves of the world had been living their lives for all this time, if not oblivious to each other's existence, certainly ignorant of most of each other's history. Maybe her friends had died in the process of making the reunion possible; maybe they'd survived. But either way, it was up to her and Imogen now, not just to preserve their own lives, but to complete what they'd started and bring the divided world together.

Chapter 21

The visitor to the house stood before them, placed his fist on his sternum, and said, "Jo plen Lados."

"What's he doing?" Imogen asked Del.

"I have no idea."

Their host copied the gesture, and said, "Jo plen Halem."

The visitor regarded them encouragingly.

"It could just be their names," Del guessed. She put her fist against her chest and said, "Jo plen Del." Imogen seemed unconvinced, but she offered her own name. The visitor – Lados? – was pleased, so they'd either deduced his true intentions, or convinced him that they'd learned some other lesson entirely.

He turned to Del and uttered a string of syllables that ended with a fair approximation of her name. She gazed back at him apologetically; he tried again, speaking more slowly. "Sere makom lemere pedra, Del."

Del supposed it was a simple greeting; she repeated the sounds as best she could, substituting "Lados." Lados rewarded her with a smile that couldn't quite hide his gritted teeth, and he insisted on another few rounds of refinement before moving on to his other pupil.

When Imogen had mastered the phrase to Lados's satisfaction, she turned to Del and whispered, "What have we done to deserve this torture?"

"We need to learn their language," Del insisted. "It's the only way we'll get anywhere."

Imogen said, "I'm willing to do hard labor in exchange for food and board. Do I really need to talk to anyone, to dig a ditch? They can just point me in the right direction and mime an appropriate shoveling action."

"Do you ever want to go home?"

"You think they're going to build a bridge for us, if we just ask them nicely?"

Del didn't reply; put so bluntly, the notion seemed preposterous. But until they understood much more about this society, they had no way of knowing whether it would require a struggle a thousand times greater than Montano had faced, or whether a better guide to their prospects was the spectacular diminution of effort involved in traveling from land to land.

Lados led them patiently through several more phrases, with Halem helping out when the lesson required two speakers, as well as supplying props from around the dining room as examples of various colors and food groups. Del hoped she was at least beginning to get an ear for the sound of the language; however impatient she was to acquire a meaningful vocabulary and understand the grammar, without the shortcuts she'd been accustomed to as a student back in Apasa – a second, shared language that her teachers could use to sneak extra information into her head – everything would depend on the clarity of this one, phonetic means of exchange.

Eventually, Lados deferred to Imogen's increasingly undisguised misery and gave them a rest. Halem handed them some fruit to eat, without asking them to name it first, and the four of them sat and chatted in their own tongues with their fellow native speakers.

"That's the most exhausting thing I've done since we left home," Imogen declared.

Del hoped this was intentional hyperbole. "It's like using a muscle. Once you grow accustomed to it, all the soreness will fade away, and you'll have the pleasure of gaining a new strength."

Imogen snorted with amusement.

"So what do you tell your underwater diving students," Del wondered, "if they hate their first experience?"

Imogen said, "I tell them not to come back."

Del had no idea if Lados was a professional teacher, or just an enthusiastic friend of Halem who had volunteered to try out some ideas, but he was not yet willing to concede defeat with either of his pupils. He produced a stack of paper and proceeded to draw the forty-four letters of the local script, then he guided Del and Imogen in their attempts to copy and memorize the symbols. Though they looked like nothing Del had seen before, they were not overly finicky or ornate; the hard part was learning their names.

"Why does it matter what order we write them in?" Imogen asked irritably. "I don't want a job sorting index cards or shelving books."

"It's easier to remember them all if you have them in a definite order," Del suggested.

"What if I find it easier to remember them if I draw all the simplest ones first, then add the ones with increasing numbers of extra strokes?"

By the time Imogen had completed her first full recitation, even Lados appeared weary. Del wished she could do something to relieve the tedium for him; she was hardly in a position to engage in a sparkling intellectual conversation, but maybe she could offer him a welcome trace of novelty.

She said, "*Draho*" (thank you), gestured at the letters while calling them "*Limna*" (yours), then proceeded to write – "*Calla*" (mine) – her own set of nineteen.

Lados watched with interest, or at least polite attention. She hadn't expected him to recognize the symbols; they had rough equivalents in many older scripts, but the resemblance grew increasingly obscure with age, and if anyone had asked her to match her own letters to a subset of the ones she'd just learned, she would have floundered.

When she was finished, Del put the sheet aside, but then she realized she'd wasted an opportunity. Quickly, before Lados decided to resume the lesson, she said, "But these are the ones the Tolleans used," and started to draw them.

She was only halfway through when Lados started whispering excitedly to Halem. He didn't interrupt her, so she kept writing; when she'd finished she slid the page across the table to him. "That's the Tollean script. Tollean. *Lim punra?*" Do you know it?

"*Punra*," he replied.

Del picked up her pencil and wrote a question in Tollean: **Did these people come here? Are they still here?**

Lados replied apologetically, "Xala depunra." He didn't know ... the words? He recognized the script, but that was all.

He must have read the disappointment on Del's face; he made a gesture with a raised hand that she took to mean that this wasn't the end of the matter. He turned to Halem and the two of them spoke for a while; Del couldn't understand anything they said, but from the long pauses and thoughtful frowns, she assumed that they were trying, and failing, to conjure up the name of someone they knew who might actually read Tollean.

Lados rose from his seat and departed, bidding them a perfunctory farewell without stopping to turn it into a lesson. Del heard his cart starting up in the courtyard. The woman who shared the house, whose name Del had yet to learn, called out to Halem, and he left the room.

Del said, "The Tolleans came here. We can be sure of that now."

"Can we?" Imogen was doubtful. "Maybe the Tolleans just used a lettering system similar to one that was once used here – thanks to some ancestral language that dates back to before the obstruction at Sadema."

"You're right," Del conceded. "That's possible." But she wasn't giving up hope that it meant something more.

"I need some air," Imogen declared. "You want to go for a walk?"

Del found Halem and managed to assemble enough fragments from her lessons to express her intention to leave but return soon, sprinkling in enough *draho*, she hoped, not to sound ungrateful that they'd been given lodgings here, or presumptuous about the duration of the arrangement. Halem, in fact, seemed to grasp the message long before she stopped talking, and gave no impression of taking offense that his guests might wish to go for a stroll on their own.

Once they'd left the courtyard and started down the street, Del found the constant flow of mechanised carts traveling beside them both

122

wondrous and unnerving. That any ordinary person here could own a device that let them travel at such speed was astonishing, but she wasn't sure if she could trust them to remain fully cognisant of the minority among them who still moved around on foot.

Most of the buildings they passed looked similar to Halem's house, constructed from the same dark bricks, in the same style. There had to be fields and springs somewhere, to feed all these people, but Del supposed there was no need for such things to be especially close, when produce could be moved so easily.

"I don't like being dependent on Halem," Imogen confessed. "He's been kind to us, but we have to find a way to stand on our own feet."

"You could give diving lessons," Del suggested.

"What if people have never done that here?"

"Then you'll have no competition, and you'll be rich and famous in no time."

Imogen laughed. "Well, they must have need of conservators too." She stopped and gazed, frustrated, at the line of speeding machines. "I still can't tell what it is they're burning."

Del said, "A couple more language lessons, and you'll be able to ask."

"That's optimistic. What if we have no word for it ourselves? I'll ask what fuel is in his cart, Halem will reply, '*Fzzbugurble*', and I'll have learned precisely nothing."

"So then you ask him where it comes from, who grows it or makes it, and how. If a child in Yerada can learn about *Fzzbugurble*, so can you."

Imogen said, "I don't have the patience to be a child again."

"We'll be fast children," Del promised. Imogen just grunted skeptically.

They didn't dare try to cross any of the streets, with their ceaseless mechanised processions, so they walked in a circuit around the land bounded by four of them. By the third time around, Del was growing weary of the lights and noise, and she believed they were approaching

Halem's house again. It was hard to be sure, when the buildings were so similar.

"What if we walk in, and there's an entirely different family there?" she said.

Imogen turned to her with an expression of horror. "You were thinking that, too? Maybe there are a thousand extra Hoops here, threading the city, so if you walk in a circle anywhere at all, you end up somewhere new."

Del felt the skin prickling on her forearms. "You're joking, aren't you?" She glanced up at the sky, but with the glare from below washing out any trace of the stars it was impossible to tell if it contained a transition line.

Imogen gave her a look that seemed to imply that her need to ask was more alarming than the idea itself.

"Dal! Imagine!"

Del turned, and raised a hand to shield her eyes. Lados and Halem had stopped a short distance behind them, riding Lados's cart. Halem motioned to them to get on.

"Oh, now comes the cannibal feast," Imogen muttered.

Del said, "They must have found someone who can help."

Imogen followed her reluctantly, and they both clambered up onto the back of the cart. Lados started the engine again, chatting excitedly with Halem as they sped away.

The cart negotiated the intersecting streets, pausing at some crossroads, rushing through others, turning left and right in a sequence that seemed far more complex than mere geometry should require, as if they were ricocheting through the innards of some huge, gleaming machine. The city was beautiful, in its own strange way, but Del could not imagine ever feeling at home here.

When they finally stopped, it was outside a building far larger than any house. Lados jumped off the cart and set off toward the entrance immediately, as if he was afraid that whoever had agreed to assist him might change their mind if he didn't rush back to assure them that the foreigners he'd described really were on their way.

His companions followed him into the building. The foyer reminded Del of the museum in Apasa, but she couldn't see any exhibits. A few people they passed in the corridors gazed at them for a moment in puzzlement before politely looking away; perhaps the Thenans' style of dress was far enough from the local norms to incite some interest, but not quite bizarre enough to induce alarm.

When they caught up with Lados, he was waiting for them beside an open doorway. Del wasn't sure why he looked so nervous; perhaps he was afraid that she'd make a fool of him by turning out to be less interesting than he'd promised. He composed himself and stepped forward, into view of the room's occupant, and spoke quietly: "Excuse me, we're here," or something close to that; Del had reached the stage where she wasn't sure whether she was recognizing words she'd learned in the new language, or merely inferring their meaning from the context.

As they entered, a woman rose from a seat beside a paper-strewn table and approached them. There were shelves all around the walls of the room, packed with books and stacks of paper.

"Jo plen Grana," she said, addressing Del directly.

"Jo plen Del. Sere makom lemere pedra, Grana."

Grana welcomed everyone, then ushered her guests into seats around the table.

"This feels like a test," Imogen whispered.

"Good," Del replied. "One advantage of telling the truth is that the more they test our claims, the better chance we have of being believed."

"You're so innocent sometimes, I can't believe it."

Del thought: *And you're so cynical sometimes, I want to punch you.*

Grana wrote something on a sheet of paper and passed it to Del: a short passage in the Tollean script. For a moment her mind was blank, then she recognized the words and translated them for Imogen: "Can you read this language?"

Del wrote beneath it: **Yes, though not very well. It's not used anymore by my people, and all we have of it are fragments.**

Grana read the reply, and spoke to Lados and Halem; her demeanor suggested a wary fascination. Del couldn't blame her for remaining cautious; after all, if Grana herself understood Tollean, merely knowing the language proved nothing about Del's other claims.

Where do your people live? Grana asked.

On the other side of the mountains at Sadema, Del replied; the Tolleans – or at least the ones she'd read – had used the same name as her contemporaries for that land. **And in the other direction, across the landless skies.** She repeated everything for Imogen, half expecting to be told at any moment that she was handling the whole encounter the wrong way, but so far Imogen was listening in silence, apparently willing to accept that this was a valuable exchange, conducted in good faith after all.

How did you come here? Grana responded.

Del struggled with her choice of words; she wanted to be precise, so as not to cause confusion, but if her Tollean had been good enough to express the relevant concepts perfectly, she probably would have known the answers to a great many questions much earlier. **My friends built a bridge,** she wrote. **It rose from the land into the sky, spanned three landless skies, then almost touched the land here. Two of us walked across it, but then it fell.**

Grana regarded her with polite skepticism. Del gestured that she wanted the sheet back; she had questions of her own.

How did the Tolleans reach this place? she asked.

They came under the mountains, Grana replied.

Is that way still open?

No, Grana wrote.

Imogen must have seen Del slump beneath the weight of disappointment, before she'd even uttered the translated reply. "What did I expect?" she said. "With people hunting for so long and finding nothing."

Why is it closed? she asked. What happened?

Grana wrote: The Tolleans who remained in their own land filled the tunnel with rocks. At that time, it might have been cleared again, with great labor. But there have been quakes and avalanches since, so I doubt that anything could make it traversable.

Del read and re-read the passage, trying to be sure that she'd understood it correctly. Some Tolleans must have migrated to this side of the mountains, raising children and maintaining their own language long enough for Grana to have access to at least as many examples of it as Del had ever seen.

But then, those who had chosen not to follow them to the Bounteous Lands had deliberately sealed the tunnel behind them.

Why was the tunnel filled with rocks? Del asked.

Grana paused to contemplate the question, and consult with Lados and Halem. Del wondered if the claim might be apocryphal, or even a deliberate reattribution. Maybe the people here decided that they'd received as many Tollean migrants as their land could sustain, or their culture could absorb without friction; she could understand that. But if it was the Tolleans who were migrating, on the most part, why would they be the ones to stem the flow?

Your side is better placed to explain that, Grana replied. Those actions were your choice, not ours.

Chapter 22

"These people must be dangerous," Imogen declared, as Lados started up the cart's engine and waited for a gap in the traffic.

"You're right," Del replied. "Just look at how shamelessly they've fed us, sheltered us, taught us their language, and spared us the effort of walking." In fact, the sound of all the carts that had done away with walking was beginning to give her a headache, but there was no point confusing the issue.

"We haven't seen their bad side yet, but clearly the Tolleans did."

"As witnessed by precisely none of their writing," Del countered.

Imogen said, "Their writing is ambiguous about everything. You were never really sure that they'd found a way through the mountains, until now. So who knows what they thought when they got here."

"Maybe it was the opposite," Del suggested. "Maybe most Tolleans admired this place so much that those in power on our side were afraid that too many people would migrate, and their empire would trickle away."

Lados finally managed to get the cart onto the street, and they set off back toward Halem's house.

"You make it sound as if that had to be self-serving," Imogen replied. "But is it so terrible to want to preserve their own culture, if their people were being seduced by all the shiny baubles on the other side?"

Del said, "If the greatest danger we face is admiring this place too much, I can live with that. And now that we know the mountains are blocked, that only leaves us with two ways to get home: a new bridge built from Celema, or a new bridge built here."

"Designed by, paid for, built by whom?" Imogen challenged her. "To what end?"

"Even if we have nothing to trade with the Bounteous Lands," Del argued, "there must be people here who are longing to see the rest of the world, out of sheer curiosity."

"You could be right about that," Imogen conceded. "But people have all kinds of whimsical desires they can't pay for."

The cart turned into Halem's courtyard. They disembarked, then Lados bid them farewell and drove away. Halem opened the door and motioned for them to enter; Del was as grateful as ever for his hospitality, but she was already cursing herself for all the questions she hadn't asked Grana when she'd had the chance. The Tollean language was like a tunnel through the mountains, but it was a narrow one; Grana might be the only person in this city who understood it.

As they walked down the corridor, she saw the woman who shared the house sitting in the living room, reading a book. Del entered the room and spoke haltingly in the local language.

"Excuse me, please. Thank you for everything. Please, what is your name?"

The woman looked up from her book and regarded Del balefully, but then the clumsy speech must have tickled her enough that she broke into an unwilling smile.

"Jo plen Raida," she said.

"Sere makom lemere pedra, Raida," Del replied. "Jo plen Del."

"Sere makom lemere pedra, Del."

Del didn't have the vocabulary to ask if Raida was Halem's wife, a relative, or just a friend, and in any case she wasn't confident that it would be considered any of her business. "Do you enjoy reading?" she asked.

Raida stared at her in disbelief, as if she'd never been asked anything so foolish, but then she replied, speaking with exaggerated clarity to correct Del's pronunciation: "Yes, I enjoy reading."

Del said, "Thank you," and left the room, unsure if she'd done more harm than good, but glad she'd at least tried to break the ice.

"What was that about?" Imogen asked her, when Del joined her in the dining room.

"Just trying to be polite."

Halem was chopping vegetables. Del approached him, and gestured that she'd be happy to help, but he waved her away.

"What do these people do for a living?" Imogen asked. "Bird watching and taking in freeloaders can't put food on the table."

"There's a vegetable garden in the back yard," Del replied. She'd seen it from the window of the room Halem had given them.

Imogen sighed. "What paid for the house? What paid for the cart? What pays for all the fuel?"

"I don't know."

Raida joined them for lunch, and Del decided not to annoy her with further attempts at conversation. She contented herself with listening carefully to her hosts, recognizing a word or two and trying to piece together the likely meaning of each exchange.

After the meal, Raida left them, and Halem wouldn't let Del help wash the plates. She sat at the table, wondering how she was going to cling to her sanity while she waited for the next language lesson. She could not expect Halem, Lados or Grana to spend all their time teaching her things that every child here knew – but if her hosts wouldn't allow her to help out around the house, what should she do? Every moment she wasn't learning something new about this place made her feel like she was standing beside a pile of timber, more than big enough to build a bridge stretching back to Celema – but useless to her, because she didn't know where to start.

Imogen rose and fetched the stack of paper they'd used for their lessons from the sideboard where Halem had placed it. She sketched a picture of a figure in a diving suit standing on a riverbed, with an air pump on the bank.

Halem had finished cleaning up; he glanced at the picture and laughed, then started to walk away, but Imogen grabbed him by the sleeve.

"This was my job!" she said, in her own language. She pointed to the immersed figure, then to herself. "This is what I'm good at. Can I do it here? Can you help me find a way to do it here?"

Del was embarrassed, but Halem looked intrigued, so she struggled to translate, stringing together the few words she knew in circuitous constructions that she hoped might point roughly toward Imogen's meaning.

Halem took a seat, and the three of them exchanged words and sketches, gradually converging toward a shared understanding.

"We don't do it here," Halem said. "But I like it."

Del translated for Imogen.

"Don't do it in this city?" Imogen pressed her. "Anywhere in Yerada? Anywhere in the Overgap?"

Del tried a sequence of crude maps, to see if Halem would assent to the presence of a diver in some adjacent land; he grasped what she was aiming at, and drew a heavy line through all of them.

"Nowhere, it seems," she told Imogen.

"Yes, I got that."

"So ... ?"

"So I'll be the first," Imogen decided. "That might not be so bad."

"And how do you plan on making this happen?"

"Didn't you just say that Halem liked the idea?"

"Didn't you just lecture me on unaffordable acts of whimsy?"

Imogen turned to Halem. "You inherited money, right? Or you made some smart investments, and now you're living off the proceeds?"

Del said, "He has no idea what you're asking, and you know I can't translate any of that."

"He might not be spectacularly wealthy, but he clearly doesn't do any actual work. He's a businessman looking for a new venture, and we're going to put this proposition to him. We just need to polish our language skills a little more."

Del laughed. "You want to direct all of our efforts into *starting a diving school?*"

"You want to sit around the house brooding, until that lady kicks us out?"

"She has a name. She's called Raida."

Imogen said, "I know you want to build a bridge. But right now, I don't think anyone even believes that we came across the gap. That's the first obstacle. If you ever get past that, then you'll have to sell people on the idea of spending time and money building something that no one here knows how to build – and which we've already told them fell apart the very first time we crossed it."

Del was on the verge of retorting that if Imogen was going to mock her ambitions, she shouldn't expect any help with her own. But then she thought: *If all of those objections are true, what would be the best way to overcome them?*

They had to find a smaller project to embark on with the Yeradans, in order to prove themselves. The only way forward was to demonstrate their competence, make new connections, and earn people's trust.

"All right," she said. "I'll help you. Let's see if we can start the best diving school from here to the mountains."

Chapter 23

Halem looked nervous as Imogen helped him into his suit.

"Are you sure this is safe?" he asked Del.

"Imogen was fine, wasn't she?" His suit was different, fitted to his size, but he'd be using the same pump and helmet.

They'd set up the pump, and a small floodlight, near the end of a jetty that extended for twenty strides or so over the river. Imogen had wanted to incorporate the Overgap's electric lights into the helmet itself, but Halem had vetoed that until they could recruit someone suitably qualified to advise them how to do it safely. "Water and electricity don't mix," he'd insisted, bemused that this wasn't obvious to his collaborators. Del had tried to explain to him that her culture had either lost, or never possessed, half the technology he took for granted, but he seemed to find that as hard to accept as any of her other outlandish claims.

Imogen said, "If you get into trouble, just release the weights then tug on the safety line." She started the pump and attached the air-hose, then Del helped her lift the helmet and lower it into place, with the corselet resting on Halem's shoulders.

He'd braced himself, and he didn't flinch. Imogen set about bolting the corselet tightly onto the suit, while Halem looked out through the faceplate, taking slow, deep breaths. Del could hear the demand valve clicking open with each inhalation.

"Is everything good?" Imogen shouted.

Halem raised a hand with his gloved fingers spread wide, which Del had learned was a sign of approval. She helped Imogen attach the weight belt, and this time Halem staggered slightly.

"If you need to release the weights," Imogen yelled, "just pull the tag." She mimed the action, and Halem copied her, touching the tag to confirm that he could reach it.

He walked slowly toward the ladder at the edge of the jetty, and began his descent. Del adjusted the angle of the floodlight; from where she stood all she could see was the reflection of the bulb in the surface of the water, but Imogen had assured her that the light really did reach down to the riverbed.

Halem disappeared below the water. Del moved along the jetty, searching for a point where she could see him instead of the glare from the light, and finally managed to catch sight of him stepping off the ladder. The water wasn't all that deep here, which made it a good choice for beginners. But as he walked along the sand, the wind rose up, rippling the surface so it caught the light again in shimmering patches and bands, making it almost impossible to see how he was faring.

Imogen said, "He'll be fine." She pointed to the safety line: the sheath lay slack on the planks of the jetty, but any relative movement of the cord within would pull on a spring attached to a bell striker. "Nothing can go wrong so fast that he wouldn't have the chance to let us know."

"And you think we could haul him up in time?"

Imogen laughed. "At this depth, I'd just jump in and cut off the weights."

"What if his helmet's filling up with water?" Its buoyancy only countered its weight when it was full of air.

"I'd cut through his suit around the edge of the corselet."

Del nodded; she could probably manage that much herself, if it came to it. But all the mechanical encumbrances, the pressurized air and the helmet's intricate valves, made the divers seem far more vulnerable than she'd ever felt as a child, just swimming down freely, holding her breath.

"How many lessons until you take your students somewhere they'll really need the equipment?"

"A dozen, at least," Imogen replied. "They need to gain confidence, and learn how to move under all these new constraints."

"It reminds me of the nub." Del knelt down and peered over the edge, trying to see what Halem was up to. He'd walked half a dozen strides from the ladder, over to one of the jetty's pillars.

"Once we get a second pump, I'll be down there with the students," Imogen said.

"Leaving me up here to panic if anything goes wrong that you can't fix on the spot."

"There are protocols to learn, rules to follow. Once you know what to do, it will all be very simple."

Del snorted. "It's funny how I'm not allowed to tell you the same thing about learning the language."

"I can make myself understood, can't I?" Imogen protested.

"Sometimes. I'm just saying you need to keep improving, instead of complaining how hard it is to improve."

The pump shuddered, and the noise from the engine shifted into a high-pitched whine. Del said, "That's not reassuring."

"I think there's a bearing sticking," Imogen replied. "That will need to be replaced, but the engine should keep running for now."

"For now?"

"If it does cut out, we still have the hand crank. So long as someone turns that, the air keeps flowing."

"I'm liking my role in this less and less." Del stared down into the water, wishing Halem would hurry up and return. "If I falter with the crank, how quickly will someone die?"

"In the old style of helmet, if the pump failed the air pressure could drop, and at sufficient depth the water pressure would push the diver's body up into the helmet, crushing them to death. But then people worked out how to put in a valve that makes that impossible."

"Assuming the valve itself doesn't fail."

Halem began to emerge from the water. He clambered up the ladder and stood dripping on the jetty, then managed to remove the weight belt himself before Imogen and Del got his helmet off.

"Are you all right?" Del asked.

"Yes." He was shivering slightly, and still breathing heavily from the effort of ascending with the weights – but he wasn't gasping, and his lips weren't blue. It seemed Imogen's system really was working, and even a novice could use it. So long as nothing broke.

"How was it?"

"Good! Strange, but good." He smiled. "I think people will like it."

"So, what do you think we'll get from each student?" Imogen asked. She looked to Del for help. "How do you say 'how much can we charge'?"

"I have no idea," Del confessed. So far, Halem and Lados hadn't talked about money in any of their lessons.

Halem seemed confused by Imogen's question. "What are you asking about the students?"

"What will they give us, for each dive?"

"Why would they give us anything?"

Del said, "As an exchange. They gain some knowledge and experience, so the teacher should gain something too."

Halem laughed. "Do you enjoy teaching this?" he asked Imogen.

"Yes, I enjoy it."

He spread his hands, as if that settled the matter. He and Lados had certainly spent a lot of time teaching his guests, asking for nothing in return. But Halem wasn't throwing that back in their faces – and, grateful as Del was, surely there was a difference between helping stranded foreigners learn a crucial skill, and teaching a recreational pastime?

"Is he saying I have to do this for free?" Imogen asked. "He put up all the capital, so he pockets all the fees?"

Del didn't think that was the plan. "Will the students give you anything?" she asked Halem.

"No. As I said, why would they?"

"Because you ... got all this equipment." Del didn't know how to say, "bought".

Halem stared at her, as if she was spouting non sequiturs.

"What did *you* give people, so *they* gave you the pump?" Imogen asked, as if speaking slowly with the right choice of emphases might overcome their mutual incomprehension.

"Nothing," Halem replied, bemused.

"Nothing?"

"They were pleased to make it."

Imogen turned to Del. "Am I losing my mind? He didn't even barter for it? Someone just handed it over?"

Del said, "Maybe we can sort this out later." The wind was rising, and though the diving suit was waterproof she could imagine the cold droplets trickling down Halem's neck. She helped him out of the suit, then shut off the floodlight.

As they walked down the jetty, dragging the pump and floodlight on their wheeled trolleys, Imogen whispered, "What if these people don't use money at all?"

"I don't know. We haven't starved yet, have we?"

"Only because of Halem's charity," Imogen protested.

"But if he has no money, maybe it wasn't charity," Del reasoned. "Maybe he didn't go without anything to feed us."

Imogen said, "Someone must have gone without something."

Del turned to Halem. "If we didn't live with you, how would we get food?"

"From the food stalls," he replied.

"Do we need to give something to the people at the food stalls?"

"No."

Imogen interjected, "But what if they don't have enough food to give us?"

"Someone will grow more food."

"Why?" Imogen demanded.

"Because there wasn't enough," Halem replied.

"But what if those people had enough for themselves. Someone else was hungry, not the people who grow food."

Halem said, "Hungry people would probably grow food."

"Not if they have no land to grow it on," Del countered.

"There's plenty of land for growing." Halem was beginning to sound a little weary, as if he suspected the whole line of questioning was just another way of feigning naïveté.

Imogen said, "This is why the Tolleans blocked the tunnel! Everyone here is insane. If we started thinking like this ... "

Del laughed. "What? It doesn't seem to have done any harm on this side."

"If people don't need to earn money, nothing will get done. Everything will stagnate."

"I suppose that's why our technology is so much better than theirs."

Imogen said, "The carts, the lights? That's all about the Bounteous Lands, not their deranged economics."

They'd been standing by the cart talking; Halem lost patience and took the trolleys himself, dragging them up a ramp onto the back of the vehicle.

"Why do you care?" Del asked her. "Your plan was to give diving lessons and not be beholden to Halem. It turns out you can achieve both those things, even more easily than you thought."

"But I won't be making money. I won't be building up wealth." Imogen sounded as distressed as if she'd just been told she had a fatal illness.

Del said, "If things don't work that way here, we have to deal with it. If you can't get rich, you can still gain a reputation that will help us."

"Help us how?"

"Help us to be believed. Help us to gain allies. Help us to go home."

Chapter 24

When Del first saw the gray silhouette blotting out the stars, she thought it was a small moon that had somehow been omitted from the atlas. As the Diving School had traveled from land to land, she'd tried to keep a clear map in her head of the features that would allow her to navigate independently, but the book that purported to do the same job had proved so convenient and reliable that she'd started to take its comprehensiveness for granted.

Then a light flared beneath the dark globe, illuminating its underside, and she realized that she was looking at something far too close to be a moon.

She came in from the balcony and called to Imogen.

"Wake up! You need to see this!"

Imogen stirred, but then mumbled something incoherent and rolled over in her sleeping bag.

Del thought of switching on the ceiling lamp, but then decided there wasn't much point rousing a potential witness to corroborate the phenomenon by robbing them of their dark-adapted vision. She knelt down beside Imogen. "They have a flying machine. No one told us they had a flying machine!"

Imogen said, "Go back to sleep, you're dreaming."

"Come and see for yourself. If I'm wrong, I'll do every task you ask me to, from now until we're back in Yerada. Cooking, washing, suit repairs, anything."

Imogen opened her eyes. "What if I'm the one who's dreaming?"

"There's only one way to find out."

Imogen crawled out of her sleeping bag and followed Del onto the balcony. Luckily, the flying machine wasn't very fast: it had barely moved from the place where Del had spotted it. The village of Dreyas was parsimonious with its lighting, and the hostel boasted lakeside views, so they were looking out at an expanse of black water, with the stars above almost as bright as they were at home.

"That's just a moon," Imogen declared. "You can start by changing the oil in the compressors."

"Wait a little longer."

"For what? Moonset?"

The light appeared again; this time, Del could see the flying machine respond, gently accelerating upward.

"So I *am* dreaming," Imogen decided. "I should have known you'd never make an offer like that."

"Why wouldn't they tell us they had flying machines?" Del wasn't angry, but it was hard to understand.

"We never asked," Imogen replied. "They have a lot of strange habits and devices here, but if they don't know how strange they are, why would they even mention them?"

The machine drifted languorously against the stars. "Because this one could carry us home," Del said.

"Except no one believes we couldn't just walk back to whatever obscure town in the boondocks we actually came from. Where, umm, you learned to read and write Tollean, while the two of us made up our own private language." Imogen massaged her temples. "No, it's simpler than that. Whether they believe us or not, if this machine could carry us home, these people would have visited Celema long ago. No one mentioned it, because they know it's not capable of crossing the gap."

"Nobody here knows the first thing about the gap," Del protested.

Imogen laughed. "Exactly! If they'd been able to reach as far as the second landless sky, they would have learned enough to take our story more seriously. They wouldn't still believe that it's just void beyond the nubs, forever."

Del couldn't argue with her logic, but she wasn't ready to treat the conclusion as final. "Maybe they've tried a few times, and failed. But that doesn't mean it's impossible; it could just mean they didn't understand what they were up against."

Imogen said, "Maybe. But right now, I'm going back to sleep."

Del left the room and went downstairs. While much of the town adhered to a shared sleeping cycle, the streets weren't empty, and it didn't take her long to find a passerby willing to answer a few questions.

"Do you know who built that?" she asked, pointing to the flying machine but not daring to name it – not because she still doubted its nature, but in case her description sounded as comical as calling a motorized cart a "rolling machine".

"The balloon? I'm not sure if she built it herself, but Tarin takes people for rides from the north pier."

"And they return there?"

The woman hesitated. "I don't think so. They just land wherever they land. It's hard to predict."

Del wanted to ask how the machine worked, and why it was so erratic, but she was too embarrassed to reveal her ignorance. "Thank you," she said. "It looks like it would be fun to take a ride."

"Absolutely!" the woman replied. "Though I'm not that brave myself, to be honest."

Del walked back to the hostel and tried to sleep. If you needed to be brave to ride a balloon under uniform gravity, what would it take to ride one through the gap?

She woke early, before Imogen, and went to the north pier. No one was about, and there was no sign of the balloon, but a note beside the ferry's schedule mentioned the balloon rides, and gave a time in the local cycle just before she would normally sleep.

Imogen had four students booked, meeting her for solo sessions at the lake's southern pier. Del forced herself to concentrate on her role, helping people don their suits and helmets, and monitoring the pumps and air-hoses.

When they broke for lunch, they walked into town, but the only decent restaurant was full. They didn't have time to cook for themselves, so they ended up just grabbing some fruit and raw vegetables from one of the stalls.

"I should ask my students to find someone to hold a seat for me," Imogen mused. "I don't think they'd refuse, so long as I didn't make it sound obligatory."

Del said, "I'm pretty sure that anyone who tries to introduce a bartering system here gets dragged from their beds and beheaded. Let alone restaurant squatting."

"I think it's more likely that there's already bartering going on," Imogen suggested. "But only the insiders ever hear about it."

"That's possible" Del admitted. "We'll never be insiders, so we'll never know."

They headed back to the pier. They'd left a note on their equipment asking people not to move it, and as ever that seemed to be enough. The Overgaps did have a word approximating "theft", which more or less amounted to ignoring such a request, but in the absence of the note people could have done anything with the pumps and there would have been no opprobrium attached to their actions, let alone any hope of redress. Del still felt anxious sometimes, not so much out of a fear of anyone maliciously taking things from her that she needed and could not easily replace, as from the possibility that miscommunication, or an honest confusion of expectations, could lead to the same result.

Perat, the last student, arrived. As Del helped him into the nearest-fitting suit, he said, "You have an unusual accent. Where are you from?"

Del gave an honest answer, to that and to all his followup questions.

"I've heard other people tell that story about you," Perat admitted. "I just wanted to hear it from your own mouth."

"Do you believe me?" Del asked.

"I can't think why you'd lie," he replied cheerfully. That was something, Del supposed. But it didn't mean he'd give up his comfortable life to cut down timber for a bridge, then drive it through ice and storms to the nub. Even with all the labor-saving machinery here, the whole endeavor remained too daunting for any sane person to want to take it on, without a better reason than a slim chance of visiting some interesting, if backward, new lands.

Perat and Imogen climbed down the ladder. Del watched the light from their helmets struggle up through the turbid water as they went through their paces on the sandy lakebed.

She waited until they were packing up the equipment to tell Imogen about the balloon rides. "Will you come with me?" she asked.

"I don't know. It's hard work down there, I'm tired."

Del bit back a rebuke. If Imogen was reconciled to never getting home, it would be pointless to blame her for that comfort. "All right. But then you'll have to put up with me spending almost as much time telling you about it later."

Imogen said, "I might be more skilled than you think at letting you talk when I'm not actually listening."

Del picked up some fish and vegetables at a stall, and cooked a simple meal in the hostel's kitchen. There was a clock in the dining room, of the kind apparently powered by electricity, though she had yet to find someone who could offer her a clear explanation of how it functioned.

Imogen finished eating and slid her plate aside. "All right," she said. "I'll come with you."

As they approached the pier, Del saw the balloon: a huge, round sack made of something like the Overgaps' tent material, which sat upside down with its mouth connected to a metal ring over a powerful flame. The hot air rising up around the flame was gradually inflating the sack; the final shape wasn't obvious from this collapsed version, but presumably, once taut, it would match the globe she'd seen from the hostel balcony.

A woman was supervising the flame, while two other people looked on. "Are you Tarin?" Del called to the woman.

"Yes. Would you like a ride?"

"We would, thank you. Is that possible?"

"Sure, I have room for two more."

Del and Imogen introduced themselves to her, and to the other prospective passengers, Mehan and Dema.

"Have you done this before?" Mehan asked.

"No," Del replied.

He said, "I can't decide if it's a good thing or not, that most of the trip will be over the water. If we come down too fast, the water might cushion the blow. But I don't want to have to swim back from the middle of the lake."

Tarin had been busy with her preparations, but she must have overheard him. "The basket will stay afloat unless the impact's very fast," she said. "I've never had it break on me so far. And we do have life jackets."

Mehan thanked her, clearly not entirely reassured, but committed to the trip regardless.

The loose folds of the balloon grew rigid, and the parts that had rested on the pier bobbed up into the air. Imogen addressed Del, in their own language: "I can't believe we never tried this back home. It's just the principle of buoyancy, in air instead of water: the hot air is less dense than the air around it."

"It must take a lot of fuel to keep it aloft, though," Del guessed.

"It must," Imogen conceded. "And their fuel oil yields more heat for the same weight than any of ours. However much the Tolleans hated the culture here, they shouldn't have cut off trade when they could have had *that.*"

The globe stood looming above them, perfectly formed now. "You can step in," Tarin invited them. Del waited for Mehan and Dema to clamber into the basket, then she glanced at Imogen.

"Could you swim back from the middle of the lake?" she asked.

"Yes," Imogen replied confidently. "And I could tow you all the way."

"All right, then."

They climbed in, and Tarin handed out life jackets. The basket was a tight fit for the five of them, with the fuel drum in the center, below the burner, taking up as much space as two or three passengers.

Tarin began lifting sandbags from the floor of the basket and dropping them onto the pier. Del couldn't detect any change in their condition – until suddenly the basket was floating, rising a few hand's breadths above the planks that had been supporting it. Tarin discarded two more bags; the basket drifted gently upward, and the breeze pushed the balloon slowly away from the pier.

"Everyone still happy?" she asked. "Ready to go higher?"

The passengers all murmured assent. Tarin turned up the flame, and they began to ascend more rapidly.

Del felt a rush of exhilaration. She peered down at the dark water, and watched the ripples glimmering in the starlight. They were probably high enough for a fall to end their lives, but she'd been far more anxious when she'd first climbed onto the uncompleted bridge. The balloon, at least, was self-contained: there were no wooden beams far out of sight that could snap and undermine its power over gravity. Perhaps the fabric could split, but even then it would take time for the hot air to leak out.

Mehan and Dema were gazing back at the village, apparently hunting for a friend's house. "That's it!" Dema exclaimed. "He said he'd make a circle of lamps in the garden!"

Del turned to Tarin. "Have people ever tried to steer a balloon, instead of leaving the course up to the wind?"

"There are versions with propellers," Tarin replied. "But the engines are heavy, so it's not really worth it, in my opinion. I'm only interested in taking joyrides, not trying to get somewhere specific in a hurry. A cart or a boat will always be better for that."

Del wasn't sure how to take the conversation further, but as she pondered her next question, Imogen interjected.

"Would you ever think of flying this thing up from a nub?"

Tarin laughed. "Do I look that crazy?"

"Why do you say that?" Imogen pressed her.

"The air's too thin there," Tarin replied, "and the gravity's too strong, and unpredictable. People have tried it, but most of them never even managed to ascend."

"And the ones who did ascend?" Del wondered.

"They either came down again quickly, or they went around the corner and never came back."

Imogen said, "My friend and I came from around that kind of corner."

"Ah." Tarin smiled. "People tell that story, about the diving teachers. But I never knew if they were making it up."

"They weren't." And Imogen wasn't wasting time gently eliciting Tarin's opinion on their origins. "Del here was hoping you could carry us home. What would you say to that proposition?"

"Actually, I'm just seeking information," Del clarified. Imogen's haste was embarrassing, even if it was advancing the matter faster than she'd ever contemplated. "We don't have these kinds of machines in our lands. It's not clear to us what they can and can't accomplish."

Tarin took the whole thing in good humor. "Given the past failures at the nubs, it's not something I'd attempt myself. The air is too thin, the lift is too weak; I'm not speaking from experience, but I have no reason to doubt the accounts I've read."

"So it's impossible," Imogen declared.

Tarin glanced over the side of the basket, and adjusted the valve on the burner. "That might be putting it too strongly," she said. "I heard about a group in Dallya that's been experimenting with a different source of lift. Instead of hot air, they use hydrogen." Del's expression must have made her confusion apparent. "You can break up water into two different gases," Tarin explained. "One of them is much less dense than ordinary air, even at the same temperature. If you use that for lift, you don't need a burner and the fuel it consumes, though of course you still need all the extra paraphernalia to move under your own power."

Del pondered this new information. "It might make a difference, then? No one's tried that method at the nubs before?"

"Not as far as I know," Tarin replied.

Del turned to Mehan and Dema. "I'm sorry, I didn't mean to be impolite. It was never my intention to take over the whole ride like this."

"That's all right," Dema replied. In fact, she seemed to be as fascinated by the foreigners' exotic plans as she had been by the aerial view of Dreyas.

Del hunted for the lights from the shore; they were still visible, but at the altitude they'd reached the wind was blowing strongly, and it had carried them far over the water. Clarissa had had all the time she needed to take sightings and measure the progress of the bridge, instructing the builders in the precise positioning of every beam. How much control could any balloon have as it moved through the gap, even if it was equipped with an engine and propellers?

But neither her anxieties nor her wishful thinking would settle the matter; it would be up to the balloonists Tarin had mentioned to decide if such a crossing was possible – and safe enough, or even interesting enough, to be worth their while.

"Dallya?" Del asked. She couldn't recall hearing of that place before; she wasn't even sure if it was a whole land or just a city. "Is it far?"

Tarin was distracted with her own navigational efforts; it was Mehan who answered.

"I think about nineteen circuits of the Hoops," he said. "With one crossing between them, but it's through Jierra. So you'd have to go soon, if you don't want to put it off for another year."

Del still wasn't sure exactly what a "year" was, but she gathered it was a considerable interval, almost as long as she and Imogen had spent in the Overgap so far. "Why would the timing make any difference?" she wondered. Was there some cultural restriction on travel she was yet to learn about?

Mehan exchanged a glance with Dema, as if he wanted to be sure he hadn't misinterpreted Del's strangely accented words.

"Because if you go too late, you can't get through," he said. "It's Jierra! It won't be long before the entrance from the Hoop there is in sunlight, and you couldn't take a step without being fried."

Chapter 25

"Do I have any choice?" Imogen asked. "I can't just stay here and give the lessons on my own."

"You could take on an apprentice," Del replied. "What about Nisha? She's your best student by far, and she keeps coming back. Don't you think she'd be thrilled to be more involved?"

Imogen didn't answer. Del walked over to the balcony and glanced out at the lake. Their trip over the water barely felt real any more; when she'd lived beside the bridge, at least she could see it all the time, but with the balloon folded up in Tarin's cart, all the evidence that the ride had actually taken place had vanished, like the implausible premise of a fading dream.

"I want you to come, though, if you're willing," she told Imogen. "Everything would be ten times harder without you."

Imogen shifted irritably on her chair. "We're stuck here," she said. "We just need to accept that, and make the best of it."

"You don't miss anyone from home?"

The question seemed to anger her. "It doesn't matter whether I miss them or not. That won't get us back."

"It won't, if it's completely impossible," Del agreed. "But if all it takes is persistence, it might."

Imogen said, "These people aren't timid, or foolish. They've explored around the nubs, as far as they could go. Do you really think a different gas in the balloon is going to solve all the problems there?"

"I have no idea," Del confessed. "I can't do those kinds of calculations. But if we share what we know about the gap with the people in Dallya, they can make their own decisions. What's the worst that can happen? We get to see a bit more of the world, along the way?"

"Getting burned to death doesn't bother you?"

Del laughed. "I doubt that's happened to anyone, for a long time."

"And I doubt anyone quite as ignorant of things every child here should know has tried it, for a long time," Imogen retorted.

"Maybe we can find another traveler who's making the same crossing," Del suggested. "Someone who's done it all before."

"And if we can't?" Imogen persisted.

"Well, we might be ignorant, but we're not helpless. The angle of the sun above the horizon at any given point is completely predictable; it's not that different from moonrise and moonset back in Thena." Del walked over to the atlas, which included some diagrams showing the progress of sunlight over the land, along with four whole pages devoted to the art of scheduling safe passage. "Jierra is not all that special or mysterious; it just happens to have one star so close to it that it moves around that star, the way a moon goes around any other land."

"Silvio always claimed that moons keep one face turned toward the land below them," Imogen recalled. "So why doesn't Jierra keep one face toward the sun?"

"I don't know," Del conceded. "But it doesn't. It's the distant stars that stay fixed there, just like anywhere else. Maybe the Hoops have something to do with that: Montano said they're hard to turn."

Imogen was silent for a while, but then she succumbed to the urge to start reasoning about the problem. "So the land around one Hoop is drenched in sunlight for half a year, while the other is in darkness, and vice versa?"

"Almost," Del said. "But not quite. The Hoops' axis isn't exactly perpendicular to the plane of the orbit, so there's a time when each aperture is only partly lit, as the dividing line sweeps over it."

"Making everything more complicated."

"Maybe, but I think it also makes the journey less dangerous. The way in or out closes off gradually; no door slams shut in an instant."

Imogen walked over to the table where Del had laid out the atlas. "The Hoops barely rise above the ground," she observed.

"Isn't that what you'd expect," Del said, "so close to Sadema? I'm almost tempted to make a detour there, just to look at the mountains and convince myself there really is no way through."

Imogen clearly wasn't tempted at all. "My point is, the Hoops won't offer much shade. Once you go through, you'll be at the mercy of the local sky."

"That's true. But if you look at the next page, you'll see that the schedules take that into account. And it's coming up to the ideal time to enter through the western Hoop: any earlier, and we'd have to cool our heels waiting for sunset to reach the eastern Hoop; any later and we'd risk stepping out into sunshine. Go now, and we can drive from Hoop to Hoop at an ordinary pace, with no delays – but even if we get held up for some reason, it's only the way back that will be blocked. The way out will stay open for half a year."

Imogen said, "What if the cart breaks down?"

"We could walk from Hoop to Hoop in less than half a year." Del caught herself. Was that true? Jierra was larger than Zeruma, and the accessible portions of the Hoops were much farther apart. She joined Imogen at the table and began checking the route on the map, comparing distances by reasoning that the full globe couldn't be more than twice as large as Zeruma, but halfway through her calculations she realized she still didn't know precisely how long a year was.

"We'll find a guide," she told Imogen. "We'll find other travelers. This is Jierra – the most Bounteous of the Bounteous Lands – not some wasteland out near the nubs. If anything, our biggest problem will be all the traffic sharing the roads. There won't be a moment that passes without another cart rattling by."

Chapter 26

"I can fix it," Imogen said. "Just be patient, will you?"

Del walked away from the cart and sat at the side of the ring road, watching the tankers go by. There were so many of them that she couldn't tell if they were the source of the incessant warm breeze blowing across her skin, or merely happened to be driving in the same direction as the natural motion of the air.

Imogen muttered curses as she tinkered with the engine. They'd found the cart in a scrapyard in Yerada, and Halem had helped Imogen restore it, teaching her as they went; it wasn't beyond the bounds of possibility that she could manage the same feat again. Del was starting to wish she'd mastered some of the same skills herself; her driving wasn't bad, but the machinery beneath the panels was still largely a mystery to her.

"Can I help?" she called out to Imogen, sincerely; she could hold things that needed to be held, while other things that would normally cause the things she held to move could consequently be moved themselves, in a more productive manner.

"No," Imogen replied. "Not unless you have a functioning dynamo coil hidden up your arse."

"We don't have a spare?"

"If we had a spare, would I be asking?"

"So ... can you fix something like that?" Del rose to her feet and approached the cart warily. Imogen had removed the coil, and Del could see a black streak that cut across its windings. The lacquered metal of the intact wire gleamed in the headlights of the passing traffic, but something had melted the strands and their insulation into a congealed mess along a full third of the coil's height.

"Probably not," Imogen conceded.

"Don't worry," Del said. "This is the Overgap."

She stood by the stationary cart and held up an arm, hoping the tableau would be self-explanatory. The tanker drivers who chose to stop were polite, and as helpful as they could be, but no one was carrying a spare coil of the right size, and all they could offer was a ride back to the nearest town, Finlaw – or various other places, more distant, but more likely to have the component.

Imogen didn't want to leave the cart. "If we go back for the coil, who knows how long it will take to get it?"

Del agreed; they couldn't risk missing the window into Jierra. But the fuel tankers filing out of Jierra were all constructed on a different scale to their own vehicle; it was hard to imagine any of them having exactly what Imogen needed.

When Del saw a cart traveling in the other direction, she was so surprised that she almost failed to act. But she stretched out her arm and waved, peering into the headlights with a supplicatory expression that she hoped was amiable enough to overcome the entirely reasonable assumption that someone else on the crowded road would help.

The cart pulled up beside them. "Having trouble?" the driver asked.

"Yes." Del and Imogen introduced themselves; the driver was named Sejan.

Imogen explained the problem.

"I'm sorry," Sejan said. "I have some tools and some other spare parts, but no coils."

"It's all right," Del said. "Thank you for stopping."

"Were you just circling, or heading for the eastern Hoop?" he asked.

"The eastern Hoop," Imogen replied.

"I'm going that way." Sejan thought for a moment. "I could probably give you a ride, depending on how much luggage you have." The back of his cart was piled high with crates.

Imogen had left all the diving equipment with Nisha; they only had their tents and sleeping bags, some books and some food. Sejan jumped down and took a look for himself, glancing back at his own vehicle, trying to judge by eye whether the problem was soluble before he committed to anything. Finally he said, "I think we can do this, if you don't mind being squashed back there."

They carried their things over. Imogen wasn't happy abandoning the cart, but she appeared resigned to the outcome.

They climbed on, and Sejan started the engine. Del hadn't realized how parched she was from the heat; she rummaged in her pack and took out her water bottle.

"Have you been through Jierra before?" Sejan asked.

"No." Del waited for him to inquire about their accents and their origins, but he gave all his attention to the traffic as he pulled out onto the road.

The edge of the Hoop emerged from the hill here at an angle farther from the vertical than Del had seen since Celema. She glanced up at the sky; with the lights of all the tankers, and the dust they were raising, she didn't expect to see any stars, but the usual gray had acquired a faint pinkish tinge.

"We're not too late, are we?" she asked Sejan.

He laughed. "That might look like dawn, but I promise you, it's not close."

"Dawn?"

"Sunrise." He glanced back at her over his shoulder, surprised that she hadn't recognized the synonym. "It wouldn't actually kill you, but it could certainly damage your eyes if you weren't careful. But don't worry: we'll have a head start, and we'll easily outrun it."

The stream of tankers began to thin out; there might still be time remaining before exiting Jierra through the western Hoop became dangerous, but clearly most people had chosen to err on the side of caution.

"Where are you headed?" Sejan asked.

"Dallya," Imogen replied.

"Ah. I've never been there, but I hear it's nice."

"Where will you be going?" Del asked.

Sejan said, "Round the other side, back to where I started."

"I'm sorry?"

"When we get to the eastern Hoop, I can take you through to the first town on your way, but then I'm following the sunset, back around Jierra."

"Why would you want to do that?" Imogen asked bluntly.

"I'm an astronomer. If you want to study Jierra's sky, you need to keep moving."

"Why not stay in one place, in another land?" Imogen persisted. "There are plenty of stars everywhere."

Sejan laughed. "Jierra's sky is special."

"In what way?"

Sejan was silent for a while, as if he was wondering whether or not he should take the question seriously. "Once it's dark enough, I'll show you," he said.

For now, the sky was only growing brighter. Del watched the red light suffusing through the air as they circled the hill; even when she'd been approaching Erema, she had never seen anything like this. Perhaps a raging fire, hidden from view behind a mountain, might produce the same effect. The heat in the air was apparent, too: still not as strong as that of the land, but steadily increasing. For a star to be so close that it reversed the usual thermal gradient was shocking. Even back in Thena, everyone had talked about this star and this land, but however plausible their arguments for its existence, a part of her had always treated it as a kind of children's tale.

A dazzling speck of light appeared ahead of them, spilling over the rocks at the side of the hill. Del raised her forearm to protect her eyes.

"Too much, already?" Sejan asked, surprised. "I suppose I'm used to it." He stopped the cart, then rummaged in a box and found two pairs of black-lensed spectacles, which he offered to Del and Imogen. "You shouldn't need them for long," he promised.

Del hesitated, but when she put them on she wasn't blinded; she could still see her companions, the cart and the road.

"You look ridiculous," Imogen scoffed, but she put on her own pair.

"You look mysterious," Del replied. "When I can't see your scowl, it's as if you're a completely different person."

"What language is that?" Sejan asked.

"Peladan," Imogen replied.

"Ah." He didn't ask where Peladan was spoken, and why he'd never heard of it. Del could see no reason not to tell him their whole story; however implausible he found it, she didn't think he'd abandon them to the perils of sunlight just because he disapproved of their urge to confabulate. But it didn't feel right to distract him with their wild claims while he was still in the process of navigating their escape from the dawn.

As they continued around the ring road, the gleaming bead unfurled into a luminous archway that stretched from the hill far into the distance. The aperture had never looked so palpable, the transition from land to land and sky to sky never so extreme.

"What if I change my mind and agree to go on to Sadema?" Imogen pleaded. "It's only five more circuits. We might get a pleasant surprise, and find ourselves face to face with some intrepid competitors from Thena after all."

"Too late," Del replied.

As they drove through the archway into Jierra, Sejan offered a warning. "Don't look back toward the west for a while; even with the spectacles you might find it painful." Del felt her stomach tighten; the instructions would be easy to follow, but somehow she'd failed to realize that the light she'd seen so far, too intense to gaze upon directly, was coming from *the opposite side of the sky* to the rising sun.

"I won't," she promised.

She peered resolutely ahead. It was hard to make out all the details of the landscape through tinted glass, but she could see a field of tall flowers nearby, and trees in the distance.

Sejan turned off the ring road, onto a highway heading east. They hadn't seen another cart for a while, and now they appeared to have the road to themselves.

"We thought there'd be more people traveling this route," Del told Sejan.

"They probably came earlier, and then took it slowly," he replied. "Waiting for the eastern Hoop to become accessible isn't that bad if you're sightseeing anyway."

Del didn't need to look back to picture the view of the neighboring land's sky rapidly shrinking away against the glare of the Jierran dawn: all around her, the ground was growing brighter. And on either side of the road, she could now see flowers the size of her hands, on stalks as high as her waist, all lined up facing west.

"How do these plants survive the onslaught?" Imogen asked.

"Dawn's not a problem for them!" Sejan replied. "They get their energy from sunlight, the way normal plants get it from heat in the ground. Later on, they'll need to close up to avoid losing moisture, but right now they're preparing for their favorite time of the year."

"What about the animals?" Del wondered.

"Some migrate, some burrow down to avoid the heat."

"Burrow down?"

"I know that sounds strange," Sejan admitted. "But it really does end up cooler deep in the ground than up at the surface."

Del noticed an odor wafting toward them. "That's a fuel lake?"

"You can't miss it, can you?" Sejan replied.

"I can't miss the stink, but I can't see it."

Sejan gestured to the right. It took Del a moment to realize that he was pointing to a solid-looking patch of green that she'd mistaken for some kind of field.

"That's *water*?"

"Water full of algae. Don't try swimming in it."

"And all the fuel comes from those lakes?" Imogen marveled.

Sejan didn't reply. Del suspected he was too polite to mock the peculiar gaps in their knowledge, but also too honest to act as if these lacunae were normal.

"You might have noticed that we're not from around here," she said.

Sejan laughed. "Even I wouldn't call myself a Jierran. It's been a long time since anyone was born on this land."

Del had been intending to segue into her and Imogen's void-crossing misadventure, but this revelation was too intriguing to ignore. "But they have been, in the past?"

"Sure. Some people lived nomadically; some lived underground for half the year. If voles can do it, why not humans?"

"But then why did they stop?" Imogen asked.

"I suppose it was because life's easier, elsewhere."

"Then why did they start?"

Sejan paused to consider his reply. "Maybe for the same reason I did. Jierra's special."

"It's not hard to come in and grab some fuel from the lakes, then go," Imogen argued. "You can get all the benefits with none of the problems."

"I'm not talking about accessing fuel." Sejan glanced back them. "You really don't know about the sky here? You're not joking with me?"

"We really don't know," Del replied solemnly.

"Then I really will show you, the first chance we get."

Sejan sped up, eager now to outpace the sun and make good on his promise. The road east was a little bumpy, but in surprisingly good repair for a structure subject to periodic blazing heat with no permanent workforce to attend to it. Del supposed that the drivers of the tankers that flocked in from all across the Overgap had learned to fix any problems they encountered, before the damage got out of hand.

Gradually the sky grew darker, and Del and Imogen removed their protective glasses. Sejan had switched off his headlights before they passed through the Hoop, but he kept them off and allowed their eyes to adjust to the deepening gloom.

"Well, there's at least one other star besides the one that wants to kill us," Imogen remarked, pointing to a faint dot emerging from the grayness.

"And you're quite sure that's a star?" Sejan asked her.

"Now you're just being rude," she replied. "We might not be Jierrans, but that doesn't make us idiots."

Sejan said, "If there was nothing but stars to be seen, would I be here?"

Del thought for a while. "It could be a small moon. High enough up to catch the sunlight."

"It could be," Sejan agreed. "Any other possibilities occur to you?"

Imogen said, "Another world. Orbiting the sun, the way Jierra does."

"Yes."

Del stared at the dot. "How could you tell? Oh ... I suppose it moves against the stars, but not the way a moon would."

"Exactly."

"But it's so small," Imogen complained. "I understand that it's worth establishing its nature, and maybe working out its orbit. But once you've done that, what else is there to do? Why keep coming back for another look?"

Sejan said, "Be patient. Just a little longer."

More lights emerged above them, until they were surrounded by constellations as bright and varied as Thena's. Del didn't ask, but she assumed that the vast majority were genuine stars. Beside the road, the flowers were closed, their heads drooping, but the sun would awaken them soon enough. "What a strange life," she mused. "To be controlled by a star as it moves across the sky."

They reached a cross-roads, and Sejan turned south.

"Where are we going?" Del asked.

"Trust me," he replied.

"I knew we'd end up with a cannibal eventually," Imogen muttered.

The track here was much rougher than the highway, sending the cart swaying and lurching. "Sorry about the ride," Sejan said. "My colleagues are getting a bit slack."

"Fellow astronomers?" Del asked.

"Yes."

Imogen said, "Why isn't the road your job?"

"This isn't my territory; I'm just passing through. Believe me, I'll do plenty of roadwork on the other side."

Del could see a structure in the distance, silhouetted against the stars. It was a large building, a little like a grain silo, but in place of an ordinary roof it was topped with a dome. There was nothing else in sight but fields and scrubland; if this was an abandoned village once used by the mythical Jierrans, there wasn't a lot left standing, at least above ground.

Sejan brought the cart to a halt beside the building, then jumped down. "Come on!" he called eagerly. "We're well ahead of the dawn right now, but we don't want it to get close enough to spoil the view."

He dragged open a sliding door and took a few steps inside. "Ah, you two had better wait," he decided. Del had no argument with that; he'd switched on no lamps, and there was no skylight, so all she could see was his heat blotch.

Del stood in the doorway while Sejan grabbed something and began hauling on it; from the movement of his limbs and the sound it made, she guessed it was a metal chain. As he dragged the chain, an even louder creaking sound issued from above, and a crack appeared in the darkness. Two pieces of the domed roof had been drawn aside; Sejan kept working until the crack was about a quarter as wide as the whole roof.

In the starlight, Del finally saw the building's occupant: an enormous white barrel, mounted on a rectangular yoke.

Imogen said, "I was going to ask if you were carrying binoculars or a theodolite, but this wasn't on my list of possibilities."

"Beautiful, isn't it?" Sejan turned toward the behemoth and spread his arms wide. "I wish I could claim some credit, but it was built before I was born."

"Have you used it before?" Del asked nervously. However relaxed people were about property here, she didn't want him damaging this exquisite instrument just to show off to his guests. "You did say this wasn't your territory."

"It's not my territory now, but it has been in the past," Sejan explained. "Where I work depends on where my objects of interest lie. I'm experienced with all the telescopes in Jierra; I wouldn't have brought you here if I didn't know what I was doing."

Del looked on as he set about turning wheels the size of her chest that connected to the mechanism that aimed the telescope. He then labored to turn the dome itself, bringing the opening around so that it was aligned with the instrument.

A more conventional looking spyglass was attached to the side of the great barrel, at its lower end. Sejan brought some steps up to it so he could peer through the eyepiece, in between visits to the wheels to make further adjustments.

When he was done, he fetched a much taller, two-legged ladder, maneuvered it over to the side of the barrel, and climbed up beside a second eyepiece that was aimed, bizarrely, inward toward the axis of the huge cylinder.

"What are you doing?" Imogen demanded.

"This is where the observations are made," he called down to her. "You're probably used to smaller telescopes, with lenses; this one has two mirrors instead." He gestured toward the base of the cylinder. "A big curved one down there, which sends the light back up the tube. Then a small flat one up here, that catches it and diverts it."

"That's absurd," Imogen protested.

"Not really. It's hard to make a lens very large without it sagging under its own weight. With a mirror, you can support it on one side, to keep it from losing its shape."

"Hmm."

"Feel free to come up," Sejan invited them. "One at a time." He shifted onto the other leg of the ladder, making room beside the eyepiece.

Imogen turned to Del. "You first."

Del ascended slowly; the ladder seemed stable, but the floor was hard cement, and if she sent the thing toppling she'd injure their guide as well as herself.

When she reached the top, Sejan grinned at her like a child welcoming her into his treehouse. "Take a look," he urged her.

Del leaned over, then realized she needed to go down a rung to bring her eye into position. She placed it against the small tube, but all she could see were her own eyelashes.

"Close the other eye," Sejan instructed her.

"Sorry." She was used to binoculars; she'd never looked through a one-eyed spyglass before.

A pallid disk sat in the dark sky. At first, Del supposed it was just a star, badly focused, but the edges of the circle were too crisp for that. She could see some stars close to it, two quite bright ones on each side, almost in a line, as well as a smattering of fainter specks in the background.

"That's another world?" she asked Sejan.

"Another world, and four of its moons."

"Moons?"

"You can't see them?"

Del said, "I thought they were stars."

"It takes a while to tell the difference," Sejan admitted. "Over time, you can see them orbiting."

"The world itself looks ... odd." Del didn't know what to make of it. There were faint greyish stripes crossing the disk, parallel if not exactly regular. "What are the markings?"

"Cloud bands," Sejan replied. "This world has no land, or none that we can see. All that's visible are its clouds, and the striations and storms that arise from its rotation."

Del struggled to absorb these claims. "This world rotates? Jierra doesn't."

"This world has no Hoops anchoring it."

The rotation, like the motion of the moons, would take time to discern; nothing on such a scale happened quickly. "Is this our closest neighbor?" she asked.

"No. But it's the largest world of the eight substantial ones, Jierra included."

"It's larger than Jierra?"

"More than a hundred times wider. Jierra is the smallest of the eight – if you only count Jierra itself, not the lands joined to it."

Del had more questions, but she was growing anxious about the approaching sunlight, so she descended.

"Take a look," she urged Imogen.

While Imogen climbed up, Del stood at the base of the ladder, holding it firm, unsettled by what she'd witnessed but not entirely sure why. That there were worlds she couldn't simply walk to, or even build a short bridge through the Hoops to reach, should not have been a surprise. Even Thena's moons more or less fulfilled that description. But this neighbor still seemed disturbingly at odds with the world she knew: it didn't orbit any land she could walk upon, but nor did it remain aloof like the stars.

"That was worth seeing," Imogen conceded as she rejoined Del. "I wouldn't make it my life's work, but everyone's different."

Sejan clambered down and began restoring everything to the way he'd found it. As they walked back to the cart, Del asked him, "So what will you be studying, from the other side of Jierra?"

"A closer neighbor – the first that's further from the sun than us."

"Bigger or smaller than the one you just showed us?"

"Much smaller. It's called Marikh."

"Does it have any moons?"

"Three," Sejan replied. "Very tiny ones, with no discernible features. But the world itself is beautiful. You can see the land, the dust storms, the ice caps."

They climbed up onto the cart. "And you're happy to watch the storms come and go on another world?" Imogen asked.

Sejan turned back toward them, exasperated. "Tell me honestly, do you not know the stories? Were you raised in a place where they're not mentioned at all?"

Del said, "Honestly, we never knew about these worlds before. Whatever stories every child you've ever met has been told, it's all entirely new to us."

Sejan scowled, struggling to accept this claim. But then he seemed to make a decision to take her at her word, or at least pretend to for the sake of politeness.

He said, "I watch the worlds I watch because I'm looking for any changes that would mean our ancestors still reside there."

Imogen turned to Del. "'Ancestors'?"

Del translated for her.

Imogen said, in Peladan, "And we're the ones nobody believes."

"You think our lineage began on a neighboring world, not this one?" Del asked Sejan.

"No," he replied. "I think our lineage began on the world that was here, right where we're standing, before the Hoops spread it across a thousand skies. But as it says in *The Book of All Skies*, many of those that had left Old Jierra returned to the remains of their home. I'm looking for those who chose not to return. Because I'm hoping they fared better than we did."

Chapter 27

Back on the highway, Sejan drove east, only stopping once they'd gone far enough to set up camp in what he claimed was perfect safety. "Even if we overslept, and woke to find the cart broken, we'd still have enough of a head start to continue on foot without any trouble."

He brought out his stove and began cooking a meal, refusing Del's offer to help. "Next time," he said. "I don't often get a chance to play host."

"At least we can't run out of fuel here," Imogen joked, as they started on Sejan's fish stew.

"I've actually got a purifier," he said. "It takes a while, but I could pour a bucket of muck straight from a lake into it, and get something out that wouldn't destroy my engine."

Del had resisted nagging him while they were driving, but she couldn't hold off any longer. "Are you going to tell us about *The Book of All Skies*."

"Your parents never read it to you?"

"No."

"You've never owned a copy?"

"I held one in my hands, for a very short time," Del said. "But someone took it away before I could read it."

Sejan said, "At some point, you're going to have to tell me about your upbringing."

"That's a fair trade," Del agreed. "But you first."

"All right," he said. "Feel free to interrupt at any time, though, and confess that you've just been making fun of me. And if I catch you giggling knowingly, I'll take that as an implicit confession."

"Understood," Imogen replied.

Sejan shut the stove off, leaving them in starlight. A hot breeze was blowing from the west.

"Long ago," he began, "our ancestors lived on Old Jierra. They'd thrived there for thousands of years, and eventually they found ways to travel to the neighboring worlds. None of those worlds were hospitable; no one could walk unprotected on the land. People built small towns on a few worlds, sealed tightly to hold in the air they needed and keep the temperature comfortable. Food could be grown with some effort, but there were no native plants or animals, and without elaborate machinery to support the towns, everyone would die.

"Back on Old Jierra, people longed to explore more widely, but the other stars were very far away. Gathering the energy to reach them in a lifetime seemed impossible. But some people thought there might be a faster way.

"No one knows exactly what happened. I doubt that anyone fully understood what they were doing, even at the time, or it would never have gone ahead. But their attempts to find a faster way to the stars led to the creation of the Hoops – and the Hoops fell into the core of Old Jierra and consumed it."

Del started weeping. Sejan stared at her, skeptical of her reaction at first, then mortified. "It was a long time ago," he said.

She composed herself, but the implications of his words continued reverberating in her skull. People in Thena had talked about the Hoops colliding with a body of rock – a barren world, she'd imagined, long before any trace of life arose. She'd pictured the event as a cosmic coincidence, and an ultimately beneficial one: it had given rise to the world she knew. But now Sejan was claiming that the people of a bounteous world had destroyed it, and destroyed themselves, and that she was living in their ashes.

"How many people were there on Old Jierra," she asked.

Sejan hesitated. "Billions."

And they were all lost? But of course they were. When the molten rock deep underground began spilling out through the Hoops, the land above

166

would have crumpled and sank, everywhere at once. In an instant, the world would have drowned in lava.

She looked to Imogen, but her face remained impassive. Either she didn't believe the story, or she was refusing to let it touch her.

"I'm sorry," Del said. "Go on."

"Life struggled on, on the neighboring worlds," Sejan continued. "The shock and grief at what had happened was hard to bear, and the colonies were unprepared for self-sufficiency. And yet they endured, sharing their resources and knowledge, finding ways to make do without the lifeline they'd once believed would always be there when they needed it.

"Over time, the ruins of Old Jierra cooled into a thousand lands beneath a thousand skies. People argued among themselves as to whether they should be left as a graveyard, or whether they should be reclaimed. The area of these lands was now ten times greater than that which had been lost, and though most received no sunlight, the heat underground remained. In the end, though there was no consensus, those who wished to return gathered the means to make life possible. They replenished the atmosphere and the water, they crafted new plants and animals, they granted themselves the power to see by starlight and heat."

Imogen whispered, "'Crafted new plants and animals'?" Del had no idea if this was possible, but if they really had made the Hoops, breeding a fish that could live in a hot spring, or an algae that made fuel from sunlight, did not seem any more miraculous.

"So the thousand lands were made habitable," Sejan continued, "and many people came to inhabit them. Life went on too in the neighboring worlds, taking its own path, and the two halves of the family became less and less concerned with each other's affairs.

"The quakes had been seen in the thousand lands from the start, and they had been seen to be growing weaker. But then the quake came that turned every city in every land to dust."

Sejan paused, and Del realized that he'd finally reached a part of the story that troubled him as much as the beginning had affected her.

"Where were the people of the neighboring worlds?" he asked. "There is no answer recorded – except that when we needed their help, the sky remained silent. Were they all dust, themselves? Had they all departed for other stars? Were they shunning us for desecrating their ancestors' graves? No one knows.

"So we lost everything we'd brought with us on the long journey from Old Jierra, except for the new life we'd sown here, our own flesh, and our uncertain memories. The ease we'd had turned to hardship; for generations we succumbed to ignorance and confusion. What's more, we were divided: the newly risen mountains at Sadema cut the world in two."

"Until the Tolleans came?" Imogen suggested.

Sejan groaned. "So you do know the story? You've been playing with me all along?"

Del said, "We only know for sure that the Tolleans came here because some people in Yerada confirmed it."

"What do you mean, *confirmed*?" he demanded. "Had you read about it before, or not?"

Del gave up, too weary to continue. Imogen said, "We come from the Tolleans' side of the mountains, but the history of their travels is garbled. Everything else you've recounted is new to us."

"You're saying you came through the mountains?" Sejan was skeptical, but he clearly did not find the idea impossible.

"Not ... as such," Imogen confessed. "We came from *behind* the mountains, but we took the other way around."

Del was numb now; she didn't care if Sejan lost trust in them completely.

But his reaction was the opposite. "I knew it!" he said. "I knew it could be done! Everyone who tried gave up too easily." He leaped to his feet, laughing with delight. "You came by balloon, across the gap?"

Imogen said, "We came by bridge, but that didn't work out so well. Balloons are how we're hoping to get back."

Chapter 28

"I can come with you to Dallya, if you like," Sejan offered, once he'd heard the whole story. "Vouch for you, back up your claims, help in any way I can."

Imogen was bemused. "Why do you believe us? No one else does."

"I always suspected that the paths around the Hoops were finite," he said. "*The Book of All Skies* is vague about the matter, and no one in modern times has been able to settle it. But it always seemed illogical to me to suppose that the succession of new skies went on forever."

"Did you ever try to make the crossing yourself?"

"No. I just heard that everyone who tried suffered setbacks; the whole business has been discouraging. But if you really did bridge the gap with *wooden planks* ... that's just glorious."

Del said, "Those wooden planks probably killed our friends."

"I'm sorry." Sejan restrained his exuberance. "I know it's still not an easy thing to do. But you've proved that it's possible by one method. That gives me hope that we can find a safer way."

Del said, "If you'll excuse me, I need to get some rest."

She lay in her tent, unable to sleep. She kept picturing a crowded city, full of ordinary people going about their lives, when the ground began to crack and they plunged into an inferno big enough to swallow their whole world.

If the architects of the Hoops could cross the void, why hadn't they traveled to a safe remove before taking such a risk? Del almost rose to seek out Sejan and demand a copy of *The Book of All Skies* so she could read the relevant passages herself, but she had no reason to expect that would clarify anything. If that part of the story was a lie, concealing a deliberate atrocity, there would be no other sources to judge it against. All these old books, and all the supposedly learned commentaries on them, were just a swamp of deceit and confusion. She should have welcomed the theft of the crumbling Tollean translation – probably full of as many newly minted lies and misdirections as the original – and got on with her life in Apasa, never thinking too much about anything in the past, or anything that was not right in front of her.

When she finally fell asleep, she was jolted awake again almost immediately by Imogen calling to her. She emerged from the tent, and packed up her belongings while the others ate breakfast.

The sky had grown visibly pale, washing out all but the brightest stars. She wandered away from the camp site, past a field of dormant sunflowers, and approached the nearest of the fuel lakes. The water was a lurid green, and the smell was almost unbearable. Perhaps Jierra was essential to life across the thousand lands, but it was no paradisical wilderness: it was more like a kind of grim chemical factory, built to endure the extremes of the sun's prolonged presence and absence.

She heard Sejan start the cart's engine, and she hurried back and climbed on board.

"Are you all right?" Imogen asked.

"Yes. I'm just tired."

They sped east along the highway, regaining the darkness. Del wasn't surprised that there was no traffic in the opposite direction, but there were no latecomers overtaking them either, nor dawdlers for them to pass. It was unlikely that they had this land to themselves, but it still felt as if they were the last people alive.

"Old Jierra would have rotated?" she asked Sejan.

"Yes."

"How often?"

"About as often as we sleep," he replied. "That's probably where the cycle comes from."

"So the stars would rise and set, and the sun, at almost the same pace?"

"Yes. And the moon."

Del searched the sky. "What happened to the moon?"

170

Sejan said, "When the world flowed through the Hoops, it took most of its gravity elsewhere. Wherever the moon escaped to, we've lost track of it; it might have ended up inside the sun, or it might have gone so far away that we can't see it any more."

Del's head throbbed. The story that every child in the Overgap learned was full of unimaginable catastrophes. Perhaps that was what the Tolleans had recoiled from: not the idealistic notions of work and property, but the casual acceptance of this monstrous history. Who would choose to believe that their own ancestors had, through malice or stupidity, killed off the vast majority of their own species, and all the others that had shared Old Jierra? The Tolleans had seen themselves as the pinnacle of civilization – but not only was the Overgap more advanced, they taught that every living person was scrabbling in the ruins of a culture whose achievements and calamities were a thousand times grander and more tragic.

"What would you do, if you saw signs of life on a neighboring world?" Imogen asked Sejan.

"Look for some way to signal to them," he replied. "Or ultimately, visit them."

"*Visit them?*"

"Why not? They got there from Old Jierra, whose gravity was much stronger than ours. We could reach the void just by burning some simple chemicals – but maintaining life and navigating safely are still beyond us."

"You could aim for that technology anyway," Imogen said. "With or without signs of life."

"We could," Sejan agreed. "I hope we will. But every journey's easier if you know you'll be met on the other side."

The sky was as black as Thena's now, and alongside all the scattered points of light, a band of faint, closely packed stars stretched from horizon to horizon.

"That's like Juthena," Del said, pointing to the structure. "The constellations aren't the same, though."

Sejan said, "As far as I know, no two skies show the same stars, but the stars often look like they're gathered together that way."

"So do the Hoops bring us closer to any of the stars we can see from here, or not?" Del asked. "The stars the Old Jierrans were so eager to reach?"

"I can't say," Sejan replied. "Maybe the other skies are so distant from each other that there's no hope of recognizing any commonality. Or maybe they're separated in a different way. Once you go through a Hoop on land, the only way to return to where you started is to retrace your path – or complete enough circuits, as your expedition proved. That could be true all the way across the void: the Hoops could change the meaning of location everywhere, in a way that only they can undo."

"So, before the Hoops existed," Imogen asked, "where would those stars have been, compared to Old Jierra?"

Sejan said, "Somewhere unreachable. Not just distant: literally unreachable."

Del offered to drive for a while, to give Sejan a rest. He was reluctant at first, but after a supervised trial at low speed he decided that her skills were adequate.

"Wait until they see me driving down the main street of Apasa," Del joked. "They'll either make me mayor, or throw me in prison."

"It might be hard to transport a decent supply of fuel to your side, with balloons," Sejan mused. "But before anyone attempts another bridge, maybe we can build some kind of pipeline."

"Let's see if we can get across at all," Imogen replied. She recounted their conversation with Tarin, who'd followed the history of experiments at the nubs more closely than Sejan.

Sejan was undeterred. "There's a path across the gap," he said. "You proved that by coming here. The gravity might be tricky, and the shifting endpoints a challenge for any solid structure ... but what matters most is that there's nothing blocking the way."

Chapter 29

They'd driven and rested four times when they began to see hints of the sunset ahead of them.

"Should I slow down?" Del asked Sejan.

"There's no need," he assured her. "Put on your glasses if your eyes are hurting, but we've taken long enough that the exit will be well out of direct sunlight."

Del drove on, using the glasses to shield herself from the glare. The air was warmer than ever, and the stench of the lakes, bloated with half a year's worth of algal excretions, was overpowering.

"What if I miss the turnoff?" If they drove too far east the sunset would be reversed before their eyes, with the motion of the cart dragging the blazing star back above the horizon.

"The highway goes straight to the ring road at the northern edge of the Hoop," Sejan replied. "Just remember to turn right there, and you can't get into trouble."

Del held up her right hand and pointed, just in case she'd got the meanings swapped in her early language lessons and never caught the mistake.

Sejan said, "Yes, turn that way if you want to live."

When they reached the junction Del paused to read the signs spelling out the dangers for travelers at different times of the year; she had heard most of the terms before, without really understanding them, but now she could work backward from the warnings to get an idea of their meaning.

"Five circuits to Dallya," Imogen announced impatiently; there were signs listing the lands in each direction too.

Del restarted the engine and made a right turn; the meniscus of darker sky ahead was unmissable, with or without other guidance. As they drove beneath the arch of the Hoop, the stars came out, forever. Imogen cheered, and Sejan started laughing.

"You two owe me a tour of your own side now," he said.

"Only if you follow local customs and do it on foot," Imogen replied.

"That sounds fair."

Del concentrated on her driving; she'd grown used to a straight course and the near certainty of having the road to herself. When a tanker appeared around the side of the hill, she panicked for a moment, but the convention of driving on the left hadn't changed, and there was plenty of room for both vehicles.

"I wonder if our old cart's still waiting for us back at the other Hoop," Imogen mused.

"It might be," Sejan said, "but if it was only missing one part when you left it, you might find that number's increased substantially."

"Cannibals," Imogen muttered disgustedly.

As they drove out of reach of the traces of scattered sunlight, Del switched on the cart's headlights, and the oncoming tankers were soon lit up as well.

"How do people decide who makes the journey to get fuel for their towns, before the Hoops become impassable?" Imogen wondered.

"I don't know," Sejan replied. "The people who want to do it, do it, but if you hear that no one's planning the trip, you talk to your friends and someone ends up going."

"What if no one does it?"

"Someone always does."

"But what if they didn't?"

Sejan said, "You could get fuel from another town, if you had to."

"Wouldn't they stop you? Wouldn't they fight you?"

Sejan pondered this scenario. "If there was so little that it would ruin their lives to share it, maybe they would. But no one ever lets it come to that."

Imogen said, "So your whole society would collapse, if there was ever real scarcity?"

"Maybe it would," Sejan conceded. "But we seem to have become more skilled at avoiding scarcity than we are at fighting over scraps. Whether you count that as a weakness or a form of resilience is up to you."

"Just admit that you'd be lost without the sun," she said.

Sejan recited solemnly, "We'd be lost without the sun."

Del counted the circuits around the edge diligently, even though there were signs everywhere. "What did people from the neighboring worlds think when they came to Jierra for the first time, and had to leave their own sky behind?" she asked Sejan.

"I think it felt like taking shelter," he replied. "Moving into a cave to protect themselves from the sun. They would have been used to that. None of them had ever walked in the sunlight on Old Jierra, with air they could breathe beneath an open sky."

Del felt a pang of nostalgia for a world she'd never known. "Back in Thena, when we talk about the Bounteous Lands, they sound more like Old Jierra than anything I've seen here." It was certainly warmer in this region, and the forests and fields were lush, but there were no idyllic landscapes of the kind she'd once imagined, bathed in light yet somehow rendered safe. And there was no point wishing she could step onto the ancestral world; though the heat would have been moderated by the rapid cycles of sunlight and darkness, when the light did come it would have blinded them all.

They reached the turnoff into Dallya, and a highway replete with its own signs listing all the towns ahead. "I don't know exactly where the balloon-makers are," Del said. "Tarin wasn't sure, but she thought they probably moved around a lot, hunting for the most favorable weather."

"So we'll stop in the first town and ask," Sejan replied. "Eventually we'll find someone who's seen them."

In Stanas, the only hostel was full, so they drove to a nearby campground. The streets along the way were empty; it seemed the synchrony with local sleep cycles Del had become used to when she and

Imogen were traveling around the western Hoop had been thoroughly severed by the trip across Jierra.

They ate, then sat together waiting for the town to wake. "You don't mind missing your observations?" Del asked Sejan.

"I'll still have a chance on the journey back," he said. "The planets don't move so quickly that they'll have gone out of sight. In any case, this is just as important. I've spent years looking for our long-lost relatives, and now here you are, right in front of me."

"Except we're the disappointing branch of the family no one really wanted to find," Imogen joked.

"Aren't we the ones who disappointed you?" Sejan replied. "So much that you blocked the tunnel and blew it up?"

"Blew it up?" Del hadn't heard that claim before.

"Filled it with rocks then set off explosives, so the roof collapsed," Sejan insisted.

Del supposed Grana and Sejan must have read competing accounts of the details, but she was in no position to try to adjudicate between them. She said, "The truth is, we have no record on our side of having done that, let alone the reason why."

Imogen said, "Maybe we can ask whoever blew up the bridge, if we ever get our hands on them."

Sejan was startled. "I thought you said it collapsed from the strain."

Del said, "That's my theory, but we don't know for sure. We were at the far end when it splintered – that's the only reason we survived – so it was impossible to tell what was happening back at Celema."

A cart rattled past on the road beside the campground; the locals were awake at last. They walked into town, and soon found a group of willing informants.

"You're looking for the balloon races? They're in Medoun!"

Back on the road, Sejan took over the driving. Del peered ahead anxiously, checking the road signs and following their progress on her atlas. Medoun was beside a lake; maybe all balloonists preferred to travel near bodies of water as insurance against a hard landing.

"I think I can see them!" Imogen exclaimed.

Del looked up from the atlas. In the distance, the beams from three floodlights, rendered visible as faint cones through the dust in the air, fell upon three vehicles moving high above the ground. They weren't globes like the balloon in Dreyas – they were flattened, almost fishlike, and their surface bore a silvery sheen. Below each body, above the passengers' basket, were a pair of propellers, while the fish itself bore a rudder in place of its tail.

And they were not merely drifting with the wind: though they were all traveling in the same direction, one was clearly speeding ahead.

Imogen said, "Now I'm willing to admit that that's worth the trip. Because if these machines can't carry us home, nothing will."

Chapter 30

A crowd of spectators was gathered by the lake, cheering and shouting, clearly invested in the outcome of the race.

"Do people gamble here?" Imogen asked Del. "What would they even bet with?"

They kept their distance from the boisterous throng, more out of fear of a random elbow in the ribs than any consequence of picking the wrong competitor. Del gazed up at the three illuminated vehicles, which had reversed direction since she'd first seen them from afar; apparently they were traversing a circular course above the water. She looked to the floodlights tracking their progress, and after pondering the mechanisms supporting them, guessed an answer to a question she'd been forming: the racers couldn't cheat, despite the lack of any physical constraint to keep them from taking short-cuts, because the lights were constrained to sweep out only the prescribed route in the sky. If an air-fish strayed, it would go dark, and presumably be disqualified.

As they approached the finish, the balloons were drawing closer together, sending their supporters into a frenzy. "Do you think the drivers can hear any of this?" Imogen wondered. "Urging them on?"

"Maybe, though I doubt they can pick out their own names from up there." Then again, when Del had been in footraces, she'd never heard her name being shouted by her friends, but she'd still felt invigorated by the general hubbub. Maybe she'd won a few races entirely from the encouragement directed by spectators at her competitors.

Abruptly, one of the air-fish turned blue, and the cheers and laments reached a crescendo. Del glanced down, confused at first, wondering if she could have missed a fourth floodlight, but then she realized that a filter, suspended high above all three lights, was positioned to mark out the winner.

Sejan said, "This might not have been the best time to try to reach the balloonists." As the vehicles descended, the mob was already repositioning itself below. The air-fish did not come all the way to the ground; they approached a tower on the shore of the lake, arriving at different altitudes, and the drivers threw anchor ropes to secure them before assistants on the tower slid out ladders to allow them to cross.

"What could we possibly offer them to compete with this much adulation?" Imogen asked. As the drivers emerged from the base of the tower, all three were seized and carried shoulder-high by their supporters.

"Tell them they'd be famous across the whole world," Del suggested. "Feted and adored everywhere, for uniting humanity."

"Like we are?"

"I'm sure there'll be a footnote for us in the history books."

"We should find a place to stay, then seek these people out when things are calmer," Sejan decided.

They drove into town and managed to get two rooms at the hostel. When Del asked a fellow guest if he'd come for the balloon races, he laughed. "Medoun is just a rest stop for me. I've seen the races a few times, but I've never understood the excitement."

Del lay down in her room and fell asleep. She was woken by Imogen and Sejan talking excitedly in the corridor; she rose and joined them.

"I didn't mean to disturb you," Sejan apologized. "But I managed to arrange a meeting with the balloonists. The three of us are invited to their house for a meal."

Del was amazed. "How?"

Sejan said, "They're really very approachable. Also, I offered to name minor planets after all of them."

"Can you do that? Name a planet anything you like?"

"If I discover one that isn't yet cataloged. And there's still a chance I'll find three very small ones before I die."

When they set out for the house, Del was expecting to encounter a throng of people at the gates, clamoring to spend more time with their idols, but upon arriving they found the place silent, and only a single window lit.

A young woman opened the door, and invited them in; two other women were waiting in the dining room. Sejan made the introductions; the balloonists were named Lena, Katka and Asha.

Asha served the food, and the six of them sat down to eat.

"Sejan tells us you come from the other side of Sadema," Katka said, addressing Del and Imogen politely, but with an inflection that Del read as noncommittal at best. "And you crossed the void between the nubs on a wooden bridge."

"That's right," Del replied. She'd grown accustomed to Sejan's acceptance of their story, and she'd hoped that his backing would count for something. "Do you believe us?" she asked. "Because we've been here for a long time, and I still don't know what it is we're meant to do to prove that we're not lying. If you found yourself in my homeland, and you could build a cart of the kind you have here, or even just a dynamo and an electric light, everyone would be convinced at once that you'd arrived from an unknown land. But we have no wonderful inventions with which to amaze you. We just look like a couple of ignorant people from some backwater town, which I suppose we are."

She hadn't meant to sound quite so bitter, but her hosts seemed to accept her complaint without rancor.

"You do have an invention that we're lacking, though," Katka reminded her. "We've never built a bridge like that, and we don't understand the gravity at the nubs anywhere near well enough to try it. If you can explain how your bridge stretched so far – even though, I understand, it fell after you crossed it – then I'll be far more impressed than anyone would be by an electric light."

Del glanced at Sejan; if he'd known this was coming, he might have warned her. "I'll need a pencil and paper," she said.

"Of course," Katka replied. "Please, relax and finish your meal first. There's no hurry."

Imogen whispered in Peladan, "My diving suits don't count for anything?"

"Of course they do," Del assured her. "But we did claim to walk here upside-down across the void, not right-way-up across a riverbed."

Imogen addressed the balloonists. "The three of you look very alike. Are you sisters?"

Lena said, "Asha and I are sisters. Katka is our cousin."

"So how serious are the races?" Imogen wondered. "Are you genuine rivals, or do you just play it up for the crowds?"

Lena was amused. "Whether you call us rivals or not, there's only one winner at the end of each race. Then we all learn from the winner, and the race becomes even tighter the next time. That's what the crowds come to see."

Imogen seemed confused, but at a loss as to what to ask next. Del said, "You all use hydrogen?"

"Of course," Lena replied. "Hot air might be picturesque, but the lift from hydrogen is far stronger."

"How do you control your buoyancy," Imogen asked, "if you can't just turn a flame up or down?"

"There's a ballonet of ordinary air inside the lifting capsule," Asha explained. "If we pump it up, that compresses the hydrogen around it, and the whole airship becomes less buoyant."

They finished eating. Katka cleared the table, then brought Del the materials she'd requested.

"Correct me if I make any mistakes," she told Imogen.

"Correct you? You were the one who watched the whole thing being built."

"And you're the one who takes carts apart, and designs diving suits. I don't have the soul of an engineer."

She sketched the bridge in sections, one for each sky it crossed. She was fairly sure she had the overall shape correct, but her memory of the cantilevers was full of contradictory cues, and it was all she could do to avoid drawing them as impossible objects.

The balloonists looked on, intrigued. "Can you draw the direction of gravity along the way?" Lena requested.

"Of course." Del hadn't tried to sketch in all the ladders and stairs, so it wasn't obvious how the orientation of the structure was related to the local sense of the vertical.

"And if you depart from this path," Asha asked, "how fast would the strength of gravity change?"

"We never departed from the bridge," Del replied. "We just traveled along it."

"Of course. But you're asking us if we can fly the same route," Asha explained, "and we can't know that if we don't know the effects of any departure."

Del gestured helplessly at the drawing. "I didn't design this bridge. I'm not a surveyor, or a gravitational theorist. If you think that means I'm lying, what do you want me to say?"

Katka scowled, exasperated. "No one's accusing you of lying! But you've experienced how dangerous these conditions are, even with a rigid platform to support you. People have died, trying to fly around the nubs, and we have no reason to think we can do better. If you want to change our minds, you need to tell us what the gravity will be *at any point between the nubs.*"

Del fell silent. All she'd ever done was watch the others calculating from afar. What did she know about the gravity around an empty Hoop?

Only one thing came to mind. "It's all about electrostatics," she said. "The Hoop is like a metal disk."

"What?" Katka appeared ready to burst out laughing and renounce the whole story as a hoax, but then Sejan said, "You start with an inverse square law for both. But where does the metal disk come into it?"

182

"If you move across a layer of charge on a disk," Asha suggested tentatively, "the potential close to the layer stays the same ... but the electric field reverses direction?"

Lena said, "That's right. And with a layer of dipoles the field stays the same, but the potential jumps to the opposite sign."

None of this sounded familiar to Del, but she wasn't going to try to steer the discussion on the basis of some half-remembered fragments of Montano's explanation.

Sejan borrowed the pencil and started sketching disks adorned with strange symbols. "Let's keep things simple, and assume we have a single Hoop and just two skies. So ... suppose that in one sky, we replace the Hoop by a disk with a certain pattern of charges and dipoles, yet to be determined."

Katka groaned. "You can't just pretend things are present in the world, when they're not!"

"You can," Asha insisted, "if you put the opposite charges and dipoles at exactly the same place in the adjoining sky. What you've added adds up to zero. You're actually changing nothing – but you're free to split up that nothing any way that helps you understand what's going on."

"All right," Katka agreed, slightly mollified. "But how does it help?"

Asha stared at Sejan's diagram. "As you travel through the Hoop, the potential and the electric field should both change smoothly. After all, there is no actual charge there! But we're trying to find out the effect of an actual charge somewhere in the first sky – a source of gravity, really, but all the mathematics should work out the same way in the end."

Sejan wrote down more symbols as Asha pursued her line of thought. "So we add up the potential in the first sky due to the real charge, the nonexistent charge and the nonexistent dipoles on one side of the Hoop, and that sum must equal what we get from the nonexistent charge and dipoles in the second sky, on the other side of the Hoop. But the potential from the dipoles is the same in both cases, because we've crossed to the other side of the disk but also switched to the opposite dipoles, in the second sky. That means the potential due to the nonexistent charge must be half the opposite of the potential we'd get *from the real charge alone*, in the absence of any Hoops." She looked up at Del and smiled, astonished. "And we can use the same trick to find the electric field for the nonexistent dipoles. You're a genius!"

Del said, "Ummm ... "

Imogen whispered, "They're making stone soup for us, just go along with it."

Sejan said, "I don't know how to work backward from the potential to the charge distribution."

"Me neither," Asha admitted. She glanced at Lena, who made a gesture of defeat. "But someone must know a trick that can get us there. This looks so close!"

Katka said, "All right. No verdict yet, but tomorrow we'll try to find someone who can help clear this up."

"'Tomorrow'?" Del asked. Katka seemed on the verge of treating the question as an objection to her plan, but then she realized that Del was just enquiring about the meaning of the word.

"You really are from another place," she said. "*Tomorrow*: after we've slept. As on Old Vierra, after the sun has risen."

Del said, "Thank you. That would be good."

Chapter 31

Upon returning to the balloonists' house, Del found them engaged with a new guest.

"Sina's helped us before, with the airship designs," Asha offered, which Del took to mean that they had good reason to trust her mathematical acumen. Del sat back and watched the four of them arguing and calculating, with occasional contributions from Sejan; she only understood a fraction of what she heard, but it was clear that they'd moved far beyond the simple construction Montano had described to her, where mirror-image charges either side of the Hoop mimicked the effects of a metal plate, and vice versa.

"You've really lit a fire," Imogen marveled. "You just muttered a few words, but by the time this is finished, they'll be able to tell us how to build a new bridge out of paper alone."

"Ha." There was enough of it on the table to make a start. "Maybe the world really should be split in two for a few generations at a time, then brought back together so we can reinvigorate each other with the things one side discovered but the other missed."

Del picked up a sudden note of excitement in Sina's voice, and listened carefully as she addressed Asha. "The total potential from the charge – if you add it up across equivalent points in all the different skies – is still just proportional to the inverse distance. That has to be true, or there'd be lines of flux disappearing for no reason. But *this* formula tells us how to split up the total into separate parts, each of them obeying the same equation that the inverse distance obeys on its own. And that's it. That's enough to be sure that the solution is correct!"

Asha gazed down at the scrawled symbols. Then she looked up and smiled. "You're right. I understand now."

"So you can calculate the gravity?" Del asked hopefully.

"For one speck of rock," Asha replied. "Now we need to add up the results for all the specks that make up the world."

Imogen laughed. Del believed that Montano and Silvio had done something similar; there were mathematical techniques to make this less like emptying an ocean with a spoon than it sounded. But it wouldn't be easy.

Del offered to cook some food for the group, and after some initial, polite refusals the balloonists agreed. Imogen joined her in the kitchen, grumbling. "We're not their servants."

"And they're not ours," Del replied, "but we're asking them to risk their lives. Gutting a few fish and chopping a few vegetables is hardly servitude – it's what they did for us last time we were here."

When the meal was ready they brought it into the dining room, and everyone took a break.

"Any progress?" Del asked.

"We have some estimates," Asha said cautiously.

"And are they good news, or bad?"

Asha glanced at her sister. "The problem is, if the strength of gravity changes too rapidly with a change in altitude, anything that disturbs the overall buoyancy of the airship could make it drop much faster than usual. It takes time to react to an event like that, and compensate for it. We're accustomed to dealing with changes in the temperature and pressure of the air, and with up-drafts and down-drafts over land and water; we know how strong these effects are, and we're confident we can adjust the buoyancy quickly enough to deal with them. But if gravity can double between the time we start to plummet and the time we've responded to the fall ... "

"Can it double that fast, though?" Imogen asked.

"That depends," Asha replied.

"On what?"

"How accurate our estimates are. But also, on how high we fly."

"The higher you fly," Del guessed, "the gentler the changes in gravity?"

"Yes," Asha confirmed.

Imogen chewed on her fish for a while, but Del could see that she was mulling over the problem. "What is it that limits the altitude you can reach?" she asked finally. "The buoyancy you can get from the balloon, or something else?"

Lena said, "Something else. Unpiloted balloons can ascend much higher than piloted ones, but engines and pilots both need to breathe. We could swap the fuel-based engines for electric ones, for a short enough trip, but people aren't so easy to adapt."

Imogen said, "You store hydrogen gas in a metal cylinder. Is there any reason you couldn't do the same with breathable air?"

"Not in principle," Lena replied. "But something like that would be completely new and untried. It might be possible to work out a safe way to deliver that air to a person, but I wouldn't know where to start."

Del waited for Imogen to respond, but she was pretending to concentrate on her meal, mopping up the gravy as if she had nothing more to contribute.

Del ran out of patience and turned to Asha. "Have you ever walked underwater?" she asked. "Because my friend has a lot of experience with the machinery that makes that possible."

Chapter 32

Del leaned over the edge of the basket and gazed down at the cloud-strewn landscape below. In between the fluffy gray streaks, she could see the lake catching the starlight, and the dark fields to the north. On the southern shore, the streets of Medoun had shrunk to a patch of luminous tracery she could cover with one hand. Her faceplate was still fogging up from the cold; they would need to do something about that.

When she looked up, she was confused for a moment; her eye-line felt perfectly level, but the horizon lay well below it. Then she realized that that made perfect sense: this high above the ground, even Dallya's entire globe would fill less than half the sky.

"Are you ready?" Katka asked. Her voice sounded thin through the rarefied air.

Del wasn't ready for anything at this altitude besides a mug of Imogen's special tea, but it was her turn to face the terror. If she wasn't willing to do this, she should have stayed on the ground. "Yes," she replied.

Katka plunged a knife into the bag of sand attached to the side of the basket, then carved out a larger wound, like an assassin making sure of her kill. As sand trickled out the balloon began to rise, sending Del's viscera twitching and shuddering. She grabbed the handle of the pump and began working it frantically, forcing air into the ballonet.

The instrument panel showed the ambient pressure, the pressure in the hydrogen-filled lifting capsule, and the pressure in the ballonets. The first was still dropping – a surer judge of rising altitude than her gut – so Del redoubled her efforts. In a real emergency where the ballonet pump's electric motor failed, she hoped there'd be at least one other pair of hands to assist her, but the balloonists were adamant that every pilot and passenger had to be prepared to stabilize the airship's altitude, unaided, if the need arose.

Finally, the first dial became steady. Del looked over at the sandbag, but it was empty; there was no more ballast to lose.

"Did I really pump in the same weight in air as you dropped in sand?" she asked.

"Not yet," Katka replied. "We're higher now, so that's shifted the balance. You need to go further, and bring us down to where we were before."

Del resumed pumping, then realized she was near the limits of both her own ability to move the handle and the physical capacity of the first ballonet. She shifted to the second pump; it was still hard work, pushing air in to squeeze against the hydrogen she'd already compressed.

Suddenly, their altitude began dropping. Del stopped pumping, but the descent continued.

"What's happening?" she asked, bewildered. "What did I do?"

"Look at the dials," Katka urged her.

Del stared at the panel, trying not to panic. The hydrogen pressure had dropped. "You vented it?" she asked Katka. "Without warning?"

"Events don't always come with warnings."

Del opened the vents on both ballonets; as the air escaped, the hydrogen pressure dropped further, but this time it wasn't being lost. Or so she hoped. She checked the lever on the hydrogen vent, but Katka had closed it after her surreptitious intervention, and she hadn't accidentally opened it herself.

She watched the three needles moving, her stomach convulsing. But gradually the altitude leveled, and she quickly shut off the ballonet vents.

She glanced down and saw Medoun revealed as a city again, the carts moving about like delicate toys. Katka said, "Between the nubs, the scale of things will be compressed. The highest altitude we can survive, and the lowest, will be ten times closer than they are here."

Del's hands were shaking as she removed her helmet. "But you think we can survive the crossing?"

"Absolutely," Katka replied. "I wouldn't try doing it if I thought otherwise. But could it kill us, if enough things go wrong? Of course. We just need to make the quantity of bad luck needed to achieve that as large as we possibly can."

Del wasn't sure how comforted she should feel. "Every time you race your cousins, one of you could die. Maybe you're more used to that than I am."

"You almost died once, coming here," Katka observed. "But you didn't."

"Twice," Del corrected her.

"Twice?"

She had no choice, now, but to recount the ambush in Zeruma.

Katka was horrified. "That's how people treat each other, on your side of the gap? They kill each other for gold?"

Del laughed. "Not most people. It's not ... generally approved." She didn't know how to say "unlawful."

Katka took over the airship's controls; when she started the electric motor, its gentle whir barely rose above the sound of the wind. "Why do you think your people blocked off the tunnel?" she asked Del.

"I don't know. I don't think of them as 'my people'; it was so long ago, and if they ever explained themselves, whatever they wrote on the subject has been lost. I'm not even sure if any of the commentary I've read about the route to the Bounteous Lands was a genuine debate, or if it was all disinformation, deliberately sown to confuse people."

Katka was bewildered. "Why would anyone do that?"

Del said, "For the same reason they blocked the tunnel."

"Why not just state their reasons for blocking it? If they could make a good enough argument for that, no one would want to dig through."

Del had been turning that question over in her mind ever since her meeting with Grana. "It only makes sense if the thing they were most afraid of from your side was an idea. If you believe an idea is dangerous,

190

you can't warn people off it by explaining it to them, since all you'll end up doing is planting it in their head."

They were close to the tower now. Katka threw out the anchor rope and managed to hook a girder, then Lena, who'd been waiting for them in the tower, stepped forward and secured the connection before sliding out the crossing ladder.

Del went first, in the hope that her fear of Katka's impatience would prevent her from freezing halfway. Staring down at the shore with just the rungs between her and a long drop made her heart race, but the trick seemed to work. The tower itself was all open girders and platforms: no more frightening than the bridge, and much less likely to collapse unexpectedly.

"How did it go?" Lena asked her.

"I'm not sure," Del admitted. "We survived the test, but I don't know if we would have survived the same kind of event in the gap."

Katka joined them on the platform. "We were close," she said. "We just need some improvements to the pumps, and some more practice to reduce our reaction times."

Del said, "I don't know if this is practical or not, but is there any way to show the volume of the ballonet on the instrument panel, as well as the pressure inside it?"

Lena was puzzled. "Why would you want that?"

"It would give me a clearer picture of what's going on," Del replied. The pressures were crucial, but they were abstract numbers to her; she wanted the means to visualize as much as she could about the changes in any structure on which her life would depend.

"I'll think about it," Lena said. "Maybe there's a simple way to do it without adding another failure point."

Back at the house, Asha and Sina were working on yet another refinement of their gravitational calculations. Del stared at the charts on the wall, which looked like topographical maps but actually portrayed empty space. The curves of constant potential progressed from lines radiating out from the edge of the Hoop, to spirals, to circles, then back again, which was in accord with her own experience on the bridge.

"If you can get everything that I know about right, how much room is there to be wrong about the rest?" she asked Asha.

Asha hesitated, but Sina answered. "Not a lot, unless we've made an arithmetical error somewhere. It's in the nature of the gravitational force that if you know how it behaves on the boundary of a region, you know how it behaves in the interior."

Asha was a little more circumspect. "That's true for an entire boundary, but we only know what things were like along one path. We can push it a bit further by assuming there was nothing special about that path – but in the end, nothing's certain until you've measured it."

Del recalled Clarissa's hope that successive measurements as the bridge grew would alert her to any failure in the calculations. But she still didn't know if it was the calculations that had failed them in the end.

Imogen and Sejan joined them, back from the food stall, and they all sat down for a meal.

"I've been thinking about the trip to the nub," Lena began. "If we take the airships apart and move them by cart, that would be faster, and less subject to the vagaries of the wind, but it won't give us much of a chance to test them after reassembly. If we fly them the whole way, we'll get to see them under stress while we still have ground to land on if we need to carry out repairs."

"That makes sense to me," Katka replied.

Sejan said, "I was hoping to get in some observations on the way back."

"You can still do that," Lena assured him. "If you're driving the cart, and we're following along by air, there'll be plenty of time for you to stop and use the telescopes while you wait for us to catch up."

"We would need to leave earlier, though," Asha said. She turned to Sina. "Are you sure you don't want to come with us?"

Sina laughed. "I can just about cope with an ordinary flight, but losing sight of the ground completely is my idea of a nightmare." She addressed Del and Imogen. "Seriously, when that bridge had no visible means of support, how did you keep going?"

"With one foot in front of the other," Del replied. "Thankful that I wasn't a carpenter."

"How soon until we'd need to leave?" Imogen asked Asha.

"About thirty days."

Sejan pondered this. "Twenty might be better."

Katka said, "That should work."

Del's chest tightened. "How many more test flights will Imogen and I have time for?"

"Maybe ... half a dozen each," Lena suggested.

"And you think we'll be ready?" Del felt like she was watching sand pouring out of a ballast sack again.

"You'll have the chance to observe all the operations on a much longer flight along the way," Katka replied. "By the time we reach the nub, you'll be experienced copilots."

Imogen exchanged a glance with Del. "How many lands have the three of you flown between, so far?"

The balloonists went quiet, but then Lena said, "We've all been through the Hoop and back once, just to convince ourselves that it was possible. We never had reason to travel very far before. But as I said, the more we have a chance to test the airships before the crossing, the better."

Del helped wash the dishes, then she went for a walk. The household wasn't short on any provisions, but out of habit she ended up wandering past the stalls in the town center where people left things they'd made, or obtained, for others to take as they wished. Most stalls were unattended by the providers of the goods, but there were always a few touts to be seen, so passionate about their creations that they harangued passersby with a constant monolog on the virtues of the product. "This mop will clean twice as thoroughly as any other design!" a man exclaimed, holding up the glorious device. "And if the head becomes worn or dirty, it's easily replaced!"

When Del came to the bookstall, there was no one speaking on behalf of the wares. She had borrowed a few volumes since arriving in town – an eclectic mix of titles she'd chanced upon, chosen mainly on the basis that the first half-page had been comprehensible to her, despite her limited grasp of the language.

She entered and switched on the light, then walked between the shelves, waiting for something to catch her eye. *The Murderer's Apprentice* and its seventeen sequels occupied a substantial portion of the stall; Del had tried the first volume, and found it quite entertaining, but she'd lost interest by the fifth killing. For a largely peaceful society with almost no concept of property crimes, the Overgaps still managed to maintain a lurid obsession with violence to rival anything from the Vitean age.

She spotted a new title on the maintenance of engines, and took it in case it was of interest to Imogen. She turned and headed back toward the exit, then paused; for a moment she wasn't sure why.

The Book of All Skies sat on a shelf beside her, the cover crisply printed with a simple illustration portraying a helicoid decorated with star maps. Del picked it up; the binding was uncreased, and it looked as if no one had opened the volume before her.

Sejan had always claimed that the book was widely available, but when she'd failed to locate it in her previous visits to the stall she'd started to wonder if that merely reflected his own experience in another land. But she wasn't hallucinating, or mistranslating the title; the words in front of her were exactly the words he'd used.

She opened the book and began to read.

Long ago, our ancestors lived on Old Jierra, a world with an uncomplicated, spherical shape from which every land we now live upon was formed.

Chapter 33

Given that the expedition would be robbing Medoun of its heroes for at least a year, Del had expected to find the crowd gathered at the shore for their departure hostile, mournful, or perhaps just entirely absent.

But when she arrived, the site was as packed as she'd ever seen it, and the people every bit as exuberant.

"Why do they love you so much?" she asked Katka, as they approached the tower. People were running in front of the cart, waving at them blissfully, as ecstatic as if some despotic ruler had just dropped dead.

"Because we fly. Who doesn't love flying?"

"Sina?" Del suggested.

"Sina loves the idea as much as anyone. She just doesn't enjoy it if she actually has to do it."

Del stopped at the base of the tower, and the mob allowed them to disembark unmolested. Asha, Lena and Imogen were already waiting for them inside.

"How are you feeling?" Imogen asked Del in Peladan.

"I'm fine," Del replied, the same way; however fluent they'd become in the local language, it was comforting to revert to their native tongue. "Ask me again at the nub."

Imogen laughed. "Yeah, this first part's nothing. Just the longest balloon trip in history."

"Unless they had balloons on Old Jierra."

"Why would they have bothered with balloons, if they could fly through the void?"

Del had no answer to that. "Stay safe," she said.

"You too."

Katka's airship was moored at the topmost berth, so she and Del took the stairs first and the others followed behind. "When I left my home town, we had a party," she told Katka. "But that seems like a different world now. Something I dreamed."

Katka said, "I hope it wasn't a dream, or we might have some trouble navigating back to it."

They reached the berth and climbed out along the boarding ladder. Del panicked for a moment, confused by the sense that her center of gravity was not where it should have been, then realized she'd never done this wearing her pack before. It wasn't even holding much: just a single book, and enough food and water to last until their first stop. She steadied herself and completed the crossing, jumping down into the basket then moving aside for Katka.

"Back home, some of the ships have names," she said. "Like a town, or a person."

"Of course they do," Katka replied, in her no-I-am-not-that-gullible tone.

Del didn't press her claim, but as she surveyed the basket and glanced up at the lifting capsule, she searched for some reassuring label. "Can we call it the *Apasa*?"

Katka replied without turning away from the instrument panel. "You can call it anything you like." She disengaged the anchor and wound in the mooring rope. "Do you want to fly the *Apasa* away from the tower?"

Del had practiced all the necessary maneuvers, but in her mind they had always been held in reserve for emergencies. "All right," she said. "But please stop me if I'm doing something foolish."

"Always."

Del reached up and switched the propeller gears into reverse, then started the combustion engine. The *Apasa* moved backward slowly, rudder first, weaving side to side a little as it went; though the propellers could be spun either way, the craft as a whole wasn't really designed for bidirectional motion. Below, the crowd began cheering them on, their voices audible even over the clatter. Del glanced back at the tower, where the other two craft were waiting on her to give them clear air.

She switched into first gear and steered the *Apasa* along a broad arc, veering away from the tower to point along the road. As she accelerated, she felt a sense of elation: nothing was certain, but she was finally heading in the right direction.

"Do you want to take over?" she asked Katka.

"You might as well keep going, if you like. The weather's fine, and there are no obstacles ahead."

"What about the Hoop?"

Katka laughed. "We're still a long way from the Hoop."

Del leaned over the edge of the basket and looked down at the road. Carts were speeding by, easily outpacing her. She'd pictured this stage of the journey as following the same progression as her first ride in Halem's cart, magically retracing the paths she and Imogen had toiled along on foot. But it really didn't matter that the airships were slower; the magic now was being freed from the ground, and seeing all the old routes anew.

She glanced behind, and spotted the second airship following along; she could just make out Imogen and Lena.

"Should we race the *Dreyas*?" she joked.

"I'd rather conserve fuel," Katka replied. "If we end up stranded, or blown off course, Sejan won't be too thrilled if he has to come looking for us."

"No."

Del followed the road, tracking the glow of the headlights as the carts came and went beneath her. The wind wasn't strong, but it was unpredictable; maintaining the course required patience and a different kind of concentration than she was used to. Any drift in their position and heading manifested slowly, but any small correction she applied also needed time to take effect, and be properly assessed. In a cart, you had to have your wits about you, but everything happened in an instant; you were never left wondering if you'd overcompensated when you found yourself veering toward the wrong side of the road, or waiting to learn if you'd steered sufficiently into a bend.

"Did your parents ever try to talk you out of this?" Del asked Katka.

"They don't live in Dallya. I haven't seen them for a while, so I don't think they even know about this trip."

"But how did they feel at the beginning? When you and your cousins started building your own airships?"

Katka said, "We talked about the dangers, and I showed them that the three of us had studied as much as we could to be prepared. I think they were satisfied in the end."

"That you'd be safe?"

"That we weren't being reckless. Hydrogen is a dangerous gas, if you're not careful with it. But if you understand the risks, they can be managed."

"Would you have done it if you had children of your own?"

Katka pondered the question. "Probably not. Would you have joined Montano's expedition, if you had children?"

"I don't know," Del replied. "I didn't really grasp how dangerous it might be, but no one could tell me how long I'd be away."

When they finally reached Stanas, Del was exhausted. Katka took over, lowering the *Apasa* and nudging it over the campground until they were able to drop a rope ladder for Sejan to attach to his cart. As they climbed down the ladder, Del asked Katka, "If all three airships stayed moored to the cart and emptied their ballonets ... ?"

"No."

"You're sure?"

Katka said, "I'm fairly sure they couldn't lift the cart, but I'm absolutely certain that we're not going to try."

Sejan greeted them, and they were soon joined by a group of curious spectators, intrigued by the sight of one tethered balloon and another two approaching.

"Are the races shifting from Medoun?" a woman asked.

"No." Katka began describing the expedition, but when she reached the part about the void between the nubs, the woman began raising objections and Katka lost patience, leaving it to Sejan to take up the argument.

The second airship, the *Dreyas*, dropped its ladder, and Del and Katka secured it. Imogen descended first, and greeted Del curtly before rushing to the bathroom.

Lena joined them, looking as weary as Del felt. "This is tougher than the races," she admitted. "I keep waiting to hit the blue light."

Other people from the campground and the town kept arriving, some to stare, some to ask questions, some bringing food. By the time the *Medoun* arrived and Asha was on the ground, there was enough to feed all the travelers.

When they'd eaten and were preparing to sleep, a fresh group of spectators arrived, with their own gifts and questions. "What's happening here?" a man at the front of the pack asked eagerly. "We've heard all kinds of rumors, but they can't be true."

Imogen said, "We're going to visit the Tolleans, flying in the opposite direction to the way you'd expect, sometimes through air with no land beneath it. If you don't understand that, go away and think about it."

Then she took the bag of fruit from the man's outstretched hand, walked into her tent, and closed the flap.

Chapter 34

With no clouds in sight and the adjoining skies indistinguishable in brightness, Del struggled to make out the arch of the Hoop. Katka was more confident that she could discern its position by watching for the stars that were occluded and revealed as they approached, but she still took the *Apasa* as low as she could without risking them running into a hillside.

They'd traveled away from the ring road in order to gain the maximum clearance, which made perfect sense but left them with no easy cues to follow. Del looked up at the stars behind them, but with the balloon blocking so much of the view, it was a while before she could convince herself that they had actually passed through the aperture.

Katka turned the *Apasa* right, back toward the ring road. At least the point where the edge met the ground was unmissable, and even if they couldn't stay close to it the whole time, so long as they kept it on their right they'd know they were making complete circuits.

"If this ever becomes routine, there'll need to be more guidance for the airships," Del suggested.

"Beacons lighting the way?"

"Yes. And safety lights hanging below the Hoop as well."

Katka laughed. "Hanging from what?"

"Some kind of gantry," Del extemporized.

"That sounds like more work than your bridge."

They reached the ring road and made a wide turn around the edge, staying well clear of the Hoop. Del gazed across at the divided ground, one version of the road being swept away while a new one was revealed.

"Do you ever wonder if we might all be closer than we think?" Katka asked. "All the lands are really sharing the same space, but the Hoops are a kind of trick to hide us from each other?"

"So I'm already home, but I just can't see it?" Del contemplated the idea. "I wish that were true, but I don't know what it would mean in practice. Could you give me a magic potion I could drink that would make me visible in my homeland again, without passing through any Hoops?"

"Why not?"

"How would the potion know which land to take me to? Or show me to?"

"Hmm." Katka thought for a while. "Maybe you carry it with you, and it remembers where it came from."

"So does a potion from Thena need to be carried to Dallya and then used there ... or can you use a potion from Dallya that you carried to Thena to bring a potion from Thena to Dallya?"

Katka said, "If you're holding a bottle of one potion while you drink from another bottle, everything you're holding comes with you."

"What if I drink two potions at once?" Del wondered. "From different lands?"

"Now you're just being absurd."

A bank of clouds had drifted into view behind the aperture, rendering the edge starkly visible. It was apparent now that it was well above them, so Katka turned the *Apasa* and brought it through. As they headed north again, Del saw a group of people below, gathered around a stationary cart, gazing up at the balloon. She leaned over the side of the basket and waved at them; there wasn't much light away from the instrument panel, but maybe they'd see her heat blotch as a chilly silhouette against the engine.

"Soon everyone will start making airships," Del suggested.

Katka laughed. "Thanks to our swift and efficient passage through the Hoops?"

"You're the one who told me that everyone loves flight. Where I come from, you have to be very lucky to do things just for the joy of it." She'd wanted to say "lucky, or wealthy", but she didn't know how.

"It does take work, as well as joy."

"That's true. But here, you're unlikely to starve while you're working on it."

"Do you really let people starve?"

"We try not to." Del was embarrassed. "If someone's in need, someone else will usually help them. But even here, there are no promises, are there?"

"No," Katka admitted. "But we make sure the springs aren't overfished, and the forests aren't over-harvested. If people don't grow enough crops, there's usually something else we can gather to make up for the shortage – and enough people who set aside more time for farming."

They were close to the ring road when Del saw the glint of another lifting capsule in the starlight, far behind them. "I think Lena's catching up," she said.

"Good."

"Are you getting tired?" Del asked. "If you want, I could steer for a while. I think I've got the hang of most of the circuit, so long as you take us through the aperture."

"No, I'm fine," Katka insisted. "We'll have a rest in Jierra, then we can take turns following the highway."

"All right." Del looked down at the divided road again. If every inhabitant of every land was here, hidden beneath her, she still wasn't quite home: the eastern Hoop was half a world away from Apasa. But once they'd crossed Jierra, it would all be a matter of the winding of her thread, and whatever forces rendered the different lands visible or invisible.

Chapter 35

When the engine above her began emitting the sound of grinding metal, Del's first thought was that she'd inadvertently bumped the gearstick and knocked it out of place. She disengaged the clutch and prodded the stick, but it was already firmly in position. The problem was elsewhere.

Katka was curled up on the floor of the basket, but the screeching was enough to rouse her. "Shut it off!" she yelled, rising to her feet.

Del complied. As the engine faded to silence, it sounded like some pitiful metallic creature screaming in pain as it was thrown off a cliff.

"Do you know what's broken?" she asked.

"Something in the drive train," Katka replied glumly.

Sejan, with all the spare parts, was far ahead of them, probably camped at the next observatory. But if they could get a message to Lena or Asha, they'd pass it on to him and he'd drive back.

Del glanced down at the highway below. She'd seen tankers and other carts passing by now and then, but no one else was going to be carrying components for an airship's engine. They would just have to be patient.

"Why is the smell of the algae so much worse when we're still?" Katka complained.

"So what's the plan?" Del asked. "Should we take the *Apasa* down while we wait?"

"Not until we've made contact with the others. It will be easier to signal to them if we're at the same level."

"All right." Del looked back, hoping they'd be able to spot the *Dreyas* as it approached. The sunset was far ahead of them, but the western sky was still noticeably brighter. Would that make an airship coming from the east more visible, as it reflected the light? She wasn't sure. But in any case, Lena wouldn't stray far from the highway.

A breeze was blowing from the north, though, and there was nothing to stop the *Apasa* from straying.

Katka caught the worried expression on her face. "Lena's not far behind. We'll still be well within sight when she passes us."

They drifted away from the road, over a field of tall, broad-leafed plants of a kind Del had no memory of seeing on the drive east. "Do you know what they are?" she asked Katka.

"No. But I'm no expert on Jierran flora."

"If every plant was designed especially for this place, you'd think it would have some use."

Katka said, "It probably has a role here as part of the whole system, but I'm not aware of people coming in and harvesting it."

The wind died down, leaving them hovering above the field. Katka fidgeted with the signaling light, then flashed it once, to be sure that it was working, but she held off sending a message into the gloom with no recipient visible. "I don't want to run down the batteries for nothing."

Del saw a speck of pale gray, high above the road to the east. She waited to be sure it wasn't a trick of her eyes, or the atmosphere, before nudging Katka and pointing it out.

"That must be them," Katka agreed. She started flashing the light, pausing between repetitions to wait for a response.

After the seventh transmission, Del saw the gray speck light up. She missed the first few letters, but then translated the code in her head: " ... received. Will ask Sejan to come back for you."

Katka signaled a brief reply. Lena responded: "Received. Stay safe."

Del watched the *Dreyas* grow nearer, until she could make out the occupants: Imogen's heat blotch was unmistakeable, standing at the side of the basket. No sooner had they passed than Del looked east and saw the *Medoun* following close behind. Katka signaled Asha, explaining the situation; Asha replied, "Understood. Good luck. See you soon."

As the *Medoun* receded in the west, Del felt a great sense of relief. There'd been talk early on of the expedition taking just one airship and two extra carts instead, but the system they'd chosen now looked like it would work at least as well.

"Now we wait," Katka said. The wind was rising, so she began lowering the *Apasa*, hoping to avoid being blown much farther from the road. The ground below them wasn't suited to a landing, though, covered with woody shrubs and patches of brambles. Further south, the prospects only grew worse: they were approaching one of the vomit-green lakes.

Del said, "What if I moor us to something?" They needed to stay high enough to be visible to Sejan, but if they remained floating freely they could be anywhere by the time he arrived. "I don't know how deeply rooted those bushes are, but it's worth trying, isn't it?" She really didn't want to end up having to disembark by wading through algal sludge.

Katka agreed, and they unfurled the rope ladder until it trailed over the ground. The wind kept toying with the *Apasa*, so Del descended slowly, unnerved by the swaying of the ladder but fairly sure that a fall into brambles would be nothing compared to her last drop.

When her feet finally hit the ground, she had to run after the airship to keep hold of the rope, but then it stopped long enough for her to twist one rung around a nearby shrub. She'd stuffed her pockets with pieces of string, and she set about tying new restraints, until she'd built an ungainly web of more than a dozen threads that shared the job of anchor between a multitude of different plants.

"Are we secure?" Katka yelled down at her.

"I'm not sure," Del replied. "I'd be happier if I could find a big rock."

Katka called back, "Just be careful."

Del picked her way through the brambles. She saw a few stones about the size of her fist lodged in the carpet of roots and moss, but nothing more substantial.

She approached the shore of the lake, wincing from the smell but convinced that the body of water would have cracked the surrounding rock in a greater variety of ways than other forms of weathering – and at the edge of the green slop, she finally saw a promising candidate. She knelt down and tried to lift it; it was half buried in the dried mud, but by pushing it to and fro she succeeded in working it loose. She pulled it out and began lugging it back toward the rope ladder.

She heard someone call out, nearby. She glanced over her shoulder and saw the speaker, standing alone, apparently addressing her. Maybe he was a tanker driver that she and Katka had failed to spot from above.

The man spoke again. It sounded like the Overgap language, but either his accent or his dialect were far enough from those Del was accustomed to that he remained incomprehensible. She put down the rock and turned to face him, gesturing apologetically.

"I don't know what you're saying," she told him. "If you're offering help, that's very kind, but our friend is coming back for us with the parts we need."

The man showed no sign of having understood her. He also seemed to be struggling to maintain eye contact, until he finally stopped fighting and gave in to the urge to stare up at the *Apasa*. As he gazed at the airship, the expression on his face was more intense than Del had seen from even the most enthusiastic spectators before.

"It's beautiful, isn't it?" she said. "We've come a long way in it, but we're hoping to travel even farther."

The man began sobbing, gasping for breath. Del took a tentative step toward him, but without understanding what ailed him it seemed unwise to try to comfort him.

She picked up the rock again and carried it back to the ladder. When she squatted down and placed it on top of the rope it formed a satisfying indentation in the ground; having fought the wind-blown airship herself, she was fairly confident that the same force wouldn't easily shift this new anchor.

She called up to Katka, "Can you come down? There's someone here."

"I saw him. Who is it?"

"I don't know, I can't understand what he's saying."

"How secure is the ladder?"

206

"It's secure."

Katka descended, frowning. "What does he want? Is he stranded?"

"Maybe. I haven't seen any carts for a while."

The two of them walked back to the shore. At first Del thought the man had recovered his composure, but then she realized that he was trembling.

"What's wrong?" Katka asked him. "Are you separated from your friends?"

The man replied. Del still couldn't make any sense of his words, but Katka was visibly taken aback. "What do you mean, you've been waiting for us?"

He pointed to the *Apasa* and spoke again. Katka addressed Del quietly. "He's talking like someone out of an old book, using words no one uses any more. I don't know if it's a joke, or ... "

"But what's he saying?"

"He says his people have been waiting for us to return. From Marikh."

Marikh was one of the planets Sejan was watching, hunting for signs that it might still be inhabited.

Katka spoke to the man. "We just came here from Dallya. We haven't crossed the void. We haven't come all the way from Marikh."

He frowned at her, confused or disbelieving. Katka tried again; Del had never heard half the words she used this time, so she assumed they were archaic synonyms that might be more familiar to someone who really had been isolated from the wider Overgap community.

The man seemed to understand the rephrased message. He looked up at the *Apasa* again, with an expression of utter dejection, as if the thought of such a beautiful vessel being nothing but a crude, barely skyworthy machine built by his own close relatives was the most crushing disappointment imaginable.

"Do you live here?" Del asked him. "Do you go underground to shelter from the sun?"

He regarded her scornfully, and muttered something, then turned and walked away along the shore.

Del turned to Katka. "Sejan told me there used to be people here all year round, but they gave it up for an easier life."

Katka said, "Maybe some stayed, or moved back later. I don't know. Or maybe he's just lying."

"People thought Imogen and I were lying." Del wished she could pursue him, and learn about his people's history and beliefs. If they were hoping for the civilization that had repopulated Jierra to return, surely they had reason to make common cause with astronomers like Sejan. Why spurn the rest of the culture, just because their interests weren't in perfect alignment?

"I should go back up," Katka said. "If it breaks free, someone has to be on board."

"All right." Del thought for a moment. "I'll wait for Sejan on the road, so I can show him how to reach us."

"That makes sense," Katka agreed. "But take some water with you."

Del picked her way through the brambles, then the field of leafy stalks. Walking among the shoulder-high plants, she saw that many of them bore stumps that ended in sharp cut marks, as if a fruit or other part had been hacked off with a machete. If there were burrowers nearby, they had to eat something.

As she waited by the road, she waved on three separate tankers that stopped to see if she was in trouble. Then there was a lull in the traffic that stretched on so long she could have sworn she'd detected the light in the west growing dimmer.

When Sejan finally showed up, she explained the problem with the engine in more detail than Katka could fit into her message; he rummaged in the back of his cart and picked out a selection of components. As they walked through the field, Del pointed out the signs of harvesting, and described her encounter. She'd expected Sejan to be skeptical; anyone could have come and cut the plants.

He said, "I've seen hints before, but I was never sure. I never met any of the people."

"You should talk to them," she replied. "Let them know what you know."

Sejan looked up, and pointed out a faint red light hanging in the gray sky. "That's Marikh."

"The most populous neighbor at the time our world was resettled," Del recalled. At least, according to *The Book of All Skies*.

"Even with our best telescopes, we can't make out any structures on the surface. *The Book* talks about all the food being grown there, but if that's still happening, it's not in large fields, out in the open, big enough for us to see. So what should I tell your burrowers? We can't prove that there's life there now, but we can't prove that it's gone, either."

"But you still keep watching," Del said.

"Yes. Because there's still a chance that they'll do something more, something bigger. These were people with the power to make the ruins of Old Jierra habitable! Who knows what they might choose to do on Marikh?"

Del didn't reply. If they hadn't come to their neighbors' aid when the quakes struck, it was hard to think of them as the same people at all.

They reached the moored airship, and Sejan ascended, while Del stayed on the ground to ensure that the rope didn't pull free. Even from below, she could hear the clanking and cursing that accompanied the repairs, but eventually Sejan came down the ladder again, looking weary but pleased.

"It's done," he said. "We'll all be waiting for you at the observatory."

"Thank you."

Del climbed up, then reeled in the ladder. Katka had a gash on her hand that was still bleeding, but she refused to let Del attend to it. "I'll just suck on it," she said, demonstrating. "Saliva is the best way to deal with small wounds."

"If you say so."

They set off before Sejan was back in his cart, but it didn't take him long to outpace them. Del looked to the side of the road, hunting for some sign of the burrowers' dwellings, but there was nothing apparent.

If she couldn't find proof of these people's existence from the modest height of a balloon, what chance did Sejan have of spotting the neighbors on Marikh, if they didn't want to be seen?

Katka had insisted on taking charge of the *Apasa*, so Del sat in a corner of the basket. With the engine running, the dynamo was making enough power for her to switch on a lamp. She took out her copy of *The Book of All Skies*.

If the book that Orsino stole from the museum had been a faithful translation of the one she now held in her hands, whoever hired him surely knew the story of Old Jierra and its fate by now. However furtive they were obliged to be about their crime, could anyone remain silent about the entire history of the world?

Perhaps by the time she returned to Apasa, she would have no news about the past to convey. The story she'd fought so hard to uncover would be common knowledge, and she could recount her misadventures to the director, take on an apprentice, and proceed to live a quiet, ordinary life.

Chapter 36

Del and Imogen hung back as Sejan made his way over to the supply dump, struggling against the gravity, huddled against the cold. He opened one of the bags of dried tomatoes and peered inside. "This still looks edible!" he announced. "Food from the other side of the world!"

He rejoined them by the cart and surveyed the scene, grinning with astonishment even as his teeth chattered. There were still pieces of wood lying on the ground where they'd fallen from the collapsing bridge. Del wasn't sure what she'd expected; thieves, or the elements, somehow erasing every trace of her arrival?

Sejan said, "I believed you from the start, but you should have taken the skeptics here and shown them all this evidence."

"It's not the easiest trip, even from Yerada," Imogen replied. "And if we really were intent on deceiving people, we could have planted anything."

"Hmm." Sejan conceded the point, but Del suspected he'd been harboring a trace of doubt himself, or he would not have been quite so excited to have it dispelled. And to be fair, if he was about to put his life in the hands of three daredevil balloonists and two dubious witnesses to the presence of a land across the void, any evidence bolstering the claim that he would *not* be floating off into an infinite spiral of emptiness would surely come as a relief.

"We should be helping the pilots," Del suggested. She climbed up the moored rope ladder into the *Apasa*, where Katka had opened a hatch in the engine compartment and was at work removing parts of the assembly that would be redundant while they were operating on battery power.

"Is there anything I can do?" Del asked.

"You can take these down to the cart," Katka replied, indicating a pile of greasy metal objects now sitting on the floor of the basket. Del obliged, one piece at a time. Removing the ability of the engines to run on fuel would leave them with no hope of flying the airships much farther than Celema, but she understood why the balloonists were intent on reducing the vehicles' weight as much as possible, especially for the first, untested crossing.

"Don't forget to leave a note on the cart, asking people not to take anything," she told Sejan as she delivered another component to him to pack away.

"Good idea," he replied. "Just because no one ate your food, that doesn't mean no one ever comes here."

Despite the cold, Del was sweating from exertion as she ascended the ladder again. When she peered over the edge of the basket, Katka said, "There's nothing more to bring down, but we can start bringing up the batteries."

On the ground, they improvised a kind of sling, attached to straps on both of their shoulders so they could share the weight of the battery. As soon as they both had their feet off the ground, the ladder tugged the *Apasa* visibly lower.

The ascent felt like the hardest thing Del had ever done; it was not just the weight pulling down on her shoulders, it was the need to synchronize her movements with Katka as they each clung to one side of the ladder. "If I have a heart attack before we get to the top," she panted, "let these be my dying words." As she struggled to catch her breath, the pause that followed stretched out much longer than she'd intended, until Katka finally lost patience and demanded, "What words?"

"Next time, bring a winch."

They made it to the basket, and heaved the battery onto the floor. Del said, "I need a rest."

"Me too." Katka detached the sling and they both sat. "If this works, then once we know exactly what we're facing, it should be possible to make the whole process easier. If it's safe to fly at lower altitudes, we can do everything with air-breathing engines, but if it's not .... maybe we could have generators at the nubs feeding electricity to the airships by cable, if there's a way to do that without the wires getting tangled, or chewed up by the edge of the Hoop."

Del laughed. "You're really thinking that far ahead?"

"Why not? You're the one who came by bridge, hoping it would remain traversable. Isn't the whole idea to let people cross at will?"

"Of course." Del tried to recall Montano's prescription for the exact circumstances that would have left his investors with a profit, but the whole concept now felt too alien for her to reason about. It had to be possible for the two sides to enter some mutually beneficial arrangement, without either of them abandoning their economic precepts, but she didn't have the energy to start quizzing Katka about the Overgap's philosophy on trading strategies.

They climbed down and brought up the second battery, and then the tanks of air they'd need in order to breathe. When they fetched the helmets, Del had to remind herself that all her bad experiences with them had consisted of deliberately induced calamities. They were not, themselves, the cause of any problem, apart from annoying constraints on her field of vision.

"I don't suppose there'll be any supplies waiting for us on the other side?" Katka wondered.

"Nothing I'd rely on." Del had imagined every possibility, from the construction village reborn and a new bridge half completed, to a barren landscape no different from the nub as she'd first seen it, save for the presence of three graves.

"So we'll need to take enough food and water to get to the nearest town on foot, if we're stranded?" Katka pressed her.

"Yes." Del had to stop and think for a while to decide what was needed; she was so used to the convenience of the cart and the Bounteous Lands' bounty. But she believed the friends she'd made among the Deremans would be willing to offer her and her companions food and shelter, if she showed up on their doorstep with stories of the world beyond the gap.

On the ground, they talked things over with the other crews, and gave instructions to Asha and Sejan on how they could seek help if the worst happened and they found themselves the sole survivors. Del stood by the cart and gazed up through the Hoop, trying to dispel her qualms. There were different strengths and weaknesses to any method for making the crossing; the bridge's anchored rigidity had failed it in the end, so maybe the airships' rootlessness was exactly the right solution.

Imogen approached her, smiling apprehensively. "I kept telling you we were stuck here, and you never believed me."

Del had no idea how much Imogen had believed that herself, or whether it was just pre-emptive pessimism. "It could have turned out either way," she said. "And it's not over yet."

"Yeah, the odds are still good that one of these four is a cannibal."

"When we get back to Apasa, please don't say that, even jokingly."

Imogen gave her a comradely embrace. "If I don't make it, tell my parents that at least I filled someone's belly."

Katka ascended into the *Apasa*. Del climbed onto the ladder, then reached down and untied it from the side of the cart. The airship, weighed down with all its new appurtenances, barely moved.

"See you on the other side!" she yelled, then she clambered as fast as the gravity and her aching limbs allowed her, up into the basket.

Chapter 37

Del followed Katka's example and put on her helmet so she'd be ready to make use of it when the need arose, while keeping the intake valve in the position that admitted ambient air. Then they attached their safety harnesses and stood side by side at the instrument panel.

"Can you hear me clearly?" Katka asked.

"Yes I can. And you?"

"Yes. Any problems with your face plate?"

"No." Del could see every dial, almost as crisply as if there were nothing but air between her eyes and the panel; the hygroscopic chemicals Sejan had recommended were sequestering water from her icy breath before it could turn to fog.

"Then here we go." Katka began venting the ballonets, and the *Apasa* ascended slowly.

Del peered over the side of the basket and watched the cart receding, with the other two airships still attached. She braced herself for the unnerving spectacle that she'd doubted her memories from the bridge would render any tamer, but then she found that the sight of the ground tilting actually left her smiling. It was still astonishing to think that Natasha's theory had foreseen this – and even more encouraging that an entirely new group of people had been able to recreate the same predictions.

She turned to Katka, who was smiling too, but had more on her mind than the triumph of mathematics. "We need to be sure that we stay on an outward spiral," she said. Following the local vertical could take them either nearer or further from the edge of the Hoop, depending on where they started, and air currents could easily push them from one case to the other. As they ascended, the edge was starkly visible: gray starlit rock on one side, star-filled blackness on the other. Nothing about the dividing line directly revealed its distance, but its bearing told them whether gravity alone would bring them nearer or farther.

Katka took a sighting with the theodolite, then started the propellers. Gradually the edge dropped below the horizontal, implying that to rise was to move away from it. Once she was satisfied that they were spiraling gently outward, she shut off the engine.

Del watched the rocky plain of the nub continue to tip as the *Dreyas* ascended, for the moment traveling almost orthogonally to the *Apasa*'s vertical.

"Start the air," Katka said. Del hesitated; she'd been inclined to ascribe any light-headedness she was feeling to the sheer strangeness of their surroundings. But then Katka tapped the instrument panel impatiently; the ambient pressure had already dropped to eighty-five percent of normal. Del turned the valve and began inhaling bottled air; there was a metallic taste to it that always threw her for a moment, but after a few breaths her lungs declared it perfectly satisfying, and her less-addled skull admitted that the switch was warranted.

The last sliver of the nub vanished behind the Hoop, leaving them alone among the stars. Del hunted for the *Dreyas*; after a while, she saw the beacon of their signaling light flash three times then go dark again, an automated sequence that caught the eye without overtaxing their batteries. The edge was harder to fix on now, but the *Apasa*'s motion and the abundance of stars produced a line of extinction and emergence that, once located and tracked against the background, she could find again without too much trouble.

She checked the ambient pressure; it was seventy-eight percent. The ballonets were empty now, so their lift could not be increased. She looked to the edge again; its bearing was almost constant. But the stars were reeling around the basket, constellations rising up as she watched, proving that the *Apasa* was still making progress.

"We're through the aperture," Katka announced, sounding about as calm as anyone could be who'd lost all sight of land for the first time in her life, while her notion of *up* turned a full circle. Del was embarrassed that she hadn't been navigating well enough to mark the event herself; she looked to the edge and watched five stars emerging, fixing them in her mind as the vertices of a pyramid.

The pressure crept down to seventy-two, then seemed to sit there; the march of the constellations became agonisingly slow.

"Have we hit the top?" she asked Katka.

"I don't think so," Katka replied. "We shouldn't be neutrally buoyant yet. But we're farther from the edge, so everything is changing more slowly." She pointed to the spring balance; gravity was two-thirds what it had been at the surface. Del had been too preoccupied to notice the burden slipping away.

Finally, the stars of the pyramid vanished one by one, replaced by a butterfly. The pressure read sixty-eight percent. Del looked from dial to butterfly and back, willing them to keep moving, but they refused to budge.

Katka said, "Now we've hit the top." She started the engine, setting the propellers whirring gently above them, sending the *Apasa* in closer to the edge.

Del had no need to check the charts they were carrying; she'd committed the level surfaces of each sky to memory. Here, the curves of constant potential didn't plunge straight into the edge; they spiralled around it, and those that were high enough never touched it, instead bottoming out as circles when they crossed into the middle sky.

"We didn't need an air supply on the bridge," she said. "I don't think the pressure dropped below eighty percent. So we must be able to make it across the midpoint at sixty-eight, right?"

"Absolutely," Katka assured her. Del knew full well that the question wasn't that simple; reaching a level that escaped the edge was one thing, maintaining it was another. But at least they had some significant leeway; if the bridge had still been standing, they would have been flying high above its decks right now.

The edge dropped down below the basket and the stars began turning again, while the pointer on the pressure dial merely trembled. Del checked the spring balance; their weight was climbing as the adjacent spirals wound together more tightly. Whatever the strength of gravity, perfect neutral buoyancy remained neutral: the weights of displaced air, hydrogen and cargo were all multiplied by the same factor, so if they added up to zero before, they would add up to zero afterward. But *perfect* was a lot to ask for, and if the balance slipped and they began to fall or rise, they would fall or rise faster.

The flashes from the *Dreyas* were no longer visible; it was probably stalled at the same point where the *Apasa* had lingered. Del didn't trust her sense of time, but as the stars flowed by it felt like the swiftest circuit she had ever made.

When they passed through the aperture again the edge ran almost directly below them, but now that she'd stopped looking for the closest segment, she could catch hints of the entire Hoop sweeping across the sky. While they raced around one point on the ring, the rest of it formed a giant arch that was toppling from the zenith, changing the stars as it fell.

This beautiful structure had killed billions of people. It had sterilized the world of her ancestors, melting and dispersing it beneath a thousand skies. She did not know what to do with that knowledge – but the ache of grief and guilt it induced was part of her now. The people of the Overgap had accepted their history. She had to do the same; there was no other choice.

"We're halfway there," Katka announced.

The whole arch had fallen below them. Del said, "Now you know for sure that the gap's not infinite." She glanced back, and saw three flashes; Lena and Imogen were catching up with them again.

The basket shuddered, and Del felt the drop in the pit of her stomach before she had the presence of mind to check the panel. The ambient pressure was rising: seventy, seventy-two, seventy-four. But there was no sign of a hydrogen leak. They'd hit some kind of down-draft, some instability in the air flowing around the edge.

She turned to Katka, who stood frozen. The ballonets were empty, they couldn't squeeze out any more lift.

"We can throw the food out," Del suggested.

"That won't be enough," Katka replied grimly.

"Then ... ?" Del's head swam. *Did one of them need to jump, to save the other?* Katka and her cousins had risked their lives for two strangers; Del was the one in their debt. There was no doubt about the rightness of it, but she had to find the courage quickly, or even her death would be in vain. She looked down toward the edge, and willed herself to accept it. *A few moments in free fall, then she'd be crushed before she knew she was in pain.*

Katka said, "We need to dump the second battery." She crouched down and pulled out the leads, then motioned frantically to Del for assistance.

Del squatted beside her and they seized the leaden block. Katka started bellowing and Del joined in, as they fought to straighten their legs and then draw the battery up to the basket's edge.

For a moment it hung cradled in their hands, high enough, but held so awkwardly that the final move sideways seemed impossible. Then Katka straightened her spine a fraction more and worked the base of the battery onto the wooden rail. With the tension on their arms relieved, Del recovered first, and heaved the thing over the side.

The *Apasa* reacted immediately; she could feel it snap upward like a bottle full of air rising through water. The pressure dial was plummeting: seventy, sixty-eight, sixty-six.

Katka was bent double with pain. She waved her hand at Del. "Fill the ballonets!" she commanded. "If we go too high, we'll burst the capsule!"

Del hit the button. The pump made a weak, sickly noise, but nothing happened to the ballonets. "Shut off the—" Katka croaked, but Del had already grasped the problem: with one battery, they couldn't run the propellers and pump at the same time. She shut down the engine and started the pump.

Their ascent slowed, and they began to level off. When Del finally stopped the pump, the pressure read sixty-one percent.

"Do you want to sit?" she asked Katka.

"That would just hurt more."

"Where's the pain?"

"I think I've pulled a muscle in my back." Katka laughed weakly. "I'll survive, don't worry. But it will be faster if you work the controls."

"All right. Should I start the engine again?"

"Yes."

Del complied. "How bad is it, losing the battery?" she asked.

"It's not a disaster," Katka insisted, wincing and trying to find a less painful position. "We can still run one motor at a time; that's all we need."

Del's arms were aching, but she wasn't injured. She checked all the dials again anxiously, then looked around, trying to get oriented. When she saw the triple flash from the *Dreyas*, she felt a surge of relief, then confusion: they seemed to be in the wrong position entirely. But then she understood what had happened, and her relief turned to elation. Their friends had overtaken them, at a lower altitude. Whatever phenomenon had afflicted the *Apasa* had been narrow or transient enough to have spared the second airship – and with luck, Asha and Sejan would come through untroubled as well.

With the *Apasa* lightened, they could probably pump more air into the ballonets and return to their old altitude, but Katka seemed satisfied with their present conditions, and Del was reluctant to start second-guessing her.

"Is there anything that would make you more comfortable?" Del asked. They didn't have a lot to work with, but maybe she could improvise some kind of brace.

"I'm all right," Katka assured her. "So long as I don't move."

"Forget what I said about winches. What we need are lighter batteries."

"You can blame the Hoops for that."

"I'm sorry?"

Katka said, "On Old Jierra, it would have been easy to find lighter metals that had risen up to the surface. Now there's more surface, so they're much more diluted."

They passed through the aperture again, entering the last of the landless skies. Looking back, Del saw a quadruple flash: the *Medoun* was not far behind.

"Do you recognize any of these constellations, from before?" Katka asked.

"I'm not sure." Del tried to think back to her time on the bridge with Clarissa. Had she seen those five stars that reminded her of bellows? The six that looked like an angry rat? "One of my friends memorized all the skies on our side of the gap, but that kind of thing was always a struggle for me."

Katka said, "It's just that ... if we threaded the second Hoop as well, by mistake, we might not be headed quite where we planned."

Del stared at her, dumbfounded, then realized she was joking. "Please don't tease me again until we're on solid ground."

"Fair enough."

When they'd almost come full circle, Katka said, "Time to shut off the propellers and descend." Del followed her instructions, knowing they made perfect sense, but it still felt more perilous to begin lowering the airship with no land in sight beneath them than it had to undertake the reverse maneuver at the corresponding point at the start of the crossing.

She pumped up the ballonets slowly, wary of the possibility of another sudden lurch, and she stopped well before they were full, giving the *Apasa* a chance to drift down to a new equilibrium. The stars kept turning around them; the edge of the Hoop moved into its expected place.

When a sliver of pale rock appeared through the aperture, she let out an involuntary sob of relief. However hard the journey, at least the Hoops were not fickle. She had found a way to unwind her thread, and they had not changed the rules and pulled the ground out from under her.

As the plains of Celema slowly tilted toward her, Del saw the flashes from the *Dreyas* again. "Imogen will never stop gloating about beating us," she said.

"We can always come down a little faster," Katka replied.

"No, I'm only joking. It's not a race." Before long, she could see the other airship by starlight alone, following its own path below them, gently spiraling toward the nub.

Something hot and bright moved across her view, much faster than the stars. She closed her eyes and saw the streak of its motion; it had started between her and the ground, crossed the sky, and then passed out of sight behind the basket. She looked to the other side of the *Apasa*, but there was nothing out of the ordinary.

"Did you see that?" she asked Katka.

"What?"

Del described the object.

Katka said, "Are you sure you didn't just catch the flash from our signal light?"

As Del watched the *Dreyas* come nearer to the ground, she saw the ruins of the bridge's foundations. There was timber strewn across the rock – far more than at the other side of the gap – but even so it did not look sufficient to account for the whole structure. The edge must have taken most of the bridge and turned it to dust. *And Montano, Clarissa, Silvio?* There was no trace of the old village, or a new one in its place.

"We shouldn't need bottled air now," Katka suggested, switching off her own supply. Del did the same; she thought about removing her helmet, but her arms were still aching, and there was no reason it couldn't wait.

A second bright streak rose up from the ground and collided with the *Dreyas*. Del bellowed to Katka to look, half out of fear and alarm, half because she doubted her own perceptions.

Katka's expression shifted rapidly from astonishment to outrage. "Some fucker's trying to kill us!"

222

There were flames on one side of the basket now. "What do we do?" Del pleaded. She could see Lena and Imogen beating the fire with a blanket, trying to subdue it, but it was showing no signs of capitulating.

"Drop us faster," Katka replied. Del started the pump, speeding the *Apasa*'s descent. Katka quickly sketched the rest of the plan; Del took the rolled up rope ladder, her hands shaking, and stood by the edge of the basket.

Katka groaned with pain as she moved toward the control panel. Del kept her eyes on the burning airship, but she heard the pump switch off and the propellers start up again. The *Apasa* was still falling faster than the *Dreyas*, and now it was closing the gap between their trajectories.

As they approached, Del started yelling, "Get ready to grab the ladder! Get ready to grab the ladder!"

Imogen turned, saw the *Apasa*, and pulled Lena away from the fire. They took off their helmets, moved to the nearer side of the basket, and stood, arms outstretched, waiting.

Del flung the ladder out, aiming high. It unfurled as it ascended, reached a peak, then the last quarter draped itself over the *Dreyas*'s lifting capsule. As the *Apasa* dropped lower, Katka steered directly under the basket, drawing the ladder back around the side of the capsule. Del looked on, her heart bursting, as Lena and Imogen reached out to seize the nearest rungs, then leaped into the air.

She watched the rope swing down as Katka started venting the ballonets. When the tug of extra weight from their new passengers arrived, it jolted the *Apasa*, but they continued ascending.

Behind them, the basket of the abandoned airship was now entirely filled with flames. Suddenly, the lifting capsule ruptured, and a ball of pale blue fire burst from the jagged hole to engulf the whole structure. The propeller housing broke free and plummeted toward the ground; the rest of the fiery wreckage drifted down after it, panels and struts brightening and fading as the rush of air rekindled smouldering portions and burned them more completely.

Del leaned over and looked down along the ladder. Lena and Imogen were clinging on, but it would be insane to expect them to climb up to the basket – least of all under this gravity, while the *Apasa* accelerated upward.

"We need to set them down on the ground," she urged Katka.

"Is it safe down there? Someone's lobbing flaming projectiles at us!"

"I'd rather dodge flaming projectiles on the ground than in a balloon full of flammable gas."

Katka said, "What else is down there? Who else, with what weapons?"

"I don't know." Del still couldn't see where the attack had come from. "But what are we going to do? Turn around and fly back, with one battery and two people dangling from a rope? Whoever's down there, I don't believe it's some great army. We're more likely to outnumber them, than they us."

"All right, we'll risk it," Katka agreed reluctantly. "This is your land, you know how things work here."

Del thought: *Not all the time*, but kept that verdict to herself. She yelled down to Lena and Imogen, "Hold on! We're going to descend!"

"About time!" Imogen shouted back.

With Katka hunched over the instrument panel, Del acted as her eyes, monitoring their approach toward the ground. As the end of the ladder brushed the rock, another blazing projectile flew past the *Apasa*, missing them by four or five strides.

The catapult's range was impressive ... but it was probably heavy, slow to redirect and aim, and close to immovable. It had not been put in place with some plan to attack the airships; no one on this side of the gap even knew what an airship was, let alone that the arrival of three of them was imminent. It had to be intended to deal with the only thing its builders knew had crossed the gap before: a bridge. Someone had camped here and waited all this time, with the goal of setting fire to any bridge that appeared, reaching across from the other side.

Lena and Imogen stepped onto the ground and released the ladder together. As the *Apasa* rebounded upward, Del surveyed the plain. She'd scrutinized the wreckage of the foundations before, but whether it was the change in angle or a change in her expectations, she could now see exactly what she'd been hunting for. The catapult itself was, mostly, a long piece of timber, but the camouflage was no longer fooling her. She could make out a single figure beside it; maybe their attacker had companions, but she doubted there was room in the hiding spot for more than one or two.

She explained what she'd found to Katka. "Can you put me down?"

Katka was past arguing; she started filling the ballonets again. Del removed her helmet then clambered out onto the rope ladder and began her descent, watching Lena and Imogen glance up at her in perplexity, but resisting the urge to shout instructions to them lest she alert the enemy prematurely.

She alighted on the rock and joined them, then quietly explained what she'd seen, and what she believed about the purpose of the catapult.

Lena looked toward the bunker. "Do you think they can see us from here?"

"It's hard to tell," Del admitted. Though the structure would have been built around the need for a clear line of sight to the region above the Hoop, there could easily be gaps in the timber that also allowed the occupants a view of the ground nearby.

Imogen said, "If your plan is to toss a lump of burning resin at an immovable target, how many people does that take? And how many people could you persuade to sit around freezing, for a year or two, waiting for the chance?"

"We don't have any weapons," Del observed. She didn't want the attacker to have another chance to bring down the *Apasa*, or to endanger Asha and Sejan, but a charge that ended with Lena and Imogen knifed in the stomach would be every bit as bad.

Imogen nodded toward the bunker. "There are a dozen wooden clubs just lying on the ground, waiting for us."

Del turned to Lena; she was shivering from the cold, but she seemed resolute. "Let's get this over with," she said.

Del had pictured them rushing toward their target, with an element of shock if not surprise in their favor, but the gravity restrained them. So they strode determinedly over the plain, prepared to confront the attacker whether or not they arrived without warning.

As Imogen stooped to pick up a hefty piece of the shattered bridge, Del heard a thud from the direction of the bunker, and then she spotted a man fleeing. He was making fair progress across the ground – he must have had plenty of time to get used to the gravity – but she wasn't going to let him slip away.

She summoned all the energy she had and broke into a steady jog. Her legs felt like they were weighted down with stones, and each lungful of frigid air left her nose streaming and her eyes watering, but she persisted. Beyond her anger at this one man's crimes, he might be the only chance she'd ever have to find the people who'd harassed her and her friends from the start: the people who'd bribed Orsino to steal *The Book of All Skies*, the people who'd sent bandits after the expedition, the people who'd arranged the destruction of the bridge.

The man wasn't faltering, but neither was she. *For Montano, for Silvio, for Clarissa.* She was growing dizzy; the plain seemed to be tilting, as if she were seeing it from above.

Del heard whirring; she glanced up and saw both the *Apasa* and the *Medoun* traveling overhead. They passed some distance in front of her quarry, then stopped and began unfurling their ladders.

The man paused, clearly confused, unsure exactly what threat these new participants posed to him. Del redoubled her efforts, even as her skull pounded, and by the time the man decided that no change in course was warranted she'd almost cut the distance between them in half.

As Sejan took the ladder down from the *Medoun*, Asha moved the airship sideways, panicking the man into a sharp swerve. Del willed herself forward, her ribs bursting, her lungs on fire. She collided with the attacker and knocked him over; he struggled to rise, but he was at least as winded as she was.

Sejan arrived, and helped her pin him down, then Lena and Imogen joined them.

Del watched bright streaks spread across her vision, jittering in time with her heartbeat. As her friends turned the man over, for a moment she was convinced that she had finally caught Orsino, but then she talked herself out of the delusion; even under the heavy beard, it really wasn't him.

When the man finally caught his breath, he was unrepentant. "What now? You think you can drag me all the way to Derema? I'll break free long before we reach the magistrate." He nodded toward Asha's airship. "And if you put me in one of those contraptions, I'll make it so dangerous for everyone you'll wish you'd just left me alone."

Del said, "You tried to kill us, for no reason. You can make as much trouble as you like; we're not setting you free."

The man laughed. "*No reason?* Where have you been? What have you brought back? Everything corrupt, everything debased, everything that turns our strength to weakness and our hopes into despair."

Del was bemused by the intensity of his convictions. "You've been there, have you? Through the mountains at Sadema? Or did you float across the gap?"

He didn't reply; he just gazed back at her contemptuously. Most of the Tolleans who'd made their way through the mountains might have been enchanted by what they'd found, but they would have been the ones who lingered – and were stranded forever when the tunnel was closed. Those who'd despised the Overgap's culture were then left, unopposed, to rewrite history, in the hope of ensuring that future generations doubted that the journey was possible at all. They could never be sure that they'd erased every record of the act – but they could bury it beneath an avalanche of disingenuous debate, questioning the veracity of everything else that had been written on the subject.

But alongside the scattered legacy of noise and distraction, another thread had endured. This man clearly believed that he was some kind of sentry, guarding his own culture against the barbarians who'd tried to drain it of its virtues once before.

Imogen glanced at Del, then addressed the prisoner.

"I suggest you come quietly," she said. "Because if you don't, my friend and I can only control the others for so long. And they're not like us; their passions aren't subject to the same restraints."

The man snorted with derision, but there was a hint of fear in his eyes. Imogen leaned down closer to him and whispered, "The worst I might do is beat you, but if you make *them* angry, they'll cut off a limb and eat it before your eyes. One more moment of struggle, one attempt to break free, and I'll let them feed on you, piece by piece."

Chapter 38

After some discussion among the balloonists, it was agreed that Asha and Lena would return to the Overgap in the *Medoun*, then make plans to start ferrying over the fuel, supplies and parts needed to keep the *Apasa* functioning. Del, Imogen and Sejan would lead their captive on foot to Derema, while Katka flew the *Apasa* above them. Katka believed it still had enough charge in its lone battery to complete the journey, and moving it to a populated area seemed less risky than mooring it at the nub.

"What about your back?" Del asked her.

"It's not great," Katka admitted. "But between crossing the gap again, walking for days, or taking a leisurely flight, the last choice sounds the least painful."

The man looked on, grim but unbowed, as the *Medoun* ascended and swung around the edge, out of sight. "You'll never defeat us," he said. Del wasn't sure if he was referring to the murderous clique he belonged to, or the wider civilization that he imagined he needed to protect, but she'd given up trying to question or debate him.

She worked with Sejan to disassemble the catapult, then they used the resin to set fire to the pieces, along with most of the timber left from the bridge. It was impossible to be sure that the attacker's comrades wouldn't find a way to rebuild the whole apparatus, but the travelers would return to the nub to check that all was clear before Lena and Asha made the crossing again.

Imogen whooped with delight as the flames from the bonfire crackled, and the smoke spiraled up through the Hoop. "This place is much nicer when you warm it up a bit!" she declared.

The fire was still smouldering as they set off, across Celema and through the Hoop. Katka brought the *Apasa* so low beside them that Del could almost have jumped up and touched it under more normal gravity. Their prisoner, hands bound tightly and feet roped together, shuffled along sullenly at first, but stepped up his pace when Imogen threatened to relieve him of his warm jacket, which was more suited to the climate than anyone else's attire.

As the four of them trudged along in the cold, Sejan couldn't stop smiling at the bleak landscape.

"What?" Del asked him.

"I'm walking on ground that none of my people have seen for millennia. This has to be the next best thing to setting foot on another world."

"You should aim higher," Imogen suggested.

"I will," he replied. "Once things are going smoothly with the crossing, I think it will be time to set our sights on Marikh."

Imogen said, "I'm in. Someone's got to come along and keep the travelers breathing."

Del laughed. It was absurd, wasn't it? But if it was possible, and there were still people up there – or even just ruins and records – what might they reveal about the history that *The Book of All Skies* had claimed to tell? At best, it contained the imperfectly transmitted stories of people whose material culture had all but vanished in the quakes, struggling to reconstruct their own past. At worst, its authors might have had their own reasons to distort the truth.

They set up camp and rested, making sure the prisoner was as well fed, and afforded as much shelter, as any of them. Then they each took turns sleeping while the other two stood guard. With the *Apasa* moored and floating above them, they would be easy to find by anyone wishing them ill – though whether Katka was awake or asleep, the airship's potential as a lookout would probably give any would-be assailant pause.

When Imogen prodded Del awake, she said "Nothing to report." If the man had allies watching over him, they'd kept their distance.

As they drew closer to Derema, Del felt a weight growing on her chest. The expedition's history could not be undone just by unwinding their path and reversing their steps. Imogen became quiet, and Del knew better than to try to buoy up her spirits with some false hope or cheerful distraction.

On the outskirts of the main town, Gathan, a crowd of children appeared, running toward them, gaping up at the impossible silver craft escorting the unremarkable travelers.

"Del?" One of the boys grinned at her. "It is you, isn't it?"

She stared back at him, hoping to reciprocate. "I'm sorry," she said finally. "It's been a long time."

"I'm Niso! Elledo's son."

Del nodded, though she'd have sworn Niso had been knee-high when she departed, wandering through the dining tent being coddled and fed by all the kitchen hands.

"Can you bring your father?" she said. "Tell him you saw me, and tell him we need the magistrate."

Niso looked up at the *Apasa*, clearly tempted to find an excuse to linger, but then he decided to accept the task. "All right." He ran off back into town.

Del kept walking, half aware of Imogen responding to the children's questions. "Of course you can ride in it, if your parents agree." "Yes, that man did something bad, we wouldn't have tied his hands if he hadn't." "No, my friend can't understand you, he doesn't speak our language."

A small group of adults approached; Del recognized Elledo at once, but wasn't sure about the rest. Elledo's expression was subdued; if he was glad of her return, he also had news that would render a celebratory attitude unfitting.

"I can't believe it!" he said. "You survived the collapse, and you made it back in ... that?" He gestured at the *Apasa*.

"We did."

"Silvio is away, still trying to raise funds for a new bridge."

Del emitted an involuntary sob of relief. "He's all right?"

"Yes. He wasn't harmed."

"And the others? Clarissa and Montano?"

Elledo hesitated. "We were hoping they'd made it across."

Del said, "I'm sorry. It was just the two of us."

Another man spoke up. "Who's the prisoner?"

Elledo introduced him as the town's magistrate, Kellano. Imogen described the attack on the *Dreyas*.

"How many witnesses do you have to this?"

Imogen said, "Four, though only two of us speak Peladan."

Kellano wasn't happy, but he agreed to accept the man into custody.

As the group walked together toward the town center, Del quizzed Elledo about the fall of the bridge. If there'd been an explosion, no one had been in a position to observe it; all that Silvio and the few remaining workers at the site had observed had been the structure tearing loose from its foundations.

Imogen said, "Something was sabotaged. It didn't just fall on its own."

The prisoner laughed. "Prove it."

Del stopped and grabbed him by the arm, swinging him around to face the *Apasa*, hanging in the sky behind them.

"They're here," she said. "Everything you hated, everything you feared, everything you lied about. And now the whole world knows that the gap can be crossed. Whatever you thought you'd achieved by killing my friends, you failed. The two sides will never be kept apart again."